What people are saying about …

THE MAILBOX

"A tend̲e̲r̲ ... lic. *The Mailbox* is a p̲o̲w̲e̲r̲f̲u̲l metap ... ̲t̲h̲e dreams we keep, year after year. A perfect beach read!"

Susan Meissner, author of *The Shape of Mercy*

"If you're looking for the perfect summer-beach read, slather on your sunscreen and pick up *The Mailbox*. Full of longing, angst, romance, and healing, this book will keep you turning pages and wishing several of the characters were your friends. A curious mixture of Nicholas Sparks and a style Whalen's own, I dearly enjoyed this book."

Mary E. DeMuth, author of the
Defiance Texas Trilogy and *Thin Places*

"The only thing I didn't like about this amazing story is that it had to end. If you are looking for the perfect chick flick in book form, this is it. Marybeth has masterfully woven together a story of second chances that women will be talking about for years. I loved it."

Lysa TerKeurst, award-winning author of
What Happens When Women Say Yes to God and
Becoming More Than a Good Bible Study Girl

"Is there such a thing as a soul mate? Can you find true love at fifteen? Do we ever get a second chance at love? Marybeth Whalen has written the perfect novel to answer those questions. A young girl, brimming with hope and promise, a young boy who can't forget her smile, and an isolated beach mailbox owned by the Kindred Spirit keep this story humming. The story takes place over several summers, and it's the perfect beach read. Unfurl your towel, plant your umbrella, and jump into this book with both feet."

Bonnie Grove, author of *Talking to the Dead*

"*The Mailbox,* a debut novel by Marybeth Whalen, begins with an isolated mailbox on Sunset Beach, North Carolina. It is a love story that begins between two teens, spanning twenty years as letters unfold the story of Lindsey's search to understand betrayal, heartache, and a God who loves her. The setting is beautiful, the story unique, and I can't wait to read the next book, and then the next from this storyteller."

T. Suzanne Eller, author and speaker

"A romantically enticing debut novel, brimming with what we all long for—those unexpected second chances. Readers of Southern coastal fiction will delight in this tale that begins with young summer love and continues over the years."

Alice J. Wisler, author of *Rain Song* (2009 Christy
Award finalist), *How Sweet It Is,* and *Hatteras Girl*

"*The Mailbox* is a great beach read. I'm left longing to leave my own letter in that salt-air-weathered box."

Rachel Olsen, national speaker for Proverbs
31 Ministries and author of *It's No Secret*

"*The Mailbox* is a best friend of a love story, with a tenderness as fresh as first love and a wisdom as old as time. Marybeth Whalen is a gifted author with an instinct for the care and feeding of readers."

Kathleen Popa, author of *To Dance in the Desert* and *The Feast of Saint Bertie*

"Marybeth Whalen is one of those rare authors who speaks the language of every heart. She navigates a journey of loss and longing with a deft and gentle hand, making us yearn for our own summers of long ago. *The Mailbox* will stay with readers long after the book is closed, a reminder of enduring friendship and love that never forgets."

Ariel Allison, author of *eye of the god* and codirector of the She Reads book club

"*The Mailbox* is an enchanting, emotional island hop. Throughout its pages you'll voyage with Lindsey Adams as, with the help of the Kindred Spirit, she transforms from a Walkman-wearing, chestnut-haired teen at Sunset Beach, immersed in '80s melodies and enamored by first love, to a strong, sure, and devoted mother given an amazing second shot at her dreams by the One who numbered the very sands on the shores."

Karen Ehman, national speaker for Proverbs 31 Ministries and Hearts at Home and author of *A Life That Says Welcome* and *The Complete Guide to Getting and Staying Organized*

"*The Mailbox* is a poignant tale of bittersweet memories, the love of a lifetime, and the God of second chances. Pack it in your beach bag for a great summer read."

Debbie Fuller Thomas, author of
Raising Rain and *Tuesday Night at the Blue
Moon* (2009 Christ Award finalist)

"*The Mailbox* takes you to the coast of North Carolina where young love begins with a promise and ends in betrayal. With characters that are like friends and themes that are true to life, Whalen captures the power of hope, the sting of disappointment, and the lure of romantic mystery. This story stays with you long after the last page is turned. I sometimes still find myself thinking about Lindsey and Campbell, wondering how they're doing."

Renee Swope, Proverbs 31 Ministries Radio
cohost, speaker, and author of *A Confident Heart*

THE MAILBOX

THE MAILBOX

—A NOVEL—

MARYBETH WHALEN

David C Cook

transforming lives together

THE MAILBOX
Published by David C. Cook
4050 Lee Vance View
Colorado Springs, CO 80918 U.S.A.

David C. Cook Distribution Canada
55 Woodslee Avenue, Paris, Ontario, Canada N3L 3E5

David C. Cook U.K., Kingsway Communications
Eastbourne, East Sussex BN23 6NT, England

David C. Cook and the graphic circle C logo
are registered trademarks of Cook Communications Ministries.

The Web site addresses recommended throughout this book are offered as a
resource to you. These Web sites are not intended in any way to be or imply an
endorsement on the part of David C. Cook, nor do we vouch for their content.

This story is a work of fiction. All characters and events are the product of the author's
imagination. Any resemblance to any person, living or dead, is coincidental.

All Scripture quotations are taken from the *Holy Bible, New International
Version*. *NIV*. Copyright © 1973, 1978, 1984 by International Bible
Society. Used by permission of Zondervan. All rights reserved.

Don Henley's "Boys of Summer," *Building the Perfect
Beast* © 1984 The David Geffen Company.

LCCN 2010923222
ISBN 978-0-7814-0369-6
eISBN 978-1-4347-0217-3

© 2010 Marybeth Whalen

The Team: Terry Behimer, Nicci Jordan Hubert,
Sarah Schultz, Jack Campbell, and Karen Athen
Cover Design: Amy Kiechlin
Front Cover Photo: iStockphoto.com
Back Cover Photo: Peter Doran, www.peterdoranphotography.com

Printed in the United States of America
First Edition 2010

1 2 3 4 5 6 7 8 9 10

032910

To

*My dear friend, Ariel Allison Lawhon, without whom
this book would not have been written.*

*And my husband, Curt: After twenty years, our love
story is better than anything I could make up.*

Acknowledgments

Abundant thanks to …

My heavenly Father, who supplied exceedingly abundantly more (Ephesians 3:20) than I could ask or imagine throughout this whole process.

My six unique and energetic children, who put up with Mom going off to write and are always faithful to ask, "How'd your writing go, Mom?"

My mom, who never failed to believe this book would be published.

My agent, Jonathan Clements, who is always in my corner.

The online groups who offer me very real support: The Writers View 1 and 2 and Writers and Sisters in Christ.

Cec Murphey for supporting the dreams of writers—especially this one.

Susan Meissner for being one of my first readers and encouragers.

My prayer posse, who prayed me through the editing of this book!

Mary DeMuth for being your gorgeous self and for making me cut the *wases.*

My editor, Nicci Jordan Hubert, who saw the angel in the marble and carved (and carved and carved) until she set it free.

The folks at Cook, especially Terry Behimer and Ingrid Beck, who championed the book from the beginning; Amy Kiechlin, who so far exceeded my expectations for an amazing cover; Jack Campbell, who had eagle eyes and a lot of patience; and Don Pape, who emailed to say he was praying for me.

Buddy Messer, PsyD, who helped me with the details of anorexia. And his sister Amy, who connected us.

The women of Proverbs 31 Ministries. I have said it before: You are family, plain and simple. I love us!

My new friends Susan May Warren and Rachel Hauck, who saw desperation in my eyes and took the time to reassure me, quote Scripture to me, and give me some great insight into how to make this novel better.

Bonita Lillie, who encouraged me to write the book I wanted to read. This is it.

My uncle Bob and aunt Frances, who open their beach house to us each summer.

And finally, Holly Drerup Ratcliffe, who first took me to Sunset Beach, North Carolina, when I was fifteen and sparked a lifelong love of the place.

Do you ever wonder, where did the summer go?

The Blue Nile, "Broken Loves"

The Kindred Spirit Mailbox
Sunset Beach, NC
Summer 2003

The Kindred Spirit waited from a safe distance for the man to leave the mailbox before she approached in the amber light of the late July evening. Because they knew each other, she would normally have spoken to him. But not here, lest he suspect her purpose. She watched until he drifted out of sight before she limped toward the mailbox tucked into the dunes, her knee aching dully. The doctor wanted to replace her knee but the recuperation would keep her from coming to the mailbox. There would have been no one to tend it in her absence, so she told the doctor the surgery would have to wait.

The sun had nearly set, as she removed her turtle-watcher visor and stowed it in her bag. No one saw her take out the notebooks and various pieces of loose-leaf paper, all dampened by the sea's spray and more than a few tears. She planned it this way, making the trek out to the mailbox only when she could come and go unnoticed, keeping her identity a mystery. She replaced the filled notebooks with blank ones, their pages crisp and smooth. She added a few new pens and took out the ones that had gone dry. Finally, she laid some extra loose-leaf paper on top of the new notebooks, smoothing it out with satisfaction, anticipating the words that would fill the pages by the time she returned.

She turned away from the mailbox and looked out at the sea. She breathed in the scent of the ocean, watched two seagulls chase each other in midair, then turned to walk slowly back down the beach, the weight of the notebooks she had stowed in her tote bag causing her shoulder to stoop slightly. She looked like the crazy old woman she had become, hunched over and limping, her hair askew without her visor, coming and going in secret from a rusty old mailbox that had started out as a mystery and become part of coastal folklore.

For years she had made this journey, taking her duty as keeper of the mailbox as seriously as a pastor takes his time in the pulpit. The Kindred Spirit played an important, albeit anonymous, role in their community. Every time she collected the notebooks, she remembered what the previous Kindred Spirit told her as she was dying of cancer—too weak to make the journey to the mailbox anymore—and asked her to step in. "This isn't just some forgotten mailbox on a desolate stretch of beach. This is a place where dreams are shared, tears are shed, and lives are changed." She remembered nodding soberly, grasping her responsibility to not only tend the mailbox but also to keep her own identity a secret. In her bag she carried the words of many strangers, scribbled in moments of grief or hope or joy, with the belief that the Kindred Spirit would guard their words, gathering them like pennies from a wishing well, protecting them like the treasures they were.

When she got home, she would make a pot of tea and sit down with the letters, reading through them deep into the night and praying for those who had written the words before she packed them away with the others, her own little ritual.

As she made her way home, she thought about the man she saw at the mailbox, wondering why he had been there, what story he had to tell. She had known him his whole life, yet didn't know why he came to the mailbox. That part, she suspected, was private. She knew that—like everyone who visited the mailbox—a matter of the heart had sent him there.

Chapter 1

Sunset Beach, NC
Summer 1985

Campbell held back a teasing smile as he led Lindsey across the warm sand toward the mailbox. Leaning her head on Campbell's shoulder, her steps slowed. She looked up at him, observing the mischievous curling at the corners of his mouth. "There really is no mailbox, is there?" she said, playfully offended. "If you wanted to get me alone on a deserted stretch of beach, all you had to do was ask." She elbowed him in the side.

A grin spread across his flawless face. "You caught me." He threw his hands up in the air in surrender.

"I gotta stop for a sec," Lindsey said and bent at the waist, stretching the backs of her aching legs. She stood up and put her hands on her hips, narrowing her eyes at him. "So, *have* you actually been to the mailbox? Maybe the other kids at the pier were just pulling your leg."

Campbell nodded his head. "I promise I've been there before.

It'll be worth it. You'll see." He pressed his forehead to hers and looked intently into her eyes before continuing down the beach.

"If you say so …" she said, following him. He slipped his arm around her bare tanned shoulder and squeezed it, pulling her closer to him. Lindsey looked ahead of them at the vast expanse of raw coastline. She could make out a jetty of rocks in the distance that jutted into the ocean like a finish line.

As they walked, she looked down at the pairs of footprints they left in the sand. She knew that soon the tide would wash them away, and she realized that just like those footprints, the time she had left with Campbell would soon vanish. A refrain ran through her mind: *Enjoy the time you have left.* She planned to remember every moment of this walk so she could replay it later, when she was back at home, without him. Memories would be her most precious commodity. How else would she feel him near her?

"I don't know how we're going to make this work," she said as they walked. "I mean, how are we going to stay close when we're so far away from each other?"

He pressed his lips into a line and ran a hand through his hair. "We just will," he said. He exhaled loudly, a punctuation.

"But how?" she asked, wishing she didn't sound so desperate.

He smiled. "We'll write. And we'll call. I'll pay for the long-distance bills. My parents already said I could." He paused. "And we'll count the days until next summer. Your aunt and uncle already said you could come back and stay for most of the summer. And you know your mom will let you."

"Yeah, she'll be glad to get rid of me for sure." She pushed images of home from her mind: the menthol odor of her mother's cigarettes, their closet-sized apartment with parchment walls you could hear the neighbors through, her mom's embarrassing "delicates" dangling from the shower rod in the tiny bathroom they shared. She wished that her aunt and uncle didn't have to leave the beach house after the summer was over and that she could just stay with them forever.

The beach house had become her favorite place in the world. At the beach house, she felt like a part of a real family with her aunt and uncle and cousins. This summer had been an escape from the reality of her life at home. And it had been a chance to discover true love. But tomorrow, her aunt and uncle would leave for their home and send her back to her mother.

"I don't want to leave!" she suddenly yelled into the open air, causing a few startled birds to take flight.

Campbell didn't flinch when she yelled. She bit her lip and closed her eyes as he pulled her to him and hugged her.

"Shhh," he said. "I don't want you to leave either." He cupped her chin with his hand. "If I could reverse time for you, I would. And we would go back and do this whole summer over."

She nodded and wished for the hundredth time that she could stand on the beach with Campbell forever, listening to the hypnotic sound of his voice, so much deeper and more mature than the boys at school. She thought about the pictures they had taken earlier that day, a last-ditch effort to have something of him to take with her. But it was a pitiful substitute, a cheap counterfeit for the real thing.

Campbell pointed ahead of them. "Come on," he said and tugged on her hand. "I think I see it." He grinned like a little boy. They crested the dune and there, without pomp or circumstance, just as he had promised, stood an ordinary mailbox with gold letters spelling out "Kindred Spirit."

"I told you it was here!" he said as they waded through the deep sand. "The mailbox has been here a couple of years," he said, his tone changing to something close to reverence as he laid his hand on top of it. "No one knows who started it or why, but word has traveled and now people come all the way out here to leave letters for the Kindred Spirit—the mystery person who reads them. People come from all over the world."

"So does anybody know who gets the letters?" Lindsey asked. She ran her fingers over the gold, peeling letter decals. The bottom half of the *n* and *e* were missing.

"I don't think so. But that's part of what draws people here—they come here because this place is private, special." He looked down at his bare feet, digging his toes into the sand. "So ... I wanted to bring you here. So it could be our special place too." He looked over at her out of the corner of his eye. "I hope you don't think that's lame."

She put her arms around him and looked into his eyes. "Not lame at all," she said.

As he kissed her, she willed her mind to record it all: the roar of the waves and the cry of the seagulls, the powdery softness of the warm sand under her feet, the briny smell of the ocean mixed with the scent of Campbell's sun-kissed skin. Later, when she was back at home in Raleigh, North Carolina, she would come right back to this moment. Again and again. Especially when her mother sent her to her room with the paper-thin walls while she entertained her newest boyfriend.

Lindsey opened the mailbox, the hinges creaking as she did. She looked to him, almost for approval. "Look inside," he invited her.

She saw some loose paper as well as spiral-bound notebooks, the kind she bought at the drugstore for school. The pages were crinkly from the sea air and water. There were pens in the mailbox too, some with their caps missing.

Campbell pointed. "You should write a letter," he said. "Take a pen and some paper and just sit down and write what you are feeling." He shrugged. "It seemed like something you would really get into."

How well he had come to know her in such a short time. "Okay," she said. "I love it." She reached inside and pulled out a purple notebook, flipping it open to read a random page. Someone had written about a wonderful family vacation spent at Sunset and the special time she had spent with her daughter.

She closed the notebook. Maybe this wasn't such a good idea. She couldn't imagine her own mother ever wanting to spend time with her, much less being so grateful about it. Reading the notebook made her feel worse, not better. She didn't need reminding about what she didn't have waiting for her back home.

Campbell moved in closer. "What is it?" he said, his body lining up perfectly with hers as he pulled her close.

She laid the notebook back inside the mailbox. "I just don't want to go home," she said. "I wish my uncle didn't have to return to his stupid job. How can I go back to … her? She doesn't want me there any more than I want to be there." This time she didn't fight the tears that had been threatening all day.

Campbell pulled her down to sit beside him in the sand and said nothing as she cried, rocking her slightly in his arms.

With her head buried in his shoulder, her words came out muffled. "You are so lucky you live here."

He nodded. "Yeah, I guess I am." He said nothing for a while. "But you have to know that this place won't be the same for me without you in it."

She looked up at him, her eyes red from crying. "So you're saying I've ruined it for you?"

He laughed, and she recorded the sound of his laugh in her memory too. "Well, if you want to put it that way, then, yes."

"Well, that just makes me feel worse!" She laid her head on his shoulder and concentrated on the nearness of him, inhaled the sea scent of his skin and the smell of earth that clung to him from working outside with his dad.

"Everywhere I go from now on I will have the memory of you with me. Of me and you together. The Island Market, the beach, the arcade, the deck on my house, the pier …" He raised his eyebrows as he remembered the place where he first kissed her. "And now here. It will always remind me of you."

"And I am going home to a place without a trace of you in it. I don't know which is worse, constant reminders or no reminders at all." She laced her narrow fingers through his.

"So are you glad we met?" She sounded pitiful, but she had to hear his answer.

"I would still have wanted to meet you," he said. "Even though it's going to break my heart to watch you go. What we have is worth it." He kissed her, his hands reaching up to stroke her hair. She heard his words echoing in her mind: *worth it, worth it, worth it.* She knew that they were young, that they had their whole lives ahead of them, at least that's what her aunt and uncle had told her. But she also knew that what she had with Campbell was beyond age.

Campbell stood up and pulled her to her feet, attempting to keep kissing her as he did. She giggled as the pull of gravity parted them. He pointed her toward the mailbox. "Now, go write it all down for the Kindred Spirit. Write everything you feel about us and how unfair it is that we have to be apart." He squinted his eyes at her. "And I promise not to read over your shoulder."

She poked him. "You can read it if you want. I have no secrets from you."

He shook his head. "No, no. This is your deal. Your private world—just between you and the Kindred Spirit. And next year," he said, smiling down at her, "I promise to bring you back here, and you can write about the amazing summer we're going to have."

"And what about the summer after that?" she asked, teasing him.

"That summer too." He kissed her. "And the next." He kissed her again. "And the next." He kissed her again, smiling down at her through his kisses. "Get the point?

"This will be our special place," he said as they stood together in front of the mailbox.

"Always?" she asked.

"Always," he said.

Summer 1985

Dear Kindred Spirit,

I have no clue who you are, and yet that doesn't stop me from writing to you anyway. I hope one day I will discover your identity. I wonder if you are nearby even as I put pen to paper. It's a little weird to think that I could have passed you on the street this summer and not know you would be reading my deepest thoughts and feelings. Campbell won't even read this, though I would let him if he asked me.

As I write, Campbell is down at the water's edge, throwing shells. He is really good at making the shells skip across the water—I guess that's proof that this place is his home.

Let me ask you, Kindred Spirit: Do you think it's silly for me to assume that I have found my soul mate at the age of fifteen? My mom would laugh. She would tell me that the likelihood of anyone finding a soul mate—ever—is zero. She would tell me that I need to not go around giving my heart away like a hopeless romantic. She laughs when I read romance novels or see sappy movies that make me cry. She says that I will learn the truth about love someday.

But, honestly, I feel like I did learn the truth about love this summer. It's like what they say: It can happen when you least expect it, and it can knock you flat on your back with its power. I didn't come here expecting to fall in love. The truth is I didn't want to come here at all. I came here feeling pushed aside and unwanted. I can still remember when my mom said that she had arranged for my aunt and uncle to bring me here, smiling at me like she was doing me some kind of favor when we both knew she just wanted me out of the picture so she could live her life without me cramping her style.

I tried to tell her that I didn't want to come—who would want to spend their summer with bratty cousins? I was so mad, I didn't speak to my mom for days. I begged, plotted, and even got my best friend Holly's parents to say I could stay with them instead. But in the end, as always, my mother ruled, and I got packed off for a summer at the beach. On the car ride down, I sat squished in the backseat beside Bobby and Stephanie. Bobby elbowed me and stuck his tongue out at me the whole way to the beach. When his parents weren't looking, of course. I stared out the window and pretended to be anywhere but in that car.

But now, I can't believe how wonderful this summer has turned out. I made some new friends. I read a lot of books and even got to where I could tolerate my little cousins. They became like the younger siblings I never had. Most of all, I met Campbell.

I know what Holly will say. She will say that it was God's plan. I am working on believing that there is a God and that he has a plan for my life like Holly says. But most of the time it feels like God is not aware I exist. If he was aware of me, you'd think he'd have given me a mom who actually cared about me.

Ugh—I can't believe I have to leave tomorrow. Now that I have found Campbell, I don't know what I will do without him. We have promised to write a lot of letters. And we have promised not to date other people.

A word about him asking me not to date other people: This was totally funny to me. Two nights ago we were walking on the beach and he stopped me, pulling me to him and looking at me really seriously. "Please," he said, "I would really like it if you wouldn't see other people. Is that crazy for me to ask that of you when we are going to be so far apart?"

I was like, "Are you kidding? No one asks me out. No one at my school even looks at me twice!" At school I am known for being quiet and studious—a brain, not a girl to call for a good time. Holly says that men will discover my beauty later in life. But until this summer I didn't believe her. I couldn't admit that no one notices me at school because, obviously, he believes I am sought after. And I knew enough to let him believe it. So I very coyly answered back, "Only if you promise me the same thing."

And he smiled in that lazy way of his and said, "How could I even look at another girl when I've got the best one in the world?"

And so now you see why I just can't bear the thought of leaving him. But the clock is ticking. When I get home, I swear I will cry myself to sleep every night and write letters to Campbell every day. The only thing I have to look forward to is hanging out with Holly again. Thank goodness for Holly, the one constant in my life. In math class we learned that a constant is something that has one value all the time and it never changes. That's what Holly is for me: my best friend, no matter what.

I wonder if Campbell will be a constant in my life. I guess it's too soon to tell, but I do hope so. I'm already counting down the days until I can come back and be with Campbell. Because this summer—I don't care how lame it sounds—I found my purpose. And that purpose is loving Campbell with all my heart. Always.

Until next summer,
Lindsey

Chapter 2

Charlotte, NC
Summer 2004

Grant stood on the porch steps with papers in his hand. More documents, Lindsey knew, that said their marriage was over. He shuffled his feet awkwardly as she stared him down with her back against the closed front door, a barrier between them and the home they used to share. "Did you need something?" she asked, enjoying watching him squirm.

She continued to stare as he shuffled through the papers. Even though this week marked the end of a year's separation, the pain was still as fresh as the day he left. They had been married for twelve years—Lindsey had given him the better part of her twenties and nearly half of her thirties—and for what? To end up divorced and confused about her future. Her hopes of an eleventh-hour reconciliation were dashed even as he stood there with papers signifying the end.

Looking at Grant with a mixture of longing and disgust, Lindsey decided that if it wasn't easy for her, she sure wasn't going to make it easy for him. She knew that wasn't a very Christian attitude, but there it was, creeping into her thoughts and actions. No matter how godly she tried to be around Grant, her best intentions lasted mere moments. About as long as it took for him to start talking.

The kids, she knew, were watching from his car where they waited for an evening with their dad. She willed herself to stay calm and civil, for their sake. Grant held up the papers. "My attorney wanted you to look through this," he offered. "It's some final stuff for our bank accounts to be separate and … well, you'll see when you look through it. No surprises or anything. Just standard stuff."

No surprises? It was still surprising to her that they had reached this point. How could he call anything he was doing "standard"? She accepted the papers and fought to keep tears from her eyes at the way their marriage had been reduced to a business arrangement, a mere contract with terms to negotiate.

"We'll need a response from you when you get back from Sunset Beach," he said. "Do you know when that will be?"

She shrugged. She wanted to stay at the beach as long as it took to clear her mind, to find the happiness she once found at Sunset. "I'm not sure, Grant," she said. "We're not really on a timetable. My uncle said we could have the house for as long as we want to stay."

Grant smiled, looking every bit like the nice guy she once thought he was. "Well, I hope you and the kids have a good time. It'll be good for you," he said.

She couldn't stop herself from saying what came next: "It would be good for us if we were going down as a family," she said. "You can't possibly think the kids aren't going to *notice* that you aren't there.

They've spent every summer of their lives going to Sunset with both of us, not just one of us. Don't insult me by pretending it's the same. That it's *good*."

"Linds," he said, using the pet name he had called her for years, which he had no right to do anymore, as far as she was concerned. "You know I would love to be there, but it just isn't the best thing. It would confuse the kids."

"Don't even try that, Grant. You don't care about the kids at all. You don't care that you have broken their hearts!" She had coached herself not to go in this direction a million times, yet there she stood, tears leaking from her eyes once again. Grant stood on the front porch, not a trace of emotion on his face. His absence of feelings confounded her.

She could feel Anna's and Jake's eyes on her as they sat in his car, waiting to be taken to his bachelor pad for the night, their packed bags sitting at their feet like obedient little dogs. They couldn't hear their parents, but she glanced over to confirm that they were watching. She knew that they were smart enough to read her angry expression and the way she swiped tears from her eyes.

She could almost read eleven-year-old Anna's lips saying, "There she goes, crying again." Jake, her sweet eight-year-old, sitting in the coveted shotgun spot of the front seat, jabbed angrily at the radio buttons, casting nervous sidelong glances in their direction every few minutes.

She turned back to face Grant, ashamed of her inability to just let things go where he was concerned. She wanted to, but years of history with him and a profound need to have a real family muddied the waters, clouded her judgment. Instead of playing it cool, she played it hot, her words and actions belying her resolve to not let him see her grief. She knew him well enough to know that he secretly loved that he could still stir up passion in her—even if it was just passionate anger.

"Just go," she said. "Be with your kids." She forced a smile. "But have them back in the morning so we can get on the road."

"Linds," he said, "I do hope you have fun at Sunset this summer. That place always seems to make you happy."

"I could certainly use some happiness in my life," she said before she went inside and shut the door. She did not allow herself to watch him drive away but turned instead to grab the phone, a reflex for as long as she could remember.

"What happened now?" Holly answered the phone without saying hello.

"I am such a fool," Lindsey rasped.

"What did you do?" Holly's baby fussed in the background. "Hang on," Holly said. She could hear Holly's muffled voice telling her husband, Rick, to take the baby. "Okay, I'm back. Josie's teething. You didn't warn me how hard this would be, by the way."

Lindsey laughed. "If I told you how hard having a kid is you never would have done it."

"Well, you always made it look so easy," Holly responded.

"Ha! You just weren't here enough." Lindsey thought about the times Anna or Jake cried all night and she and Grant snapped at each other the next day. Is that when their relationship started to crumble?

"Well, it's too late now." Holly laughed, unwittingly echoing Lindsey's own thoughts about her and Grant. "So tell me what happened and make it fast. The clock is ticking with Rick and Josie."

Lindsey smiled, then sighed deeply. "Well, I *might* have asked him to come to the beach with us."

Holly made a tsking sound. "Let's play a game," she said. "It's a little game I like to call 'How Many Times Will Lindsey Humiliate Herself with Grant?' You don't even want to know what the score is."

"I knew I'd have your support," Lindsey said, looking at the clock. Her thoughts flashed to where Grant and the children would be by now. Probably dinner. Did her place at the table look as empty to him as his did to her?

"So what did Mr. Congeniality say when you asked him?" Holly interrupted her thoughts.

"Well, he said no of course or I wouldn't be calling you."

"Please.... You'd definitely be calling me if he said yes. I can just hear you now, declaring that this time it would be different. This time he wouldn't cheat. This time he'd be the father and husband you always imagined he'd be."

"He was a good father and husband once," Lindsey spoke a little too quickly.

"Well, that stopped awhile ago, Linds. And he hasn't changed. He isn't going to change. He's not going to be what you hope he'll be. And throwing yourself under the bus for him isn't going to make your wish come true."

"Wow. So glad I called," Lindsey said, rolling her eyes even though Holly couldn't see her. "How do you talk to people you *don't* like?"

Holly laughed. "You know, it's because I love you that I say these things. I just want you to believe you're worthy of someone to love you."

"I do think that!" Lindsey said, her voice rising an octave.

"If you thought that, you'd quit putting yourself out there over and over for Grant to hurt. And you definitely wouldn't have just asked him to go with you to the beach so he could humiliate you further. We both remember how well that worked last year." Holly's voice got louder at the end. "Do we need to review what the definition of insanity is again?"

Lindsey held the phone away from her ear with a grimace on her face. She counted to three before putting the phone back to her ear. "Doing the same thing over and over expecting to get different results," she supplied the well-rehearsed answer. "I just—"

"*I* just want you to realize what a treasure you are," Holly interrupted.

"Thanks, Holl. But … I just want my family to stay together," she said. "It's all I ever wanted." Holly knew that better than anyone. She had been there when Lindsey's mother stayed out all night, brought strange men home, and left her to make her own meals day after day. Holly had also been there when Lindsey vowed that if she ever had kids, they'd have a different, better life. So much for that vow.

"I know, Lindsey. I want your family to stay together too. And it hurts my heart that Grant's turned out to be a total louse." She paused. "But he is. A total louse. A total cheating louse, I will add. Not to mention an idiot for letting you go. By the time he figures that out, it'll be too late, because you will have moved on."

Lindsey looked toward the ceiling. She didn't like Holly bringing up Grant's extracurricular love life or her moving on. The divorce was final, yet the idea of moving on with her life seemed about as likely as being suddenly able to perform a heart transplant operation. Come to think of it, a heart transplant sounded like exactly what she needed.

"Listen, I gotta go." Lindsey could hear Rick's voice in the background and Josie's faint cry. "Don't forget where you're going tomorrow. Your favorite place in the whole world." Holly's words were rushed as the sound of the baby's crying got closer.

Lindsey smiled. "I know. I am looking forward to it."

"Even without Grant you can still have the best trip you've ever had."

"At this point just surviving it sounds good."

Holly laughed. "O ye of little faith. I am going to pray that this trip is life changing for you."

"Sounds like a good plan. I'll pray for that too." Lindsey laughed along with her best friend. "I'll be sure and tell you how it goes when I get back."

"I'm counting on it!" Lindsey heard Rick's voice. "I really gotta go now. Have a great trip! I love you! Bye!" and she was gone.

Lindsey hung up the phone and thought about what Holly said. As much as she hated to admit it, her friend had a point. She had to get over Grant. Sunset Beach sounded like the place to start doing just that.

The drive to Sunset the next morning had seemed longer than Lindsey remembered. The kids, who normally contented themselves with music and movies, poked, elbowed, and annoyed each other and took turns tattling. Lindsey had resorted to playing the silly road games she used when they were little. "Look, kids! Cotton growing! Did you know that's where cotton comes from?" Of course, that hadn't worked now any more than it did then.

They had barely unloaded the car when the children had settled into their usual positions: Jake played video games, and Anna watched *Pirates of the Caribbean* for the hundredth time. Now, with the kids settled, Lindsey stood in the sunny kitchen of the beach house and tried to avoid a single, persistent memory: One year ago she had watched Grant lay his house key on their kitchen counter back home. When she looked at him, his eyes had flitted away.

"I didn't think you'd want me to have this anymore," he said, standing close enough to her that she could smell his unique scent—a combination of the laundry detergent she washed his clothes in, the soap she purchased at the grocery store, and the cologne she picked out for him. He looked at her for a moment, leaning in close as though he were about to say something. She backed away.

"Just go already," she mumbled.

He stood, still and silent for a moment. "I …" he said.

She looked up, breaking her resolve to not make eye contact, feigning more strength than she felt. "I want you to leave," she said, a lie. "Why are you still standing there?" Holly had coached her, made her promise not to cave until he was gone.

Shrugging, he turned and walked out the front door while she watched his retreating back. The sunshine filtered through the window over the front door and streaked his T-shirt with bars of light, a shirt she didn't recognize from a place they'd never been together. She thought of his T-shirts, once precisely folded in his drawer in their room upstairs, now packed in a suitcase he stowed in the trunk of his car earlier while she pretended not to watch. She restrained herself from running after him, from asking him what he almost said, as if it would have made a difference.

As she looked around her, she consoled herself with the thought that she stood hours away from the place where her marriage had quietly ended. The beach house spoke to her of fresh starts and possibilities. She put the bags of groceries she brought into the small pantry and unpacked the cooler. The bottled water and cheese and juice went into the refrigerator. She held the door open with her foot as she deftly moved the final contents from the cooler into their temporary home on the refrigerator shelf, her thoughts disobediently wandering back again to the day Grant left. She thought of all the firsts they celebrated in their life together. The first kiss. The first dance at their wedding. Their first night as a married couple.

But she hadn't found a way to mark the lasts that inevitably also occurred. It seemed tragic that the lasts just slipped by unnoticed, unmarked. The last breakfast he ate at her table. The last time they saw each other naked. The last kindness he extended for no reason at all. The last kiss he gave her, his scent as familiar as her own skin as he pressed his lips to hers. With sadness she realized she did not even remember the last time he kissed her. In spite of their problems, she had mistakenly hoped that his kisses were renewable resources, a lifetime supply. Like a fool she had hung on to the bitter end.

"Get a grip, Lindsey," she scolded herself. "You are on vacation. So act like it and stop this pity party."

She closed the refrigerator door and considered venturing to the mailbox. But at that moment, the idea sounded overzealous. Still, she felt the urge to go. Perhaps a walk would clear her head and reset her brain. She usually waited until later during her stay at the beach to go to the mailbox, savoring the anticipation and composing her yearly letter in her head. There had never been a better year to break with tradition than this one, she reasoned.

She shut the cooler lid and headed toward the bedrooms in the back of the house. Engrossed in her movie, Anna did not hear her mother's approach. It gave Lindsey an excuse to study her daughter without her whining, "Mo-om, you're so weird!"

Lindsey watched her for as long as she could, taking in the way her cheeks were losing their childish roundness, her eyes losing the expressive innocence and wonder they once carried. She couldn't tell whether Anna's burgeoning maturity had resulted from age or Grant's departure. Anna looked up and caught her staring, removing her headphones and imploring her to state her reason for the interruption with one of her patented tweenage looks.

Lindsey wondered what she had been doing when Anna morphed into this hormonal, exasperated preteen.

"I'm going to go for a walk," she said and—though she knew the answer—added, "Do you want to come?"

Anna shook her head reflexively—"No thanks"—and wedged her earbuds back into her ears.

Lindsey signaled for her to remove them again.

Anna did, with an added roll of her eyes. "Yes?"

"Are you sure you're okay to stay here without me for a little while?" she asked.

"Mom, I'm almost twelve. My friends stay by themselves all the time."

"Okay, honey. I trust you. Keep an eye on your little brother."

"As if I wouldn't," she said, keeping her eyes on the movie.

Lindsey turned to talk to Jake.

She found him in the den, his whole body engrossed in a football video game, his thin shoulder blades hunched together like little bird wings underneath his T-shirt, a leftover from vacation Bible school two years earlier that still, miraculously, fit him.

"I'm going for a walk," she said from the doorway of the den. The decor of the house hadn't changed since she first came there in 1985. Jake sat on the same This End Up couch she used to sit on that first summer. "If you need anything, ask your sister."

But Jake kept playing the video game as though she hadn't spoken. She moved in front of the TV, blocking his view.

"Mom!" he yelled, suddenly capable of responding.

"Yes?" she said with an authoritative smile while whistles blew and lights flashed behind her.

"I can't see the game!" he said, waving his hand at her to move as he spoke.

"I told you I am going for a walk," she said.

Seeing that she had no intention of moving until he responded in a way that she liked, he huffed and said, "Okay." Emphasis on the "kay."

She moved out of his way and exited the den, and he resumed playing as though she had never been there. She used to require respect from her kids at all times, but she had relaxed about that quite a bit after Grant left. Both her children's attitudes showed it.

Pick your battles, she reminded herself as she headed out the door.

She made her way down the porch steps and into the street, which led to the beach. And the beach would take her, just as it always had, to the mailbox.

Chapter 3

Sunset Beach
Summer 2004

The funky techno-beat ringtone of Campbell Forrester's cell phone went off, jarring his thoughts about the errands he had to run and the oppressive heat that overworked his truck's air-conditioning. After his daughter, Nikki, chose the ringtone for him a year ago, he hadn't had the heart to change it, even though it drove him nuts. "Every time my phone rings," he had said to her with a smirk, "I will think of you."

With teenage sarcasm she had shot back, "Well, that won't be very much, seeing as how the only people who call you are me, Grandma, and Minerva!"

He scrambled for the phone as he drove, feeling around for it without taking his eyes off the road. Just before it went to voice mail, he found it and answered quickly. In the scramble he didn't check the caller ID, and he cursed himself for picking up when he heard the voice on the other end.

Ellie.

It was a voice that had the power to ruin a perfectly good day.

"I'm so glad I caught you," his ex-wife said with that deceptive blend of smoky sexiness and Southern charm that has fooled a great many men. But now it had the opposite effect on him.

He forced out the words, willing himself to sound more polite than he felt. "What can I do for you, Ellie?"

"Campbell, listen. Nikki passed out at work and they rushed her to the hospital here in Charlotte. I don't know any more than that. I am on my way now and I just thought—"

"What hospital?" he broke in. Even as he waited for her to tell him what hospital and what floor, he turned the truck around and headed toward home to pack a suitcase. Nikki lived with Ellie in Charlotte, a three-and-a-half-hour drive from Sunset. His mind raced with possibilities of what had happened to his daughter. At seventeen years old, she was healthy and thriving as far as he knew. He pushed the thought from his mind that what he knew about his daughter wouldn't get him very far.

He dialed the number to work, a land surveying company that his father had started and he now ran. Minerva—his mother's oldest friend and also the secretary he inherited when his dad died—answered the phone, sounding bored. "Campbell," she sighed. "Thought you were going to the store and would be right back." She didn't bother to mask her frustration with him.

He found it difficult to be the boss of someone who had rocked him to sleep and changed his diapers. Minerva had been a second mom to him and didn't mind throwing in her two cents about most everything Campbell did, including business decisions, lawn care, personal purchases, his wardrobe, and his love life—which was admittedly lacking.

"Listen," he began. "I don't want you to worry, but something has happened to Nikki." He plunged on before she could comment. "I'm not sure of any of the details, but I'm going to head to Charlotte right away."

"What happened?" she asked, her voice weighted by her words.

"Ellie called and said she passed out at work. That's all we know for now. I'm going home to pack a few things. I will call you just as soon as I know more."

"Well, I guess you'll be needing a room when you get there, then. I'll look into hotels near the hospital and get you a reservation." She paused. "You going to tell your mother?" He knew she would like nothing more than to be the one to tell his mother. Even bad situations weren't off limits for Minerva's meddling.

"Yes, Minerva. I'll tell her just as soon as I get home. Okay?"

"Well, then, other than the hotel, I guess there's nothing else for me to do but wait and pray. Of course, that's the best thing I can do." She paused. "Isn't it?"

"Yes, Minerva," he said as if talking to his Sunday school teacher. He hated that Minerva had to remind him to pray.

"Okay, then, I will let you get on home to pack. You tell your mama I will call her if I don't hear anything, so she better keep me posted." Campbell knew he was in trouble when his mother and Minerva became armed with cell phones.

Soon enough, as he drove, he let his thoughts drift into a prayer. He prayed for protection over his daughter and especially that he'd keep his cool—he didn't want to expect the worst when her passing out could be the result of any number of benign things.

He drove down the highway toward the bridge probably a little too fast, leaving Shallotte and heading for Sunset. All the cops that patrolled through the area knew him, so all he would have to do is tell them about Nikki and they would let him off. He loved the small-town security that came from knowing everyone—the good, the bad, and the ugly. Truth was he had grown up with most of the cops on the force and knew dirt on nearly all of them. It worked in his favor whenever he pushed the speed limit.

The dog days of summer had descended, and the heat rose from the asphalt in shimmery waves. Tourists were out in force, making him miss the calm quiet of the off-season. He could still remember when people called Sunset the "best kept secret of the Carolina coast." Not anymore. It seemed every Yankee in the free world had discovered the place, with license plates from Ohio, Pennsylvania, and New York outnumbering the ones from North or South Carolina during the months of June, July, and August. They showed up in droves, smiling at the "cute" accents and talking about Southern charm. Campbell laid low and tried not to make eye contact with any of them. Of course, Nikki loved the tourists. She said that visitors from other parts of the country were exciting. She got that from her mother. All he ever wanted was his own little corner of the world, right there in Sunset Beach.

He steered his truck through the town, past the Pelican bookstore and the Food Lion, past the planetarium where he and

Nikki liked to waste time on rainy afternoons, past the liquor store/miniature golf place—a combination he never quite understood. Thankfully, he didn't have to wait long for the bridge to begin cranking open. Sunset's dilapidated drawbridge sometimes worked and sometimes didn't, only allowing one-way traffic and opening on the hour—stopping traffic on both sides—to let boats get through the Intracoastal Waterway. A lot of people complained about the bridge and said it kept Sunset behind the times, turning away frustrated tourists from visiting again. From a business perspective, he understood the push to build a new bridge, but from a personal perspective, he loved the bridge. Just one small way, at least partially, to hold on to the past.

To take his mind off Nikki, he cranked the radio as the DJ announced the "All '80s Lunch Hour." A song came on—"Boys of Summer"—that took him to a time before Nikki, before Ellie. A time when one face and one face alone got him up in the morning and kept him going all day. A simpler time, indeed. For that moment, Campbell let himself remember what he spent most of his time trying to forget. The image of Lindsey as a teenager filled his mind, and he wondered, as he always did, where she was at that moment, what she was doing. He focused on the memory of her face—her kind blue eyes, her chestnut hair blowing on the windy beach. Her smile.

An unscheduled trip down memory lane didn't fit with his agenda, and he banished the images that played in his mind. He had to get to his daughter. Anything else would have to wait.

As his tires crunched over the shell and gravel drive, he saw his mother sitting on the front porch, a packed suitcase perched by her feet on the weathered gray boards, her purse in her lap. Even though the temperature gauge in his truck said 97, her trademark cardigan sweater was pulled over her shoulders. She owned a rainbow of colors and never left the house without one.

"You just never know when you might get chilled, Campbell," she had said when he teased her about it. "People keep their air conditioners cranked down entirely too low." Today's cardigan, a pale pink, reminded him of the baby blankets she used to knit for Nikki. She wore a white T-shirt that said "Sunset Beach" in matching pink lettering, a sign. She only wore that T-shirt when she left the island, claiming it was good advertising.

"No need to advertise the place," he often said. "Let's just keep it to ourselves."

He walked up the porch steps, silently cursing Minerva. He nodded at his mother and looked pointedly at the suitcase.

"What's all this?" he asked, playing dumb.

She got that look on her face that told him she didn't intend to play along. "Campbell," she said, all business, "don't go using that old charm of yours on me right now. Go get your things, and let's get on the road."

He nodded his head and trotted obediently inside like a nine-year-old. As he walked inside, he inhaled that familiar scent of home, wishing he could plop down on the porch swing with a glass of something cold for a while. He took the house in with fresh eyes; knowing he wouldn't be back for several days made him want to linger even though he couldn't. He threw clothes into a duffel bag, not paying attention to whether the clothes matched or even how many pairs of underwear he included. He had no idea how long he would be gone.

His mom sat waiting on the porch for him in the same spot, staring past the other houses toward the inlet. Campbell wondered if she was remembering when his father used to fish over there. Once, Campbell had tried to take Nikki to the inlet and fish with her, but she wasn't into it. She cried when they caught one and begged him to let it go. For the rest of the day she talked about how the hook must have hurt the poor fishy.

His mom lumbered into the truck cab and sat beside him. He didn't even try to talk her out of coming along—he knew there wouldn't be a discussion. As he turned the key in the ignition, he looked at her. "So … how's Minerva?" he said with a wry smile. "I told her I'd tell you myself."

She looked back at him, unblinking. "Oh it wasn't Minerva who told me, Campbell. Ellie called."

"Ellie?" he asked, lightly hitting the brakes in reflex. His ex-wife and his mother never spoke.

She nodded. "She said that she thought I deserved to know."

"Well, you did—you do—deserve to know," he said, looking back as he reversed out of the driveway. "I just … you know. I never expect Ellie to consider other people …" He paused to take his eyes off the road and look over at her with his most mischievous grin. "I just didn't know she could have thoughts like decent people."

His mother smiled back, obviously reluctant but unable to help herself. Ellie had made both of their lives miserable at times.

Campbell knew his mother didn't expect kindness from Ellie any more than he did.

They continued on their drive in silence. Campbell switched off the '80s music for his mom's sake. While he might have enjoyed driving for three hours with Van Halen and Journey blasting out the songs of his youth, his mom would not feel the same.

About an hour into the ride, she finally spoke, interrupting the silence of his thoughts. "Ellie said she passed out at work. You don't think she's gotten involved in drugs, do you?"

"No, no, Mom. Nothing like that. I'm sure it's no big deal." He refrained from admitting that he wasn't informed enough about his daughter's life to adequately answer that question. The image that flashed in his brain of his little girl in pigtails evoked his defensive response. He repeated it for emphasis. "Nothing like that."

"Then what, Campbell?" she answered. "A brain tumor? A seizure? 'Cause the way I see it, there's not much good that could cause a healthy girl like Nikki to collapse."

He felt frustration mounting—misplaced frustration that he knew he shouldn't aim at his mom. She asked legitimate questions. "I'm sure she's just been working too much, that's all. I'll bet she's just exhausted after such a hectic senior year and working that job. Ellie said all that activity was good for her, but maybe it's not." He slammed his hand down on the steering wheel like a judge with a gavel, rendering his verdict as final. "She'll get some rest and be good as new," he pronounced.

He looked at his mom to see if she bought his confidence. "We should offer to let her come back to the beach with us," she said.

Campbell agreed. Ever since she hit her teens, Nikki had been coming to Sunset less and less. These days, almost never.

"She's just so busy," Ellie had said to Campbell each time she called to say their daughter wouldn't be coming to Sunset. Somehow, the news always left Campbell feeling like a wallflower at a dance.

"I hope you're right," his mom replied to his overconfident statement, then turned to look out the window. Silence filled the car once again as he reached over to turn the radio back on, shutting out his own thoughts. He hoped he was right too.

Chapter 4

Sunset Beach
Summer 1986

At first, things seemed okay during Lindsey's second summer at Sunset Beach. She had eaten at Campbell's house almost every night, and they had fallen into a routine: the same warm hug at the end of his workday with his dad, a meal with his parents, and a walk on the beach. Twirling her hair around her index finger, she waited at Campbell's house for him to get home from work as though it was just another night.

Tonight was different, though, and they both knew it. When Campbell suggested a walk on the beach while his mom finished dinner, this time their normal conversation had turned into something else.

"You must think I'm stupid, Campbell!" Lindsey yelled. They were alone on the beach so she felt free to shout and gesture wildly. Campbell was still wearing his work clothes: a pair of worn khakis and a polo shirt with the name of his father's company, Forrester

Surveying, embroidered where an alligator might normally sit. Lindsey was wearing cutoff denim shorts and a bathing-suit top. She had spent the day laying out at the beach and waiting for him to come home. While she waited, his mom taught her how to slice up vegetables for a salad. The two stood side by side at the sink, and Lindsey felt a feeling she could only describe as family. And now the night was going horribly wrong.

"I know she came to see you at work today. She called your house last night when I was there. I haven't said anything until now, but I have had it with this girl. Ellie? Is that her name?"

Campbell nodded soberly and sat on the sand. "Lindsey, I promise I don't like her. She annoys me. She shows up all the time, and she can't seem to take the hint that I am not into her." He reached up and took Lindsey's hand, pulling her onto the sand beside him. "I'm into you," he said with a smile.

"Then why is she throwing herself at you?" Lindsey was undeterred. "Does she have no shame?"

"Baby, I don't know. She's crazy. Everyone at school knows it."

"Yeah, well," Lindsey scoffed, "crazy about you. Campbell, you forget that I know other people who know her. Your friend Billy warned me about her. And Scott said she's—" Lindsey fumbled for the right word, "easy."

Campbell laughed out loud, forgetting that he was supposed to be serious. He covered his mouth and tried to look apologetic. "Sorry, it just cracked me up to hear you talk about someone being easy. You, who wouldn't—"

"Wouldn't what?" Lindsey's eyes flashed, challenging him to make fun of her choice to wait until she was married.

He had stepped into that one. "Um, you, who wouldn't think of being easy." He grinned.

"Is that what you want? An easy girl? Because I hear there's one for the taking. She's probably lurking in the dunes right now. After all, she always seems to be wherever you are. Want me to go check?" Lindsey made a visor out of her hand and looked around as if on recon.

He laughed and took her hand, pulling her close even though she stiffened against him at first. "No," he whispered. "I want you to stay right here with me. I want to enjoy the time we have left together before you go home. I want to take you back to the mailbox tomorrow so you can write about our time together like you did last year. Okay?"

She nodded. "It just scares me. Because I know Ellie is going to be around when I'm gone."

"But you forget that she has a major negative working against her," he said, tracing his finger around the outline of her face.

Though she knew the answer, she needed to hear him say it. "And what is that?"

"She isn't you," he said. "And you are all I want. Always."

Summer 1986

Dear Kindred Spirit,

This summer I looked for you everywhere I went. I wondered if you would know me if you saw me. Were you the lady who smiled at me on the beach when we passed each other? The fisherman on the pier who talked to me that day I went out there alone? I couldn't wait to come here this year and tell you what's been happening in my life. I hope you looked forward to hearing from me again. Something tells me you did.

Last night Campbell took me dancing. But not to a club or a wedding or any of the places you might think. He took me dancing at the pier. We were the only ones there. He held me close and said he had a surprise for me. He pulled out his Walkman and held one earpiece up to my ear and one earpiece up to his as he played Don Henley's song "Boys of Summer." We danced cheek to cheek as I cried, because I knew our time together is winding down and because I am powerless to stop it.

Don Henley sang, "I can tell you my love for you will still be strong, after the boys of summer have gone." With the lights of the pier shining down on us, I smiled into Campbell's eyes. I was thinking: After all the other people in our lives fade away, we will still be together. Right?

He nodded, answering my unspoken question. "Yes," he said. He pulled me closer and whispered, "I love you and I always will."

We rewound the song and held each other close as it played at least half a dozen times. The song is a bit too fast to slow dance to, and I teased him that we were slow dancing to a fast song. He said he could slow dance with me to any song, that we were made to dance through life together.

Standing there on that pier, Kindred Spirit, I tried not to think about the fights we have had the last few days over Ellie. I think it is just the stress of knowing that our time together is ending, that soon, reality will hit and I will go back to Raleigh and he will stay here. With Ellie. I try not to think about what could happen to us. That, even though Campbell is my soul mate, life could intervene and pull us apart. I know that and I suspect he knows it too, even though he never says it. Won't even hear of it.

Will you watch him for me, Kindred Spirit? Can you make it so we don't fall apart? If you see things going wrong, you could let me know somehow. I think that would be okay. I mean, I don't know the Kindred Spirit rules very well, but it feels like helping me out might be part of your job. I feel like you are rooting for us to make it. Holly says I should pray about our relationship. That I should ask God to guide us. I want to believe that there's a God who does guide us, but I'm not sure I can. For now, I believe in you, Kindred Spirit.

When we get back from the mailbox this afternoon, I am leaving. My aunt and uncle will have the car packed, and my cousins will be breathing their root beer breath on me the whole way home. They will ask their mother why I am crying and embarrass me by pointing it out for the whole car. My aunt will offer up some excuse. "She's sad to be leaving her friends," she will say. Friend, I will think. I am sad to be leaving my friend—the one person I trust more than anyone. The person I was made to be with. If I could change one thing about my life, I know what it would be: I would move to Sunset so I could be with him all the time.

Until next summer,
Lindsey

Chapter 5

Sunset Beach
Summer 2004

Lindsey made her way back to the house from the beach, ashamed of her inability to simply journey a few miles to a stupid mailbox that she had been to so many times before. She had only gotten halfway there before turning around and heading for home. As she walked, she made excuses in her head.

It was getting close to dinner and the kids would be hungry.

She needed to finish unpacking.

Why rush a visit to the mailbox when she had so many days ahead of her to do it? She had all the time in the world, she told herself.

But the truth was that she just wasn't ready to go. She pushed aside the thought that for the first time in many years, when she got back home, there would be no one, no Grant, to ask her about the mailbox visit.

As she approached the house, she looked for signs of life,

movement, anything. Even though she knew two children were
holed up in there, the house looked empty. She wanted to see the
detritus of family vacations past—discarded sand pails and lone
flip-flops littering the yard, dripping swimsuits tossed over the
porch railing, little people keeping watch for her return while their
daddy sipped Diet Coke on the porch swing.

But instead of facing what she lacked, she continued to walk
past the house. The kids would be fine, she knew. She headed
straight to the "downtown" area of Sunset Beach, home to a few
beach shops, a place to get ice cream on warm summer evenings,
and the Sunset Beach pier.

She smiled as a memory of that pier crept back into her
mind—and for once, she let it. After all, she was no longer a married woman. She could remember old loves, relish the long-ago
feeling of a summer romance, and savor the sweet memory of a
handsome boy's kiss. She remembered dancing slow to a fast song,
clinging to each other as though they were drowning when really
they stood far from the danger of the waves that crashed below. She
remembered the tickle of his voice in her ear, singing the words to
the song like a promise.

Take that, Grant, she thought to herself and smiled without
meaning to, the warmth of hope flooding her body. A thought skit-
tered through her mind: *Is this what healing feels like? What moving
on looks like?*

The town bustled with families and teenagers enjoying the evening breeze after a long day on the beach or being cooped up inside
with napping children. Soon it would be time to go back to their
rentals, eat dinner, then collapse after too much sun exposure. The

pace at Sunset is slow—there are no amusement parks, no water slides, no tourist traps. There is not much to do other than enjoy the ocean and take it easy.

Someone had propped open the door to the Island Market so that the steady stream of customers could make their way in and out. She wished she had thought to bring money. She could have picked up some things to make dinner instead of ordering pizza.

Although her kids would probably whine if she proposed anything else. "But it's tradition to order pizza the first night," they'd say. Thinking of this, she realized pizza was the right choice after all. Over the past year, she had learned to hold to the traditions her kids treasured even though their family felt very untraditional without Grant. Sometimes it physically hurt to go on with the traditions, but she found that, in doing so, she actually felt better. And she knew the kids felt better too. So they would have pizza their first night at the beach, just like they always did. And she would avoid looking at the empty place at the table and ignore her forced-sounding laughter that had replaced the natural flow she used to take for granted.

Even though she had no money with her, she wandered into the market. It hadn't changed much in the years she had been coming to the beach. It was still a place to pick up eggs, milk, and bread for those folks who didn't want to leave the island. People still had to stock up on the mainland because the market didn't carry everything families needed for vacation. But its size was part of its quaintness. Lindsey loved biking there in the early mornings each summer and picking up a bag of miniature powdered-sugar doughnuts for her family when they woke up. Back in her "real life" in Charlotte, she couldn't bike to a grocery store to pick up breakfast. But at Sunset, she could.

She stood in front of the doughnuts, staring idly at the packages of Sweet Sixteens, daydreaming, when she heard a voice behind her.

"Excuse me, but you wouldn't happen to be Lindsey Porter, would you?" The sound of her maiden name shocked her, making her feel like he asked for someone else entirely, someone long dead. She turned to look at the older, balder, more weathered face of a young man she knew many years ago. He wore a name tag that said "Bill."

She pointed at the name tag and smiled. "I can remember when that name tag used to say 'Billy.'"

The familiar face broke into an even more familiar grin. "It's so great to see you!" he said a bit too loud. Several customers looked over at them as Billy wrapped her into a hug.

"You too, Billy! What in the world are you doing here?" she asked as she pulled away from him, feeling suddenly self-conscious. She smoothed down first her shirt and then her hair, wondering what she looked like after her walk on the beach. Though she didn't worry about impressing Billy, she wouldn't want word to get back to the people they once knew that she had let herself go and roamed Sunset Beach in dirty capris with hair askew.

"I guess I could ask you the same thing," he replied. "You on vacation? With your family? I didn't know you still came here."

She nodded, smiling. Seeing Billy—a living, breathing reminder of just how far back she went with the place—made her happy. "Yes, I'm here with my kids." She paused to let that sink in. *With my kids, not my husband*, she wanted him to hear. "What about you? So you're working here again? Decide to get in touch with your past?"

He nodded. "Yeah, I guess you could say that." He lapsed into a godfather impression: "My uncle who owned the place sold it to me for an offer I couldn't refuse."

"The Sunset Beach mafia?" she teased. Was this flirting? Whatever it was, it felt safe to practice on Billy.

He laughed. "Yeah. Something like that. I left here years ago, moved to my wife's hometown. We were happy. Working hard, the American dream and all that. Then this opportunity came up and we both thought, why not? Let's live here, raise our kids here. Be beach bums, you know." He gestured to the rest of the store. "So, I run this place and it turns out it's a nice life." He smiled at her, and she could see him at sixteen so clearly; it broke her heart just a little bit to think of how much time had passed.

"Wow. Billy married, with children. I guess we're both grown-ups now."

"Huh! Whatever that means. I see kids in here goofing around and it feels like yesterday that was us. Me and Scott and Campbell all looking for trouble—and usually finding it." He laughed. "You ever hear from any of those guys?" She could tell he was trying to make the question sound nonchalant.

She shook her head no, looking down as her face colored with embarrassment—or longing—she couldn't tell which.

"Well," Billy mercifully went on, "they're both still here. You hang around long enough, you just might see one of them." They both knew which one he referred to. He put his arm around her shoulder, pulling her close enough to whisper. "I'll be sure to tell him to keep an eye out for you." He let go of her, ignoring her red face and gesturing toward the deli counter where a worker waved for his help. "It was great to see you, Lindsey. Really great. Don't be a stranger, okay? How long you here for?" he asked.

She turned back to look at him before she left. "As long as it takes," she said.

Chapter 6

Sunset Beach
Early Fall 1986

Campbell sat in the car while Ellie cried quietly in the passenger seat beside him. The tears, he thought to himself, were just for show. He didn't get the feeling she was all that sorry.

He looked out the windshield at his parents' house, imagining walking inside and telling them the news. "Are you sure?" he asked her again. "I mean, shouldn't you go to a doctor or something?"

"Why, so you can dodge this bullet and be free of me? So you can cover up this dirty little secret with your precious girlfriend?" She turned to face him, mascara making raccoon rings around her gray eyes. She was still beautiful even when she was an emotional wreck. "This is real, Campbell. This is happening. You've been sleeping with me and now I am pregnant. You can't just have a fling and then pretend like everything's fine again when she comes back next summer." She sniffed. "By next summer, the baby will be here anyway."

He nodded, his mouth set in a grim line. His sins, as his mother always said, had found him out. Lindsey knew that something was wrong. He had written her only a few times since he finally succumbed to Ellie that first night, and he had called her just twice, keeping the conversations brief, feeling like a miserable excuse for a human being. He looked over at Ellie, feeling nothing for her. And yet, she would have his child. How did he get here? Even as the thought made his stomach turn, he knew what would be expected of him.

"So, do you, like, want to get married?" The words were out of his mouth before he could take them back. He prayed she would say no, be a modern woman who wanted to do this on her own. But it was too late for prayers.

Ellie shrugged her shoulders and used a fast-food napkin to wipe her eyes. "Campbell, aren't you supposed to love the person you marry?" she asked.

He didn't miss the note of hope in her voice as she said it. "Well, there's such a thing as growing to love someone," he said. "And," he added, "we'll love the baby. We'll have that for starters."

She looked at him with a smile. It felt good to make her smile, and he hoped that was a good sign. "You think you really will love the baby?"

"It's my baby, right?" he asked. As soon as it was out of his mouth he knew that, even though he didn't mean it like it sounded, it was the wrong thing to say. He steeled himself for her response.

"Of course it is, Campbell!" she yelled. "How can you even ask that?"

He thought of the things he had heard about her but still put his hand on her shoulder. "I will love my baby. And we will figure this out."

She looked at him like he was her hero. Lindsey's face popped into his mind, but he pushed the image aside. "So," he heard her ask, "does this mean we're getting married?" She giggled like a little girl, but she wasn't a little girl anymore. She was going to be a mother. "I mean, how is this all going to work?"

He remembered Lindsey asking him the same question that first summer. As he promised Ellie that they would make it work, he couldn't help but think of his broken promise to Lindsey. The realization of what he was throwing away made his heart ache.

Sunset Beach
Late Fall 1986

Campbell sat in the sand beside the mailbox alone. It was nearing November, and most of the tourists were long gone. He liked being there alone. It was a good place to think.

He tried to absorb the fact that he would never go to the mailbox with Lindsey again. He held a loose-leaf page from the mailbox in his hand and shivered a bit in the crisp ocean breeze. He sat with the pen poised above the paper, using a notebook as his writing surface, waiting on the words to come. This would be the letter he would mail to Lindsey, a letter telling her what had happened with Ellie. It was time to confess, as much as he didn't want to. It was time to admit the kind of guy he really was.

He looked down at the ring he now wore on his left hand. He hadn't talked to Lindsey in weeks, and he knew she sensed something was wrong. Just yesterday he had received a letter from her that read simply, *Just tell me. Did we break up?*

How do I explain, he began to write, *what I don't understand myself?* He wrote the letter as quickly as possible. *I am sitting here at the mailbox,* he continued, *a place I promised would always be ours.* He wrote down all the things he regretted, all the things he would change, and explained why he had married Ellie, why he felt it was the right thing to do even as the words made his gut clench. His baby would have a family, a father. Something Lindsey herself had always wanted.

He stood up and folded the letter, slipping it into his pocket. He placed the notebook back in the mailbox, along with the pen, hoping that whoever came and used the items next would have something happier to write about. He pictured Lindsey coming here in the future and hoped that she still would. As he closed the mailbox, he had an idea that brought a smile to his face. He walked away whistling the tune to "Boys of Summer," feeling closer to Lindsey than he had in weeks.

Chapter 7

Sunset Beach
Summer 1987

"Hey, Holly, wait up!" Lindsey yelled at her friend, who was riding far ahead of her. They had gotten in the habit of riding bicycles each evening that summer just after dinner. Holly liked to ride fast, while Lindsey tended to get lost in thought, her memories slowing her down as she pedaled aimlessly down Sunset Beach's streets.

Holly turned around and waved back, motioning for her to catch up as she neared the Island Market. The two girls were deeply tanned and had turned sunbathing into something of a science during their time at Sunset that summer—to great effect. Lindsey could tell by the appreciative glances she and Holly received any time they were out together. But there was one appreciative glance she wouldn't be receiving this summer and, of course, it was the one that mattered most.

Holly was already inside the store by the time Lindsey arrived. She leaned her bike beside Holly's up against the building and took a deep breath before she walked in. As always, she had a simultaneous fear and hope that she would run into Campbell. Part of her wanted the thrill of slapping him in the face, and part of her wanted the satisfaction of just seeing him again, being close enough to breathe the same air. But another part of her was terrified of seeing him at all. "Girl, you have it bad," Holly chided her when Lindsey had admitted her feelings aloud.

Lindsey scanned the inside of the store for Holly and found her by the freezer selecting an ice cream. She watched as a young man started talking to Holly. It took her a moment to register that the young man was Billy, Campbell's best friend. She marched over to them, determined not to look brokenhearted. "Billy, you snake, hitting on my friend!" she said, teasing him. Her eyes darted around the store, expecting to catch a glimpse of Campbell. In the past wherever Billy was, Campbell wasn't far behind.

Billy's eyes widened. She realized he was embarrassed to see her. He blinked at her a few times. "Uh, hi, Lindsey. It's, um, great to see you," he sputtered. He gave her a half-hearted hug.

"You too, Billy," she said. *Act normal. Don't give him anything to tell Campbell. Just act like everything's fine and your heart's not broken into a thousand pieces.* "I see you've met my friend Holly."

Billy extended his hand to Holly. "Very nice to meet you, Holly," he said.

Sensing the unspoken tension, Holly plucked a Nutty Buddy cone from the freezer and held it aloft. Holly hated Nutty Buddies. "Nice to meet you too, Billy. I got what I came for!" she said. The two girls turned toward the register to pay for the ice cream.

"Wait—" Billy said.

Before turning around to face him, Lindsey grimaced. "Almost a clean getaway," she muttered under her breath.

Holly elbowed her and raised her eyebrows before turning back to face Billy. "This should be good," she said.

Billy closed the gap between them in a few steps, leaning into her as if he was about to deliver top-secret information. "Look, you didn't hear this from me, but I just want to tell you what a bonehead my friend is," he said. "What he did was stupid and what she did—" his face colored slightly—"was lousy."

Lindsey nodded, a knot forming in her throat. Billy knew everything. Billy, if pressed, could answer some of those questions that had kept her up nights ever since Campbell's letter arrived. "So I guess they have a baby now?"

"She's just a few weeks old," he said.

"A little girl," Lindsey said, her voice stronger than she thought it would be.

"Yeah. They named her Nicole. But Campbell calls her Nikki. She's a cute little thing." He looked over at Lindsey. "I mean, if you're into babies, which I'm not really." He looked over at Holly, who laughed.

Holly clapped Lindsey on the back. "Well," she said, holding up her ice cream, "we better be going before this cone melts!"

Billy took it from her and put it back in the freezer, pulling two new ones out. "These are on me." He smiled at both of them. "You girls have a nice night."

⁓

Lindsey waited until Holly was asleep to slip out of the bed they shared and steal up to the roof deck of her aunt and uncle's beach house. In her hand, she clutched Campbell's last letter to her. The paper was worn, and the ink was faded.

She loved having Holly at the beach with her this summer. She had been a great distraction, a buffer from the reality of Campbell's absence. Originally Lindsey said she would not return to Sunset, but it was Holly who talked her into coming. "You have to face it one way or another. You love Sunset—and not just because Campbell lives there. Tell you what." Holly grinned. "Why don't I come with you? That way if you see him or you just need someone by your side, I will be there."

Lindsey nodded and took a deep breath. "Deal."

But Holly's constant presence had also kept her from having the time to remember Campbell, to mourn what was lost, to confront the betrayal that simmered just below the surface of her skin. She had taken to coming up to the roof deck late at night to watch the moonlight bounce off the ocean and hear the sound of the waves crashing, to wonder if maybe at that moment Campbell was sitting on the roof deck of his house as well, missing her as much as she missed him. It helped her to feel connected to him, however tenuous that connection was. She tried to push aside the image that intruded on her pleasant fantasies—an image of Ellie holding Campbell's baby. A baby that, she now knew, was a little girl. "Campbell calls her Nikki," Billy had said that evening. The thought made her want to throw up.

She unfolded the letter.

Dear Lindsey,

How do I explain what I don't understand myself? I am sitting here at the mailbox, a place I promised would always be ours. Just like the pier where we danced. Two places, both special because of you.

I came here to write this letter to you, the hardest letter I have ever had to write. I knew that coming here would make me feel closer to you. And I need to feel close to you right now, because so much has happened to push us away from each other and it's all my fault.

I know that we fought about Ellie before you left. I guess you knew more about the way things were going than I gave you credit for or even realized. The night you left, Ellie and I were at the same party. I was really sad about you leaving and she listened to me talk. She kept giving me beers that she had snuck out of her house and I guess I got pretty drunk. I don't even remember most of that night, but I do know that I slept with Ellie before it was all said and done.

It was stupid. And what's worse, I kept seeing her. I know you sensed that something was wrong between you and me because I stopped calling and writing. I felt so guilty over what I had done, and how I had betrayed you. I couldn't face you.

The worst part in all this is that what I really want is to ask your forgiveness and try to move forward with you, but that can't happen. Because Ellie is pregnant. As crazy as it sounds, I married her. I hope it was the right thing. I won't go into all my reasons for making that choice. Just know it wasn't what I wanted, but it was what I felt I had to do.

I do not have the right words to say how sorry I am for hurting you. I am a stupid guy who threw away the best thing he ever had and I know I can't ever get it back. I want you to go on with your life, to find someone to love you the way you deserve to be loved. I am just sorry I blew my chance to be that guy.

And one last thing—not that I am in a position to ask anything of you—but I want to ask you to please keep coming here to the mailbox. I would hate to think of you not coming back here because it reminds you of me. I like to think that you will still come here to pour your heart out to the Kindred Spirit. It makes me feel close to you to think of you coming here, sitting on this same sand and maybe thinking of me from time to time as you do.

I will never forget the time we spent together here or what it felt like to hold you in my arms as we danced on the pier. I will hold you in my heart forever and, I know it's hard to believe after what I've done, but I do love you. Always.

Campbell

Lindsey wiped the tears from her eyes. As she folded the letter and tucked it back into the pocket of her sweatpants, she gazed out at the ocean and wondered when the hurting would stop and if it was possible for her to not love Campbell Forrester anymore.

Sunset Beach
Summer 1987

Campbell sat outside holding the baby, who shifted uncomfortably in his arms and let out a howl. His mother said it was colic and that no one knew how long it would go on or how to cure it. Ellie was inside the house sleeping, again. He never knew a tiny person could wear out so many adults. He and his parents and Ellie all moved around like robots, worn out from lack of sleep and the high stress brought on by a colicky infant. He rocked Nikki in his arms and felt sorry for himself, then felt guilty for feeling sorry for himself.

All of this was his doing. Had he just told Ellie to take a hike that night like he should have, none of this would have happened. He wouldn't be married. They wouldn't be living with his parents and causing them stress. He doubted he would even know Ellie at all. He stared off down the street, willing Lindsey to walk down it. He couldn't help but wonder if she was on the island at that very minute, if she had already gotten over him or if she was still sad about their breakup.

He looked down at Nikki, at her little scrunched-up face. Everywhere they took her, people commented on what a beautiful baby she was. He loved her, but sometimes wished her away. What a dog he was. What kind of father wished away his daughter? Maybe a father who wanted his old life back. One who wasn't ready to be a dad. He kissed the baby on her velvet cheek. "I do love you, little one," he told her.

He looked up to see Billy's truck pulling into the drive. Billy had been coming around less and less since Nikki was born. Campbell waved and shifted Nikki up onto his shoulder, patting her back as she rooted around and bobbed her unstable head. Billy took the stairs up to the deck two at a time, just as he always had. Campbell couldn't help but notice how carefree he looked. He looked away, jealous, pretending to be interested in the top of Nikki's head. Just the night before, Campbell's mother had showed him how to scrub it gently for cradle cap.

"Hey, buddy," Billy said, clapping him on the back and peering down at Nikki. "Whatcha doing out here?"

He yanked his thumb in the direction of the door. "Ellie's taking a nap, so I'm trying to keep the baby quiet."

Billy shook his head. "She was asleep the last time I was here."

Campbell shrugged his shoulders. "Well, she gets up with Nikki a lot at night so she tries to sleep during the day." He wondered why he was defending Ellie. The truth was, they all took turns getting up with Nikki at night. Ellie just whined about it more than anyone else.

Billy nodded, satisfied. "Well, I just wanted to check on you. Make sure you were still alive." He laughed. "Guess you are, barely."

Campbell smiled back at him. "Yeah, barely is right."

They sat in awkward silence for a few minutes. Nikki had fallen asleep, her little mouth working her pacifier. Campbell stared down at her and wondered how he could resent her and love her all at the same time.

Billy cleared his throat. "Um, look, dude, I just wanted to tell you that I saw Lindsey. Yesterday."

"You did? She's here?" Campbell tried not to look overanxious.

"Yeah, she was with some friend of hers. Holly?"

Campbell nodded. "Her best friend."

"Yeah, well, she's hot. Wish Lindsey had brought her last summer so we could have double-dated. Of course now I'm like a leper to her because I have the misfortune of being your best friend." He grinned. "But I forgive you."

"So did she ask about me?"

"Not directly, but I could tell she wanted to know how you are." He pointed to the sleeping baby. "I told her about Nikki."

Campbell nodded, wondering how she took hearing about his life from Billy. "How'd she seem?" he asked.

"Sad," Billy said. "I'd say she's still pretty hung up on you, if I had to guess. But she played it cool."

He felt bad for being happy with Billy's response. It was unfair of him, he knew, to want her to pine away after him. Billy sprang up and spun his car keys around on his key ring, something he made a habit of doing every time he was preparing to leave.

"Going already?" Campbell knew that his disappointment showed. It felt good to spend time with someone from his previous life.

Billy nodded and shrugged. "Yeah, meeting Scott and some of those guys at the arcade. See what kind of trouble we can get into."

"Okay," he said, dying to join his friends. "Thanks for coming by," he managed to add as Billy loped back down the steps.

"No problem!" Billy hollered as he jumped into his truck and backed out of the drive, kicking up gravel. Campbell resumed his position on the porch's rocking chair with Nikki in his arms, watching the sun go down and wondering if, wherever she was, Lindsey was seeing the same sunset.

Chapter 8

Sunset Beach

Summer 1988

"Lola! L-O-L-A Lola! Lo lo lo lo Lola!"

The boys Lindsey and Holly had gone out with that night screamed the lyrics to the Kinks song in unison as their little group made their way down the beach in the dark. Though they swore they hadn't, Lindsey thought they had been drinking before they picked Holly and her up for their date. They were way too happy.

Jeff, the guy Holly was with, came over and put his arm around Holly. "Just like cherry cola!" he sang to her, loud and off key. Holly laughed though Lindsey didn't find it funny. She thought he was especially obnoxious. What Holly saw in him, she couldn't understand. She suspected Holly didn't see anything in him but was only going out with him to force Lindsey to go out with his friend Joel.

She tried to catch Holly's eye, but it was too dark to see her features. Holly would be disappointed if she asked to go home so early anyway. She watched as Jeff took Holly's hand and turned to

Joel. "What do you say we split up for a while?" he asked. Just the question made her stomach turn a complete flip.

Joel looked at her and shrugged. "Guess so," he said, his voice not sounding as optimistic as Jeff's did. Jeff and Holly walked ahead as Joel slowed down.

"Can we sit for a minute?" Joel asked Lindsey. It was her turn to shrug. But she really wanted to say no.

"Jeff's got the wrong idea about my friend," she said as she sat down in the damp sand beside him.

"What do you mean?" Joel asked, grinning, his straight white teeth showing up in the darkness like little beacons.

"I mean, she likes him, but she's not going to do anything with him."

"I wouldn't think that Jeff expects that," Joel said quietly. "Jeff likes Holly. He's a good guy." He paused. "And I like you," he added.

She smiled. "Thanks," she said. She could think of nothing else.

"So no, 'I like you too, Joel'?"

"I do like you, but—" She shook her head.

"Not like that," he said and smiled again.

"It's just … there's someone I broke up with awhile back and I'm not ready—"

"Campbell?" Joel asked, his name cutting through her like a knife.

She nodded. "Do you know him?"

"No, but Holly told me about him. She warned me you might still be hung up on him. She said it's been over for a while though?"

It wasn't really a question. Joel knew that she was spending her second summer pining away for a boy who had clearly forgotten all about her. She was glad it was too dark for him to see her blush. "I guess I'm a pretty sad case," she acknowledged.

He patted her knee. "No, I get it. I've only recently gotten over someone who broke my heart. But you know what helped me?" He leaned in, she could smell the mint gum he chewed on his breath. He kissed her tentatively.

She wished for a moment that at the touch of his lips the spell Campbell had cast on her would be broken, that her body would respond to the touch of someone new and she would not long for Campbell anymore. Instead she felt repulsion, and something like anger, well up inside of her. She pulled away.

"Sorry, couldn't resist," he said. "I was hoping—"

She smiled at his earnestness. "Apparently I'm not your girl," she said.

"But you're someone's. And even though he doesn't know it, he's a lucky guy." He stood up and brushed the sand from his shorts. He extended his hand to pull her up. "Come on. I'll walk you home. Jeff'll bring Holly home if you think that won't bother her."

She smiled in the darkness. Holly had already arranged with Lindsey ahead of time that if the opportunity came up for them to be alone with the guys, they'd eventually meet back at the beach house. Lindsey knew that Holly wasn't interested in starting anything physical with Jeff, but she wanted Lindsey to spend time alone with Joel and could take care of herself where Jeff was concerned. "Thanks, Joel," Lindsey replied. "I'd love it if you'd walk me home."

She wondered if she was stupid for overlooking a guy who was obviously interested in her, and the thought surprised her. Maybe it was a sign, a glimmer of hope that she would eventually move past her love for Campbell. That someone wonderful was waiting just around the corner. As she walked underneath a star-filled sky, she ventured a prayer asking for that to happen. Holly had encouraged her to pray that God would send someone else for her to love, that she would heal. She looked heavenward, in awe of the multitude of stars, and tried to believe that God really did listen to her prayers like Holly had promised.

Summer 1988

Dear Kindred Spirit,

Holly made rules for this year's beach trip: No pining away. No listening to sad songs that remind me of Campbell. No sneaking up to the roof deck to cry. She says I did enough of that last year to last the rest of my life.

She also made me go out with a guy that we met on the beach. His name was Joel, and he was very good looking and polite and charming. But there was no chemistry. I endured my one date just so Holly would quit bugging me. So I could say that I was moving on with my life. The truth is, I want to move on, and I can feel myself straining to break the hold Campbell has on me.

Holly keeps preaching at me about it. She says I need to get back on the horse, that there are other fish in the sea. She's a storehouse of clichés. She's always talking to me about God's plan for my life and how it's been made clear by Campbell's choices that he isn't a part of that plan. I am not sure I want to believe in a God who makes a plan that is so obviously contrary to what makes me happy. I am not pleased with God's plan, I guess you could say.

I made some rules of my own:

Rule #1: No walking past Campbell's house. I haven't been down Campbell's street since we broke up. I just want to see his house, to see his truck pulled in the drive and know he's in there. But I am also afraid I would see Ellie on the front porch rocking the baby, who I guess is over a year old now. I am sure Ellie would be only too happy to wave at me and rub it in that she won Campbell and I am the big loser who can't let go.

Rule #2: No going to the pier. I can't stand in the spot where we danced together that last night. So I avoid the pier entirely. Even when we are hanging out at night and a bunch of people go up there, I just go home.

At first I made rule #3 that I wasn't going to come back here to the mailbox and write to you. But after I thought about it, I decided that would be foolish. I love coming here, and I love writing these letters each year. It makes me feel like there is someone out there who really cares about what I think and feel, who is sad with me about what happened with Campbell and who is cheering me on, believing that someday I will be happy again and this time in my life will be a distant memory. I guess I need to still believe in you, Kindred Spirit, whoever you are.

Most of all, and I don't admit this to anyone, but … I need to come here so I can feel close to Campbell. In spite of what he did and how bad he hurt me, I still want to feel close to him. No matter what happens to me—if I marry or how far I go in life—I will always equate this place with him. He introduced me to the mailbox and he encouraged me to write to you. In his last letter, he asked me to come here so that we could stay connected. So I will keep coming and keep writing. As silly as it is, it's all I have left of him, of a time in my life when I still believed in love. I am glad this mailbox is here. I don't know what I would do without it, or you. Thank you for reading my letters each year. It's nice to know you're there.

Until next summer,

Lindsey

Chapter 9

Charlotte
Summer 2004

"Campbell." He heard Ellie's voice before he saw her and still cringed reflexively. He swung his head around to see her striding down the hospital corridor, all business, her mouth set in a grim red line. She wore a tracksuit, periwinkle blue with black and white lines down the sleeves and legs. Her long blonde hair was pulled back into a severe-looking ponytail—not a strand out of place—and her jewelry, while simple, still managed to be expensive looking. Though she wore what most would consider workout clothes, he got the feeling that she would never actually work out while wearing that outfit. She looked every bit the wealthy suburban doctor's wife. It suited her much better than "teenage mother living in a beach town with her teenage husband's parents." That role hadn't lasted long anyway.

Ellie swept Campbell's mother into a dramatic hug. "Thank you so much for coming, LaRae," she said. Ellie gave Campbell a pat on the arm. "You too, Campbell," she offered.

He skipped all the pleasantries. "What's going on with Nikki?" He noticed that Ellie's son, Garrett, lay down his video game to listen in. He guessed Ellie noticed too, because she motioned for Campbell and his mom to walk down the hall, out of the boy's earshot. They followed dutifully, and Garrett turned back to his video game, the barest hint of a sigh emerging from his lips.

"I just spoke with the doctor who admitted her," Ellie said. "The good news is she was only out for a few seconds and she's totally awake and alert now. They are giving her IV fluids and running some tests on her liver enzymes and electrolyte levels. Once they know more, they will get back to us." Ellie paused, glancing over at Garrett to make sure he couldn't hear them talking. "They are saying she most likely has … anorexia. She passed out … because she hasn't been eating." Ellie paused again, longer this time, looking past them toward the windows of the waiting room. Tears had collected in her eyes, threatening to spill over. "I mean, she had gotten pretty thin, but she kept saying she had it under control," she offered, her voice sounding as weak as Campbell felt.

Without warning, anger welled up within him. "So, let me get this straight. She starved herself right under your nose? And you just let her?"

His mom put her hand on his arm, a signal: Not here. Nurses at the station glanced nervously in their direction. He saw a few of them confer with each other, determining if they should suggest the trio go somewhere more private.

He lowered his voice. Yet even in a whisper, his anger still rang. "So the … anorexia made her collapse?"

"Well, it's an indicator that something dangerous is going on.

She hadn't eaten a thing in twenty-four hours, best we can tell." Ellie paused. "Her friend at work filled me in. Seems she was going for some kind of personal record." Ellie looked at him, and he could see the challenge in her eyes. She dared him to come back at her again, to land all the blame on her when they both knew he should get in line for plenty of it. "Of course, we won't know the whole story until we can talk to her."

As much as he wanted to blame everything on Ellie—that it happened on her watch—he had to admit he hadn't seen his daughter in a very long time. He didn't know how much she weighed, what her life was like, what she was struggling with, or what she thought of herself. Yes, she had been the one to bow out of visiting him over and over again, but he had let her. And he hadn't come to visit her either.

You didn't fight for her, a voice in his head said. Instead of arguing with Ellie, he turned and walked away from her and his mom, needing a moment to collect himself. He would let Ellie see his anger but not his tears.

He walked over to the bank of windows that made up the back wall of the waiting area. From where he stood, he could see Charlotte stretching for miles. The emergency helicopter slept on the helipad below where he stood, blissfully unneeded. Seeing that helicopter made him think about the terrible, devastating things that happened to people every day. About the people who had watched someone they love be carried away, praying they would survive. He was thankful he wasn't in that place. It occurred to him that maybe God was giving him a second chance to be a good father, even if he wasn't sure he deserved one.

———

A nurse entered the waiting room. "We're finished with our testing. The doctor says you are allowed back in," she announced to the group. No one else sat in the waiting area but their family. "You can go in two at a time."

Ellie stood up automatically, brushed the crumbs from the pretzels she had been chomping on from her pants, and took her husband Oz's hand. She looked pointedly at Campbell, baiting him to challenge her decision to go first.

Two minutes later Ellie walked back into the waiting area, distraught. She singled Campbell out and pointed toward the direction of Nikki's hospital room. "She wants to see *you*," she said sarcastically. She sank into the nearest chair with a flourish.

"Apparently I'm not what she wants at all," she sobbed into her hands. LaRae moved to pat Ellie on the back and make soothing noises while Campbell made his exit. He left the scene to his sweet, forgiving, gentle mother. She had a lot more patience with Ellie than he did.

He entered the room quietly, even though he knew she wasn't sleeping. Nikki lay on her side, her back to the doorway. She looked so tiny in the bed, wrapped in white sheets, her silhouette not much bigger than an elementary school child's. His face registered how much his daughter had shrunk since he saw her last. Had she seen his expression, she would have noticed his fear, his uncertainty as to how to proceed. He took a moment to collect himself before he spoke her name, mentally smoothing out the worry lines on his face. He wanted to *appear* capable of handling this situation—which was pretty much how he had approached every aspect of fatherhood since he stumbled into it seventeen years ago. He tried to act the part.

"Nikki?" he asked into the silence of the room, his voice sounding as ragged and broken as he felt. She didn't answer. He moved to her bedside and placed his hand on her shoulder. "Nikki?" he asked again, a bit louder but still barely above a whisper. She shifted a bit under his hand as though it bothered her, resting on her thin shoulder. She did not roll over to face him.

"I go by Nicole now," she said flatly. "No one calls me Nikki anymore," she added.

He left his hand on her shoulder and bent down to kiss her cheek. Her skin smelled like the hospital. "Well," he added, hoping she would take it right, that he did not overstep his absentee-father bounds, "I do."

They remained still and quiet for a while. Campbell shifted his weight awkwardly from foot to foot, feeling like a nervous suitor struggling to find the right words, make the right move. She wiped several silent tears from her eyes. He wondered how long they would stay in silence.

"Do you need anything?" he finally asked her, hoping she would order a double cheeseburger with fries. He felt like he needed a break anyway. He needed to escape for a moment, to collect himself. Then he realized it: All his life he had taken the escape route.

She held up her arm with the IV. "They are pretty much force-feeding me," she said as she rolled over to face him.

He could see the bones of her face, a thin layer of skin covering them; her eyes sunken, black circles accentuating the hollows. She was still, oddly enough, quite beautiful, a helpless waif in need of rescue.

Her voice sounded shaky when she spoke again. "I'm sorry you had to come all this way." She looked away from him, ashamed, mumbling a word that sounded like "stupid" to herself. He didn't dare ask if she meant him, or herself.

He knew he had a choice in that moment. Step away and maintain the distance between them, cheapening what they once had even further and giving her permission to separate herself from him even more. Or step in and wrap his arms around her, tell her he wouldn't want to be anywhere else. His reaction would tell the tale of where he and his daughter were headed. He thanked God for this insight even as he stepped into the gap between them—which felt something like jumping off a cliff—and buried his head in her shoulder, the closest thing he could get to a hug with her lying in a tiny ball. He half expected her to push him away and roll back over, but she didn't. Slowly, she brought her arms up and around him, carefully navigating around the IV line and laughing self-consciously as she did.

He pulled back slightly to look her in the eyes. "I don't know how this happened," he said, gesturing at the bed and room. "But I am going to do whatever it takes to help you get better."

She nodded soberly, her eyes filling with tears that this time she didn't bother to wipe away. "Will you get me out of here?" she asked in a little-girl voice he hadn't heard in a long, long time, music to his ears. In her eyes he saw his potential to be her hero. The trouble was that he saw himself as the opposite of a hero—a failure at everything he had ever done that mattered—loving Lindsey, being a husband to Ellie, and a father to Nikki.

He found it within himself to tell her what she wanted to hear. "Yes," he told her. "Yes, I will get you out of here. And I will help you get well." He smiled at her, willing her to smile back, to reassure him that they would be okay, that time lost would be restored, that if they both tried they could fix things.

"Campbell?" he heard his name being called from behind him. Ellie's voice grated on his ears like sandpaper and steel wool. He turned to face her briefly before turning back to Nikki. He would not let Ellie make this about her. "Sorry to interrupt this father-daughter moment, but the doctor needs to speak with us," she said. He heard the whoosh of the hospital door being closed and intuitively knew it was a good thing that hospital doors could not be slammed.

He looked down at Nikki as she rolled her eyes at her mother. "Well, I guess I need to go talk to the doctor now. I am going to see about getting you out of here, okay?" He tried not to sound like he was speaking to a small child. He wanted to pretend he saw her as the adult she believed herself to be.

She nodded and closed her eyes, an unspoken permission for him to go.

"I'll be right back," he told her as he backed out of the room, keeping his eyes on her tiny form.

Ellie waited for him in the hall, all but tapping her foot. He brushed past her, determined to ignore her theatrics. She followed on his heels, nervous energy emanating from her as they walked down the corridor toward the waiting room.

"Did she say anything?" Ellie asked.

He slowed down and looked over at Ellie. Her hair fell from the slick ponytail. Her eyes were red-rimmed. Most of her carefully applied makeup from that morning seemed to have melted away. She looked more … human than normal. He couldn't help but feel sorry for her—the only other person in the world who sat in the same boat he was in. She was the parent of a young woman who had been hospitalized for reasons she didn't quite understand but nevertheless felt guilty for. She just wanted to know why and how and what. Just like him.

"No," he told her, willing his voice to sound as kind as possible. "Not really."

She shook her head, not believing him. Campbell could tell that Ellie thought he and Nikki had been trading secrets, swapping jokes. Bonding.

Just before they reached the doctor and Oz, he put his hand on Ellie's shoulder. "I think she just wanted to know we were both really here," he told her. "She knew you would be here. She wasn't sure I would be."

Ellie sized him up for a moment, then her eyes flickered over to Oz, who had stopped talking and watched them, his eyes narrowed.

"Okay, Campbell," she said. She glanced at him, a flash of something old and long dead passing between them. "Thanks for the reassurance." She paused. "I hate that I needed it. From you." She added the defensive jab before going to stand beside her husband, who wrapped his arm around her waist proprietarily and nodded smugly in Campbell's direction. Campbell walked over and joined them.

The doctor told them that Nikki would be released the next day. He explained in a grave voice that she was at 82 percent of what would be considered normal body weight for her height, a classic indicator of an eating disorder. When she was admitted, her liver enzymes were elevated and her electrolytes were imbalanced, telling them she had been starving herself for a while.

He gave treatment options and recommended that they discuss them with Nikki, advising that treatments work better with the patient actively involved in her own recovery. There were a variety of programs to consider, both inpatient and outpatient. Campbell could tell by the way Ellie shook her head that an inpatient program was not up for discussion. He would not fight her on that. He hated the thought of his daughter living in a hospital. Oz just nodded his head, acting the supreme expert in all things medical. Campbell suppressed the urge to deck him.

The doctor bustled away, on to other important business. Campbell's mother came up behind him and whispered, "Let's go see our girl" before heading in the direction of Nikki's room. He followed her without looking to Ellie or Oz for approval. His mother knocked lightly, and he heard Nikki's faint voice say, "Come in." She sat in the darkened room with only the TV for light. The sound was off, but she stared at it blankly, the colors flashing on her face, blue then green then pink. When she saw her grandmother, her mouth bent into a smile that he knew melted his mother's heart.

He hung back as the women hugged. "Oh my sweet little sunshine girl," his mom said, a nickname she had given Nikki when she was a ponytailed toddler with chubby cheeks.

Both women looked over at Campbell. "Can you get me out of here?" Nikki asked.

"The doctor said you can go home tomorrow," he told her.

She nodded, pleased with this information. She looked up at her grandmother and over at him. "I've had a lot of time to think today," Nikki said, scooching herself up to a sitting position, looking more like the Nikki who lived in his head—sweet, calm, confident, and in control. "And I don't want to go back home with Mom." She paused and looked at their faces for a reaction. He willed his face to remain expressionless. "I've been thinking about how long it's been since I've been to Sunset," she continued, "and how that's like my real home, you know? Where I was born?"

They both nodded their heads vigorously, like a set of bobble-head dolls.

"So, I think that I would like to go there to just hang out and get, um, help or whatever the doctor said I needed. Do you think there might be a place that could help me around there?" she asked, her face betraying her purported confidence, a little girl thrust into a scary situation. Not nearly as capable and in control as she would like others to think.

Campbell knew he couldn't change their situation. He couldn't make his daughter not have anorexia or go back in time and become a good husband to Ellie. But he could do something now. He realized that God gave second chances whether we deserve them or not. He looked over at his mom, a plan forming in his mind as they made eye contact. *We will do this together,* she said with her eyes.

He walked the three steps over to his daughter's bedside and took her hand. "I think I know just the place," he said.

Chapter 10

Sunset Beach
Summer 2004

Lindsey and the kids' second day at the beach was rained out, much to the disappointment of Anna and Jake, who were all suited up and ready to bodysurf when the skies suddenly turned gray. Lindsey eyed the novel she brought in delicious anticipation of a few hours of sun and escape, but no such luck today. Anna slumped on the couch, her face a mixture of sadness and anger. Jake shrugged his shoulders and reached for a fourth doughnut. Lindsey was glad that she had biked up to the market early that morning when the weather was nice to pick up Sweet Sixteens as a surprise. Thankfully, she didn't spot Bill.

Lindsey's mind reached deep into its catalog of "Plan Bs" and scanned through their rainy-day options. A movie in town? A trip to the grocery store on the mainland to pick up supplies they needed? She envisioned the mad dash for the car in the pouring rain, arms laden with packages while the children complained about getting drenched. That did not sound like a good option.

She hoped the morning rainstorm would pass soon and the sky would clear in time for them to be at the beach by lunch. She remembered the board games she had packed in hopes that they could play together instead of relying so much on electronics for their entertainment.

"How about we play a game of Sequence?" she asked, willing her voice to sound excited and eager about the option.

Anna and Jake shook their heads in unison. "You don't play Sequence with us, Mom," Jake said. "That's Daddy's game."

Lindsey bristled defensively. While Grant did play the game with them more often than she did, she *had* played it with them before.

"Oh, come on, it'll be fun," she said, false brightness edging her voice. "Besides, what else is there to do?"

She looked from Jake to Anna, daring them to come up with a better alternative than the one she had proposed. Jake shrugged again and seemed to think better of the idea. He looked over at Anna, deferring to her leadership as always. *Please,* Lindsey willed her. But instead of answering, Anna got up and left the room, slamming her bedroom door. Jake looked back at Lindsey, his eyebrows raised.

She laughed at him in spite of herself. "Well, we can still play, can't we?"

Lindsey managed to win one game, but Jake won the next two. "I'm just getting warmed up," he said after the first round, giving an evil chuckle as he rubbed his hands together.

"Hey, what about showing your old mom some mercy?" she teased.

"No can do, *Mamacita*!" he replied, smiling at her, looking so much like his daddy that her heart broke just a little bit more.

She remained resolute though, and to her son's credit, she didn't let him win. He beat her fair and square. By the time they finished their last game, it was time for lunch. Jake sat by the window, staring out at the rain forlornly. "I wish you could make it stop raining," he said to Lindsey, his lip poked out like a three-year-old's would.

There were many moments in her life when she realized that nothing made her feel more helpless than wanting to change the world for her kids yet knowing that she was powerless to do so. There were a lot of things in life that she wished she could change for them. Like the weather. Like the bullies who pick on them on the playground. Like freckles or curly hair or whatever they disliked about themselves. Like a daddy who had decided he wanted to "pursue other options." But Lindsey didn't say any of those things to her son. She simply nodded and said that, if she could, she would certainly make it stop raining.

She made them grilled cheese sandwiches for lunch and whispered a prayer for it to stop raining, just in case the Lord felt like orchestrating a miracle for a desperate single mom. She knew He had wars to stop and sick people to heal, but sometimes He still paused for her silly little requests. Gratefulness filled her heart when He did. She went to Anna's room to tell her to come to lunch, not expecting to hear her crying on the other side of the door.

"Go. Away." Lindsey heard her muffled reply, but Anna had to know Lindsey would do no such thing.

Surprisingly, Anna's bedroom door was not locked. Lindsey entered to find her daughter splayed across the bed, all long arms and legs like a little colt. She hated her long legs and often complained about being too tall and gangly.

"I wish I was short, like Emily," Anna had said more than once, comparing herself to her friends just like Lindsey used to do. Emily had a tiny and compact body, with the beginnings of a figure already. The boys had started to notice Emily, asking her to be their girlfriend; her newest admirer changing so often that Lindsey had stopped trying to keep up. But no one noticed Anna. She had never been asked to be anyone's girlfriend. So she looked at Emily and wanted what she had, wanted to be Emily instead of herself. Lindsey struggled with how to help her daughter see her own beauty. She had struggled with that when things were normal—even more after her father walked out. In the best of circumstances, parenting was hard. In the worst, well, sometimes it just felt impossible.

Lindsey lay down on the bed beside her daughter, not saying a word, though she wanted to ask her a million questions. She had learned that waiting silently often yielded better results, to let her daughter take the lead in the conversation; a gentle dance they were still picking up the steps to. Sometimes she stepped on Anna's toes, sometimes Anna stepped on hers. Lindsey picked up the end of Anna's long ponytail, wrapping it around her fingertips like she used to when Anna was little.

In the quiet, Lindsey counted the dots on the ceiling, listened for sounds in the kitchen—the water running in the sink, a bag of something being opened, the sound of the TV being turned on, then Jake's laughter following. When she was not much older than Anna, she had slept in the same room, stared at the same ceiling, listened to her aunt's and uncle's voices from the kitchen and wished in vain that they were her real family. It seemed hard to believe that her daughter was nearing the age she was when she first came to Sunset Beach.

When she met her first love. Just as her thoughts were about to carry her back in time, Anna turned to face her.

"I hate being here without Daddy," Anna said, not so much wiping her eyes as swiping at them angrily.

There it was.

Lindsey had tried to read books about single parenting in the months since Grant left, listened to advice from experts and took advice from other moms who had walked in her lonely shoes. Some suggested telling the kids everything, while others recommended telling them nothing. But lately she had learned to go with her gut. She answered from her heart.

"Me too, honey," she said.

Anna looked surprised. "Then why don't you invite him? Maybe if he knew we missed him …" her voice trailed off, already knowing the answer but refusing to lose hope that her real dad still existed somewhere and this other guy was just an impostor. Lindsey knew how she felt.

"Sweetie, your dad knows that he is welcome here. He knows we came down here just like we always do. I would love to tell you that inviting him would help but it just wouldn't. I can't explain it any better than that. Because the truth is, I don't understand all that has happened either. But one thing I can tell you. Your dad still loves you very—"

Anna stopped Lindsey, putting her hand out in the space between them, like a crossing guard. "Mom, please stop saying that. 'Cause it's not really true. If Dad loves me like you say, he wouldn't hurt me like this. I don't think that he really loves any of us. I think that he loves himself and doing what he wants is all that matters now.

But that's not what real love is. If he loved me, he wouldn't make me feel this bad. 'Cause when you love someone, you care about how they feel too."

Out of the mouths of babes.

Grant didn't witness the ugly parts of their divorce like Lindsey did. He didn't hold his daughter while she cried or try to handle her anger when it welled up to the point of spewing out, usually at Lindsey. Anna didn't feel comfortable enough with Grant to lash out at him. Lindsey got the ugly part of it, and he got to live in denial. Hardly a fair bargain seeing as how she never wanted any of it.

She pulled her daughter close, kissed the top of her head. Her older child. Her only daughter. She had vowed she would make life different for her. She had done everything right—taken her to church, gone to parenting conferences, and been involved with every bit of her child's life. She had given up on dreams of a career so she could pour herself into her daughter's life, never missing a moment. And yet she still couldn't save her from heartbreak. Outside forces still blew into their lives and knocked them off course. Lindsey shuddered to realize once again just how helpless they all were when it came down to it.

"Sweetie, I'm going to pray for you—for us—okay?"

Anna looked up, her expression a combination of hesitance and anticipation. "Okay."

Lindsey wrapped her arms around her daughter and offered as honest a prayer as she could. She confessed their sadness about Grant and asked for better times in the future, even for a good time at the beach. Even if Anna wasn't listening, or participating, the prayer felt necessary for Lindsey. She felt closer to her daughter—and to God—at that moment than she had in quite some time.

She finished praying just as they heard a knock at Anna's bedroom door. "Hey, guys," Jake said as he burst in the room, hopping from one foot to the other in a little dance that was "so Jake." "The rain stopped! The sun's out! Let's go!"

Anna looked at Lindsey with wide eyes. Gratitude for this simplest of gifts flooded Lindsey's body. As she began to once again gather their beach paraphernalia, she added a PS to her prayer. "Thank You," she whispered.

⌒

The beach felt amazingly bearable for a late July day. The morning rainstorms had cooled things down, and the sun peeked through the clouds just as Lindsey settled down on her beach chair and put on some SPF 15. As she rubbed the lotion into her skin, memories filled her mind of other times on the beach, times when she was younger and the scent of suntan oil was an aphrodisiac. She could remember a time when she would slather herself with baby oil and spray her hair with lemon juice, spending whole days cooking herself in the sun's warmth, transforming herself to a deep brown color, the ends of her hair kissed by sunlight. But that was before all the news stories about the harmful effects of the sun's rays. She had since learned to play things a lot safer.

Shielding her eyes from the sun, she looked up just in time to watch Anna catch a wave on her boogie board. She rode it almost all the way into shore before being wiped out by another, stronger wave.

Lindsey couldn't save her from that wave any more than she could save her from the other waves in life. But she could prepare her for those waves. Just like the sunscreen lotion she covered her with and the swim lessons she gave her, she could try to protect her from the things that came along and threatened to pull her under. And she could be there when she fell. She could cup her chin with her hand and tell her that she was still beautiful and treasured. By Lindsey and by God. She wondered how things in her life would have turned out if her mom had done that even once.

Anna came running up to their little compound of towels and toys and chairs on the beach, dripping wet, her nose running and eyes tearing. She reached out blindly for a towel, expecting her mom to provide it as she did. "You took quite a fall out there," Lindsey mused, her voice teasing as she added, "think you can go out there and try it again?" Anna looked up from wiping her eyes, a resolute look on her face, nodding vigorously as she threw the towel to the side and raced back to the water. As she ran, she called out over her shoulder, "Watch me, Mom!"

Jake waved at Lindsey as he straddled his board, waiting for his next ride from a wave. She waved back and picked up her book, hoping to get in some reading. But as the day unfolded—with her kids drawing her attention away between every few lines—Lindsey eventually realized she averaged a page an hour and put the book down. She resolved that she would read later, when the kids were settled down watching the Disney Channel back at the house.

At 4:00, she waved Anna and Jake in. They had had enough sun, wind, and waves. Even they knew it was time to call it a day and came without argument. Wrapped in towels, they made their way to the beach house with Lindsey pulling the wagon full of sand toys, the cooler, and the boogie boards—all piled on precariously. She led their slow procession down the street; the kids besting each other with stories of who rode the longest and got the highest wave.

"Mom, what's for dinner?" Jake asked, a question that still came faithfully every evening, no matter what changed in their lives.

"I thought I'd make hot dogs," she replied, reaching out to stop the top boogie board from falling off the wagon.

He pondered that for a moment. "Can we have mac and cheese too?" he asked hopefully.

"Sure, why not?" she answered.

"Yesss!" he said and waved the towel he carried in the air.

After they were inside and dressed in sweats, the kids settled in with a movie while she made hot dogs and macaroni and cheese. She realized she had barely thought about Grant all day. While at the beach, she hadn't worried about the future or wondered if they would ever work things out. She hadn't begged God to restore their marriage or change Grant's heart. She hadn't wished Grant was there, and she hadn't wallowed in her own sadness. With the change in weather had come a change in attitude for both her and her children. Their hope had returned with the sun. Her prayer, she knew, had been heard.

As she stirred the neon orange powder into the macaroni, she realized that she would never get away with serving a meal like that if Grant were with them. If he were there, she would have stressed about putting something delicious and nutritious on the table. But the kids couldn't have cared less. In fact, they preferred hot dogs with lots of ketchup and boxed macaroni and cheese. For the briefest moment—the barest flicker—she felt a little bit happy to be there without Grant, in her favorite place in all the world, with her children, enjoying a quiet evening. A smile spread on her face. And as she settled into bed that night alone, she determined that the place was already working its magic.

Chapter 11

Chapel Hill, NC
Fall 1989

College wasn't everything Lindsey had hoped it would be, but it was better than living at home. She could even tolerate occasionally talking with her mother once they no longer lived in the same house. Her mom seemed to derive a vicarious thrill out of her daughter's college life. Lindsey could hear the longing in her voice as she asked her to describe the classes, the campus, the parties.

Lindsey looked around at her surroundings and wondered how she could make this one sound exciting. The dark basement of the fraternity house was hardly the scene for a romantic encounter. And still Lindsey scanned the crowd. Though she went on a few dates in high school and college, no one she had met made her heart hammer the way Campbell had … yet. She still held out hope at every party, every mixer with her sorority, every new class she walked into. That somewhere, waiting for her, was a man who would bring her the happiness she used to feel.

Her roommate, Heather, walked up to her and bumped her shoulder. "Hey," she said. "This party is lame. This fraternity is lamer. You wanna leave?" Heather yawned for emphasis in her drama-major way.

Lindsey cast another glance around the room and saw a guy standing beside the keg, dispensing drinks, smiling right at her. It was a smile filled with possibility. "You can go," she told Heather. "I'm going to stick around."

Heather shrugged her shoulders. "Ohhhkaaay. See you back at the room?"

"I'll be there," Lindsey said over her shoulder, already walking toward the guy, whose gaze still held hers. As she gave him a demure half-smile, she added, "Eventually," though Heather was already gone.

She handed him her empty cup. "More, please," she said.

"Wow. Polite!" he said, taking the cup from her hand and filling it with a flourish. "I like that in a girl."

She accepted the full cup from him, their fingers brushing as she did. She felt what could only be described as an electrical jolt.

"Thanks," she mumbled, trying not to slurp the foam and staring into her beer. She didn't really like beer, but it was the drink of choice in college. Holly, who was tucked away at a Christian college, chastised her for drinking at all. Holly's wholesome world was filled with mission-trip meetings, rousing games of cards, and Christian concerts. Lindsey's was filled with parties like these, each one like the one before. She missed Holly and was already thinking of what she would tell her about this encounter. That Lindsey was deigning to talk to him was an improvement. There was something about him. Something … different that she couldn't put her finger on, yet.

"I'm Grant Adams," he said, interrupting her thoughts. "And you are?"

"Oh sorry." She sheepishly extended her hand. "I'm Lindsey Porter." He took her hand in his warm, soft one. The electricity was there. "Are you a brother here?" she asked.

He nodded and looked around. "It's not much, but we call it home." His tone was genuine as he gestured to the nearly empty room, and her eyes followed his hand. A few chairs lined the walls and a decrepit pool table had been shoved into the corner where a few guys were playing. One of them poked the other with the end of his pool stick and then waved in their direction.

She smiled at Grant and noticed again how attractive he was, and how familiar he seemed. "Have we had a class together? I feel like maybe we've met," she ventured.

He shook his head. "I don't think so." He took a sip of his own beer and handed the tap off to a fraternity brother nearby. Taking her elbow, he steered them away from the keg. "But I have to say, I had the same feeling when I saw you across the room a minute ago. That I already knew you somehow." He shook his head and smiled. "I guess that sounds crazy."

"No," she said, smiling back. "I know exactly what you mean. It's not that you look familiar, you seem familiar, like I knew you—"

"In another life?" he offered with a smile.

"No," she said. He looked back at her with an intensity she hadn't seen in another person's eyes in a long time. "Definitely in this one."

The music changed to the Dire Straits' "The Sultans of Swing," a song she would forever equate with the moment she knew she would marry Grant Adams.

"I hope you'll let me get to know you in this life, Lindsey Porter," he said. He grabbed her hand to lead her to the makeshift dance floor, in a basement that no longer seemed dark and dingy, but as bright as a brand-new day.

Sunset Beach
Summer 1990

Dear Kindred Spirit,

I think I have found "the one." Did you already know that? Could you sense it was coming? I like to think that you could. You have become a trusted friend to me, Kindred Spirit, even though we have never met. I actually like the mystery of wondering who you are. That way I can imagine you the way I want you to be. There is no disappointment in imagining.

Sometimes I imagine that you are watching this all unfold, somehow making sure that I do the right thing and that I don't miss opportunities that come my way. Holly says that I give you too much credit … that God is the only one who can orchestrate our lives. Part of me believes it—I see Holly's faith and there's something so … true *about it. But I guess I haven't caught the bug or something. Yet you seem familiar to me—more familiar than God. Most of the time, God seems very far away.*

Anyway, my boyfriend's name is Grant. We have been dating for nine months. I have known since we met that we would get married. It's just a matter of when. Grant says he knows it too.

He is so sweet and attentive. I am discovering that love doesn't have to blindside you. It can be a sweet experience. Falling in love doesn't have to feel like jumping off a cliff. It can feel like gliding on a porch swing: gentle and easy. Grant makes it easy for me to trust him. I can sit beside him and see our future spreading out in front of us, dependable and steady: kids, house, bills, the whole thing. We are blessed to have found each other.

Someday I will come back here and tell you I am engaged. And then I will come and tell you about my wedding. And my first child. I see you sharing in my whole life and I am thankful that you are a part of it. It doesn't seem like it happens until I tell you.

Until next year,
Lindsey

Chapter 12

Charlotte
Summer 2004

That night, long after Campbell's mom fell asleep in the hotel suite's king bed and he settled in the sofa bed, Campbell sat awake, surfing through TV channels with the sound turned off. In the next room, through the closed door, he could hear his mom softly snoring—something she always denied doing, but his father teased her about. Campbell wished that his father was there, that he could ask him what to do, how to be a good father in this situation.

As he looked out the window, he saw the skyline of Charlotte. He felt further from home than he really was, miles from where he belonged, as though Charlotte were another country and not just a three-and-a-half-hour drive away. And yet, he was where he was supposed to be, where his father would want him: making amends for his own failures the best way he knew how. As he thought about Nikki, about the phone calls he would make in the morning and the certain argument he would have with Ellie when he mentioned taking her back to Sunset with him, somehow his thoughts, as they always did, wandered back to Lindsey.

He knew that his feelings for her had always been wrapped up in his story, in the story of Ellie and Nikki and the choices he had made, one big tangled mess that he couldn't escape. He thought of the irony that he had been called away from Sunset the very week he knew she would be there. He thought of how her yearly trip was also part of his story—he always knew she'd be there, but they always kept their distance. He had never run into Lindsey at the beach, and he knew it was intentional not only on his part, but on hers too.

He clicked off the TV and stood, still wearing his khaki shorts but no shirt. He dug around on the floor and found the T-shirt he had worn all day, slipping it on and tiptoeing out of the room, pocketing the card key first.

The hotel lobby was nearly deserted, save for a young couple sitting close together on the sofa, her leg draped across him, his arms wrapped around her. He thought about making a joke: "Get a room." He doubted they would think it was funny. The front-desk clerk, a young, pimply faced kid who didn't make eye contact when he checked them in earlier, glanced up from a gaming magazine as Campbell strolled through the lobby on his way to the "business center," which was basically a glorified closet with one computer and a printer in it. The printer had a hand-lettered sign that read "All copies, 5 cents each." The handwriting looked like a kindergartner wrote it, but he suspected it was the front-desk clerk's penmanship.

He logged on to the computer and accessed his email account, then skimmed through the emails he missed for the day—all work related except one note from a woman in his small group at church, who he knew would like to be more than friends. She asked him to have coffee, which, in the grown-up dating world was code for "Let's meet somewhere that is not as formal as dinner and see if we're compatible."

He didn't feel like composing a reply to her, one that skillfully said, "I am not a jerk" but also "I am not interested, but please don't take it personally because you are a great person."

He thought briefly about just writing her the truth: "Dear Veronica, you are really sweet and pretty and seem to be a lot of fun. In fact, because you are all of those things, you probably should not get involved with me. For character references who will verify this fact, please contact Ellie Kessler or Lindsey Adams. They will be happy to fill you in on the details of how I will not live up to your expectations. Sincerely, Campbell Forrester."

He pushed the thought away and scanned his contacts to find Michelle Parrish's address, then plugged it into a new email form. Michelle, on the other hand, had been someone he had considered getting involved with. She was a counselor who used to go to his church. They had gone on a few dates before she moved away to start a new counseling center at a bigger church in another town. Though their relationship hadn't worked out, they had stayed in touch. In the subject line, he typed "help" and in the body of the email he wrote:

"Hey, it's too late to call as I write this, but I need some help—some professional help—for my daughter. Please call me on my cell whenever you get this."

He hit Send and leaned back in the chair, satisfied that he had done something to get the ball rolling. He knew Michelle could help him formulate a plan of action, to make a case for him to take on the responsibility of taking Nikki home, to convince Ellie and Oz and even his mom that he could handle it. Never mind that he didn't know if he could.

As he stood up to make his way back to his room, his cell phone rang, the techno beat shattering the silence of the lobby. The happy couple looked his way, startled. He raised his hand in apology before snapping the phone open. *Michelle, bless you.*

"Hey, that was fast," he said.

"What? Is this Campbell?" For the second time that day he had answered one of Ellie's calls without checking first. A stellar way to start and end the day.

"Oh, hey, Ellie. Yeah, it's me," he said. He exhaled loudly, not bothering to hide his frustration. Willing himself to sound kinder than he felt, he asked, "What's up? Is Nikki okay?"

She lowered her voice. "I'm sorry to call so late. I'm glad I didn't wake you. Were you waiting on your girlfriend to call or something?"

He detected the barest hint of jealousy in her voice. It was so like Ellie to not want him, yet not want anyone else to have him either.

"No, nothing like that. I was making some inquiries … about Nikki, actually," he said, wondering as he said it if it was a mistake to admit that yet. If she would pounce on him, accuse him of sticking his nose where it didn't belong, or degrade his efforts at being a father as being too little, too late. All accusations he probably deserved.

"Oh, well, that's why I called. I had to wait until Oz fell asleep. I didn't want him to hear me, because I know he will disagree with what I am about to say. That's why I didn't want to discuss this at the hospital tomorrow with him around."

He found himself nodding as she spoke, even though she couldn't see him.

"I talked to Nikki tonight, and she told me that she asked you to take her back to Sunset with you." He steeled himself for the onslaught of her rage, the how-could-you-tell-her-that-you-would-take-her-without-talking-to-me-first explosion. "And I just wanted to say that, actually, I think that's a great idea. I think she needs some time with you and your mom, needs the slower pace of the beach. She could spend the month of August there and, depending on how things go, go to college at the end of the summer."

Campbell stood in silence for a moment, his mouth left open in utter shock. He exhaled again, this time out of sheer relief. He never expected it to be that easy.

"I have to say, Ellie," he answered, "I'm surprised to hear that. And I really do think that going with me will be best for her. And I am not just saying that because I want to be with her." He paused for a moment, weighing whether to reveal his fear. "Frankly, it scares me to death."

"The whole thing scares me, Campbell. Nikki needs help. She needs counseling."

He paused in the lobby, not wanting to lose the call by stepping into the elevator. With his back to the desk clerk, he thanked Ellie for letting him take her without a fight. "I won't let you or Nikki down," he promised her.

"Oh, Campbell," she replied, a trace of wistfulness in her voice, "you never have let me down. I did enough of that for the both of us. Just take care of her," she said hurriedly, and then she was gone.

By the time Campbell arrived at the hospital the next morning, he had arranged for Nikki's counseling at his church to begin the next day. Michelle agreed to make some phone calls and found a counselor who had specific training in dealing with teens with anorexia, a woman he had volunteered with at an event once, never realizing that in the future she could save the day. Although, over the years, he had grown used to God's little coincidences, he wondered if God took distinct pleasure in those moments, if He rubbed His hands together in anticipation, enjoying the drama as it slowly unfolded.

Ellie hugged Campbell's mother, thanked her again for coming, then looked at him. Her eyes looked tired, weak, missing the storm that usually brewed within them.

He followed Ellie into Nikki's room. As he watched Ellie embrace Nikki, telling her good-bye through tears, he felt the closest thing to real love he had ever felt for Ellie. He grabbed the suitcase of Nikki's things and followed Ellie, Nikki, and his mother—three women he'd be forever connected to—out to the parking lot. His mom cried a little as they pulled away; she, Nikki, and Campbell crammed into the front cab of his truck—his mother in the middle. A buffer. Nikki remained stoic, staring out the window. She sipped quietly on a Diet Coke he bought for her at a gas station, but otherwise she didn't move.

He could remember once, right after Nikki went to live with Ellie and he drove to Charlotte to pick her up. According to Ellie, Garrett had been intolerably colicky and she couldn't even meet Campbell halfway on the drive. Ellie had shouted at Campbell over

Garrett's crying in the background, "I realize you want time with Nikki, Campbell. But if you want her, you will just have to drive here and get her." The conversation left him feeling bitter about the long drive—he really hated leaving Sunset—but also the slightest bit vengeful that Ellie and Oz's baby was a screamer. They deserved it. *Ha ha,* he mouthed to the receiver after she had hung up, feeling childish as he did.

As he drove with his seven-year-old daughter in the backseat, he asked Nikki if Garrett cried a lot, though he already knew the answer. He admittedly took sadistic pleasure in hearing the realities of the life Ellie had chosen for herself. Nikki chattered on incessantly about how much she hated that baby, how he had ruined everything. She hardly stopped talking the whole way to Sunset. When they arrived, he handed her off to his mother and went out to stand by the ocean to gather his wits. He wondered if taking Nikki off Ellie's hands was a blessing to her instead of the sacrifice he thought—one less noisemaker in her house.

That night they ate in Calabash with Campbell's parents, a town famous for its abundance of restaurants specializing in fried seafood. They stopped for ice cream on the way home, a tradition Nikki wouldn't ever let them forget. He and Nikki sat in the backseat like the children they were while his mom and dad drove them around, proud of their impish granddaughter, never tiring of her chatter. They delighted in her off-key singing, the made-up lyrics, the songs repeated over and over while he tired of them. They cleaned up her messes without complaint while he wanted to tear his hair out. They didn't get flustered when she made demands or threw fits. He wondered how they did it, where they got the calm, unflappable state of mind he seemed to be missing in dealing with his daughter. He felt like a failure.

The night before he drove the seven-hour round-trip to take Nikki back to Charlotte, his father sat down beside him on the couch where he had flopped, unmoving—exhausted from Nikki's bedtime routine. One more story, one more song, one more drink of water. She had worn him out.

Campbell's father patted his arm. "I know you don't believe it," he said, "but it goes so fast. You may be in your early twenties now, but soon enough, you'll be forty. You'll look up and suddenly your kid is an adult. And then you wish you could go back and do it all over. And do it right."

Campbell gestured toward Nikki's bedroom, where he hoped she was sleeping. "Is that where you get your patience? The benefit of hindsight? A chance to have a do-over?"

His dad laughed. "I'd say so, yeah." Sobering, his father added, "One day, you'll wish for these days back. You'll think that they were the simple days, when you had no worries."

Campbell had just shaken his head then, unbelieving. But now, in the truck with his mom and daughter sandwiched beside him, he knew that what his father had said was true. He longed for his little girl back—the girl full of life and words and mindless chatter, a smile always on her face, her feelings visible for all to see. He mourned that she was now locked away from him in a place he couldn't reach. He wished he could do it all over again, and appreciate it this time around. He wished he could see being a parent as a blessing he entered into knowingly instead of being thrust upon him by simple biology.

As they approached Sunset, he pushed aside the thoughts of what had been, or what could be, and focused on what was—something he had started learning to do. *Be here*, he told himself. *Be present. Don't miss this.* Turning to see the back of his daughter's head and seeing the reflection of her sad face in the window, he thought of the most important reminder of all: *Don't miss her.* He was painfully aware that it might just be his last, best chance.

Chapter 13

Sunset Beach
Summer 2004

Early that morning, before the kids woke up, Lindsey's cell phone rang. She reached for her purse atop the nightstand and fumbled around for her phone. As she searched the overfull bag, her heart threw out a word: *Grant.* Her brain quickly overrode the thought. It wouldn't be him. He never called her anymore, and he only called the children on a cell phone he had bought for Anna, breaking his own rule about her not being allowed to have a cell phone until she turned fifteen. He had started relaying messages for Lindsey through Anna—a practice she found both repulsive and immature, but also heartbreaking. She remembered the days when she and Grant could spend hours on the phone, dreaming together of a future that looked nothing like the one they were in now.

She found her phone just as it stopped ringing. It was Jane, Grant's mother. Lindsey held the phone in her hand, staring at it like it might bite her. Should she call her back? Avoid her altogether?

After all, Jane's son had left her; "good daughter-in-law" rules didn't apply anymore. And yet, she and Jane shared an unusual relationship. Unusual in that it wasn't fraught with the bitterness and territorial battles that existed between many in-laws. Jane called their friendship "mutual admiration," which was something that didn't change with the divorce. Losing Grant meant losing much more than a husband—it meant losing the only other real family she had ever been a part of. Unlike her aunt and uncle who only welcomed her during the summers, this family had been hers every day.

After he left, to her credit, Jane had kept calling. She told Lindsey she didn't agree with Grant or support his decision. She confessed that she struggled with some serious anger toward him for breaking up his family. But she also told her that he was her son and that believing the worst about him was hard for her to swallow. "It's hard to believe he could cheat, Lindsey," she said. "I raised him better than that."

"I know you did," Lindsey had answered, rubbing Jane's shoulder as she said it, baffled that she was acting as comforter to Grant's mother. But Jane was right. Grant *was* one of the good guys. He was dependable, steadfast, honorable. He came from a good, stable family and promised to deliver the same. No one counted on him changing—morphing into someone who was unrecognizable. As time went on, she and Jane talked about Grant less and less. They talked instead about safe subjects: the kids, Jane's infinite knitting projects, the weather. Grant had reduced them from loving family to awkward acquaintances.

With a deep sigh she called Jane. While she listened to the ringing on the other end, she wondered idly, was it duty that made her call, or devotion? Probably a strange mix of both—one just as likely to outweigh the other at any given moment. She found out that, in the aftershocks of her family breaking apart, she had to sort through the pieces like a jigsaw puzzle without the picture on the box to guide her. So many shapes, so many colors, all supposed to somehow connect to form something. But what that something was remained a mystery.

Jane answered as she always had. "Hello, dear." The sound of her voice brought tears to Lindsey's eyes, but she blinked them away, pressing the heel of her hand to the bridge of her nose. The week at Sunset was about making progress, not faltering.

"Hi, Jane," she answered. "It's so good to hear from you." Was it possible to keep Jane but lose Grant?

"I just called to make sure you and the children made it to the beach safely. Are you all having a good time?"

"Yes," she said. "We are having a lovely time." She knew she didn't sound like herself. She never used words like *lovely*.

They talked for a few minutes about the beach, and Jane asked how the kids were holding up. Lindsey put on her best happy voice, trying to keep Jane's worries at bay. Jane, as it were, was not the one who had hurt the family, so Lindsey had no problem protecting her. But after awhile, Lindsey decided it would be wise to cut off the conversation before she started to break down.

"Thanks for checking on us, Jane," Lindsey said, trying not to falter. "It's nice to know someone is concerned for us."

"Honey, I always will be. You don't have to wonder about that. My son's choices don't affect my love for you or the kids."

"Thanks," she said, her voice catching in her throat. "If you talk to him," Lindsey added, feeling foolish and desperate, "please tell him we're okay. I mean, if he asks."

"I will, darlin'." She detected a note of pity in Jane's voice. "If I could just give you a word of advice." Jane charged on without waiting for her permission. "Move on with your life. Find someone to love you. Stop waiting on Grant to notice what a treasure he's lost. One thing I know: By the time he figures that out, it will be too late. That makes me sad for him, but happy for you. Because I know that there is something great waiting out there for you. Give yourself permission to be open to it, whenever it comes along. Will you promise me that?"

"Yes," Lindsey managed in a weak voice. "I'll try." A memory came to mind of Holly giving her the same advice after Campbell had married Ellie. Lindsey couldn't help but feel an intense moment of grief—she had to let another love go. How was she to ever welcome love again?

～

After the conversation with Jane was over, Lindsey padded out to the kitchen to make coffee, staring out the window like a zombie while it brewed. She tried to think of what she needed to do that day. Mile-long to-do lists filled her days back at home—phone calls to make and errands to run, children to shuttle to activities, cleaning to do. Here, her schedule was swept clean. No routine whatsoever: just her life, stripped of the fat, down to a skeleton. It occurred to her that she liked the skeleton life much better than the fat one.

As she sipped her coffee, she decided that she would go on a run while the kids were still sleeping. She pulled off a piece from the pad of paper her aunt had long ago hung on the refrigerator door, the silly words scripted elegantly across the top, "To Do." The fact that the pad had hardly been used in ten years, other than to dash off a quick grocery list, was further proof that there was just not much "to do" at Sunset. She scrounged through the junk drawer and found a tiny pencil hefted from a golf course long ago, the point barely sharp enough to scratch out her message. "Gone running," she scrawled. "Back soon. Love you, Mom." She left the note on the kitchen counter, beside a box of cereal, a hint to make some breakfast while they waited for her return.

She rummaged through her suitcase to find her running shoes, thick socks, shorts, T-shirt, and exercise bra, wondering how far she would be able to go. She had only recently gone back to running, discovering anew the freedom and energy she gained from making herself hit the pavement regularly. Two days after Grant left, she decided to run instead of cry. The weight and sadness she felt in his absence were lodged inside her—like something caught that needed to be loosened—and she hoped that the running would shake it free. That first day she ran until she nearly fell down from exhaustion. Pushing herself through exercise yielded a better release, she discovered, than sobbing. When she returned home, the sadness hadn't disappeared, but the weight she felt before she left had lessened considerably. She had missed only a few days since, craving her runs like chocolate.

Heading out the door of the beach house, she smiled as she thought about the exhilaration of running along the beach. *If this is all there is*, she thought, *it could be enough. Maybe.*

She turned up her headphones and let the music fill her ears and heart. She breathed in the salty air, letting it seep in like a promise. Her legs pumped, and her feet hit the pavement in a melodic rhythm. In a moment of spontaneity, she changed her course and turned in the direction of a house she had avoided for the last twenty years. Feeling young and alive, she ran toward it with all of her might.

Lindsey felt like a stalker as she made her way down Campbell's street, still not fully understanding why she was there. Perhaps it was because Jane's words to her about moving on had spurred thoughts of him. What was the harm, she reasoned, in taking a detour down memory lane?

She ran by with her eyes trained on the house like a spy, taking in the changes, looking for signs of life. She didn't bother to pretend that she was not looking for him, was not studying the house to see some evidence that he still lived there, which was ridiculous to think, considering the amount of time that had gone by. She felt certain that he and Ellie and their child—or children by now—had moved on.

The thought of Ellie still made her cringe. It was like she was in high school all over again. Her mind unwittingly called up the image of Ellie when they were sixteen years old, skulking around Campbell everywhere he went, pretending to be Lindsey's friend that summer so she could be close to Campbell. She remembered Ellie's long blonde hair with its spiral perm, her ankle bracelet made of puka shells, the way she giggled every time Campbell cracked a joke.

Random play on Lindsey's MP3 player brought up Peter Gabriel's song "In Your Eyes." She smiled as the music filled her headphones. So many times she and Campbell had listened to that song. She had to admit it still had an effect on her and the timing was perfect—it played just as she approached Campbell's house. She decided that a little dip in the pool of nostalgia was refreshing. She just had to make sure not to drown in it.

The house looked much the same as it did all those years ago, still white with a wide gray plank porch across the front. Someone had hung a second porch swing and the rockers were new. She guessed his mom had been the one to put red geraniums in the planters, adding a burst of color, a woman's touch. She remembered going to his house, climbing the porch stairs holding his hand, wondering what it must be like to live at Sunset all the time, to have paradise as your backyard. She remembered that Campbell seemed not to notice, crossing the porch without even looking up.

Someone had painted it recently, the white and gray paint too fresh and vivid to be the paint he coated the house with that second summer. Unbidden, a memory surfaced: Campbell on a ladder with a paintbrush in his hand, turning to grin at her, flicking white paint in her direction.

"You better not hang around here too long," he said, his smile a playful warning, "or my mom will put you to work too."

And her response, so cheesy yet, in memory, sweet, "That would be just fine if it meant I could stay with you."

She remembered standing there unself-consciously, smiling at him in her cutoff denim shorts and bikini top, the smell of the ocean perfuming her skin and the glow of a day in the sun making her radiant. She was, she could recognize now, beautiful.

She didn't notice the car slowing down behind her until she heard the crunch of tires on gravel. The driver didn't notice her standing in the driveway, causing her to jump out of the way quickly, her heart wildly hammering in her chest. Whether from the fright of nearly being hit or the embarrassment of being caught standing in Campbell's driveway, staring at his house like a lunatic, she couldn't tell. As she caught her breath, the elderly woman driving the car got out slowly, never taking her eyes off her.

"Phew!" Lindsey said to break the awkwardness. "That scared me!" She smiled as genuinely as possible, hoping the woman wouldn't think she was a weirdo. She willed her heart to slow down so she could speak normally.

The woman nodded slowly, her eyes boring into Lindsey. She wore a neon green T-shirt that said "Sunset Beach Turtle Watchers" in bold blue writing, with a big picture of a loggerhead turtle. A matching Turtle Watcher visor tamed her curly silver hair. Just the year before, Lindsey had taken the kids to one of the Turtle Watcher beach tours at night, hoping to spy some hatchlings. They didn't have any luck. She wondered absently if the woman had been there.

The woman narrowed her eyes. "Are you looking for something?" she asked.

Lindsey waved her hand in the air, feeling like an idiot. "Oh no!" she offered. "I knew someone who lived here a long time ago, and I was just walking by." She laughed for good measure, hoping to show how harmless, how totally not crazy, she was. "Guess I'll

get back to my run now," she said. "Have a nice day!" She started
to jog away.

Before she could make her exit, she heard the woman's voice,
halting her. "You're looking for Campbell." It wasn't a question,
Lindsey noticed. With her back to the woman, she grimaced before
she turned around.

The woman crossed her arms over the turtle on her T-shirt. She
acted like she already knew Lindsey. Or perhaps lots of women had
stopped by to stare at Campbell's house through the years.

Lindsey decided to play it cool, nonchalant. "I'm Lindsey," she
said and extended her sweaty hand, embarrassed to be meeting anyone in that state. She should have thought twice about stopping by
the house in her exercise garb—sweaty and smelly was not the kind
of impression she would have wanted to make.

The woman, obviously undeterred by a little sweat, shook
Lindsey's hand emphatically. "I knew it!" she exclaimed, the visor
perched on top of her head waggling up and down with her rapidly
bobbing head. "You haven't changed a bit, girl!"

"I … haven't?" she asked, confused.

"Oh no! The minute I saw you, I knew exactly who you were.
You probably don't remember me, though. I'm Campbell's mother's
oldest friend, Minerva. I used to see you all the time when you would
stop by to see Campbell. His mama and I would be playing cards
or making dinner? You were always so polite." She paused, seeming
to replay a memory in her mind as she smiled. "We liked you," she
added and smiled.

The thought of two middle-aged women playing cards floated
past her. "Oh yes! I remember now! Minerva! How great to see you!"

Minerva grinned at her conspiratorially. "You here to see Campbell after all these years?" She giggled like a schoolgirl.

"Oh no, no, nothing like that." Lindsey glanced down self-consciously at her left hand with the wedding ring she hadn't had the courage to remove yet. She slipped her arm behind her back. "I was just going on my regular run, just like always, you know, and thought I'd pass by…. Just a little walk down memory lane and all that. Or run, I guess I should say!" She laughed as though her joke was hilarious. Could she have been more transparent?

Minerva just smiled. "I see. Well, he's not here, sweetheart. Though I don't suspect you would want to see him after all these years looking like that." She gestured dismissively at Lindsey's gray knit shorts, faded church camp T-shirt, and sweaty ponytail.

A glutton for punishment, she followed up Minerva's question with a question of her own. "So, Campbell still lives here … in this house?" She wondered if a middle-aged man still living in the house he grew up in was a good thing. Where she came from, it was a sign of dysfunction.

"Yep," she said, clearly proud of Campbell for still living at home. "He stayed on with his mother to help take care of his daddy when he got cancer the first time—Lord, did his daddy give cancer a run for its money, God rest his soul! For three years he just refused to die. He was such a fighter. Do you remember him?"

Lindsey nodded. But what she remembered most wasn't the man himself, but how much Campbell looked up to him.

"Anyway, Campbell just never left after his daddy died. No reason to, I guess," she added. "His mama likes having him around to take care of things. You can imagine."

Lindsey nodded sympathetically, warning her mouth not to ask the next question even as her lips formed the words. "And his wife and daughter?" she asked, trying desperately to sound like she couldn't care less. "How are they?"

Minerva didn't seem to be worried about protecting Campbell's privacy as she gladly filled Lindsey in. "Oh that woman! She ran off and left him with that little girl years and years ago, just before his daddy got sick. Boy, was that a terrible, terrible year. She eventually came back to get Nikki and took her to live with her. Now she's married to some hotshot doctor back in Charlotte." Minerva paused, seeming to weigh her next sentence. "In fact, that's where Campbell is now. He and his mama left just yesterday to go to Charlotte. Something with his little girl—though she's not so little anymore, you know. She's quite the young lady now, about to start college."

Lindsey nodded in agreement. She sensed there was more that Minerva wasn't telling her but let it drop. Campbell's life now was, she knew, none of her business.

"Well now, you don't want to hear any more from a crazy old woman!" She held her index finger in the air as an idea seized her. "Here's what we'll do. You come back this way soon." She cut her eyes over at Lindsey, waving her hand at her running attire dismissively. "But not in that getup. Why don't you try to walk by in the evening? Just act like you were out taking a walk and I'll figure out how to make sure Campbell's outside. Just leave that to me!" Minerva smiled broadly, revealing a set of teeth that had yellowed with age. She giggled again. "I sure would love for Campbell to see you again. It'd be good for him!" She paused, as if mulling something over. "But now you should get back to your run. Great to see you!" Minerva waved quickly before turning back to her car to remove a large watering can. Lindsey noticed the hitch in the woman's step as she walked toward the porch.

Obediently, Lindsey turned and ran, shaking her head and chuckling at how odd life can be. She wondered if she would ever have the guts to do what Minerva suggested.

Chapter 14

Sunset Beach
Summer 1991

"I'm sort of surprised that you wanted to come down here with me," Lindsey said, raising her voice to be heard over the rough surf as she and Grant walked hand in hand down to the water's edge.

He smiled shyly. "Well, it's important to you so it's important to me. I keep hearing you talk about the mailbox, and I wanted to see this place for myself." He stopped walking to kiss her. "Why? Don't you want me to come with you?"

"Of course, silly. I'm glad you're with me. I want you to come along." Lindsey walked on for a few minutes in silence, wondering why after five years away from Campbell, she would still feel as if she were betraying him by bringing another man to the mailbox with her. Even someone who had become as close to her as Grant had. They had talked about getting married after graduation next year. She wanted to share everything with him. And who would Campbell be to complain about betrayal, anyway?

"So," Grant said, "what's his name?"

Lindsey looked at him, confused.

"The guy you're thinking about right now … his name?" Grant gave a patient smile.

Her eyes widened. "How did you—"

"I'm just smart that way. I can sense things, especially things about you."

She smiled at how well Grant knew her. But she couldn't help thinking about Campbell's last letter to her. He had told her to move on, to find someone to love her, someone who would know her well. Grant was that person. "His name was Campbell," she said. "And I was fifteen." She waved her hand in the air. "It was a long time ago. And he and I didn't last but two summers." There was much she was leaving out, but did that really matter?

"But the mailbox lasted a lot longer," Grant said.

"Yes. This place is very special to me. I have come back every summer. I leave a letter here this same week every year. I like to think—" she broke off, blushed—"I like to think that the Kindred Spirit looks forward to my letters every year." She laughed. "I know that sounds silly."

He pulled her to him. "If it's something you take seriously, then I take it seriously."

She pointed ahead of them. "We're almost there. I tried to warn you it was a long walk."

"So, who is the Kindred Spirit?" Grant asked as they walked the last few feet to reach the mailbox.

"That's what's so cool. No one knows. Someone comes and takes all the old notebooks out and puts in new ones, replaces all the old pens, and takes the loose letters people write. But the person's identity is a secret. It's all very mysterious, which makes it that much more fun, I think. Of course, I feel like I know her after all these years."

"Her?" Grant asked. "How do you know it's a 'her'?"

She grinned. "I don't. I just suspect it is. It's like—I don't know— It's like I can feel her here, cheering for me. It sounds stupid, I know." Lindsey made a funny face to deflect her admission.

Grant nodded but said nothing in response as he followed her up to where the mailbox stood in the dunes. She pointed to the notebook and paper in the box, taking a sheet of loose paper for herself and giving Grant the option. He took out a notebook.

"You can write about how much you love me," she said, teasing him.

He grinned. "Oh, I already have a pretty good idea of what I am going to write," he responded. He leaned in and kissed her.

Lindsey took a seat on an old log someone had set up as a bench and began to write, while Grant planted himself in the sand. She was thrilled to be there with him. She even felt a bit like the curse of Campbell was being broken once and for all by having him there.

It wasn't long before Grant walked over and sat down beside her. "I wrote down what I wanted to say," he said. "Will you read it?"

She looked at him. "Well that was quick," she said, hoping he wouldn't ask to read what she had written. Her letters were private, between her and the Kindred Spirit only. "You sure you want me to read it?"

"Absolutely." In one fluid motion he laid the open notebook on her lap and got down on one knee in the sand in front of her. There, written on the notebook page were the words "Will you marry me?"

She looked up, aghast, as he opened a black velvet box to display a diamond solitaire set in gold. She looked over at the open mailbox and smiled. Grant was perfect for her. He couldn't have chosen a better place to propose. As she nodded and said yes, she blinked away an unbidden image of Campbell's face, pushing him back to the past where he belonged.

Summer 1991

Dear Kindred Spirit,

How many years I have dreamed of the day I will write this to you: to share the exciting news that I am getting married! As I look down at the ring on my finger, how it sparkles like it is winking at me, I can hardly believe it's real. Grant brought me here under the pretense of wanting to see the mailbox, but he had something bigger planned the whole time. Do you see why he is so perfect for me? He knew the perfect place to propose to me. I love that you were part of it and that you are the first person I am telling.

Leave it to me to be a complete klutz as I am being proposed to. After he put the ring on my finger, he pulled me down toward him to kiss me. I lost my balance and fell over onto him, knocking us both into the sand. Talk about graceful! I was laughing and crying at the same time! At one point, I reached up to wipe my tears away and got sand in my eyes. But Grant, still chuckling at my clumsiness (I am so glad he finds it "cute"), reached over with his shirttail and wiped my eyes so gently and lovingly. I knew at that moment I would be safe with this man forever. I am letting myself trust him, believing that he really loves me and that this time it will last.

Well, this letter is going to have to be short because Grant is waiting on me to walk back home. I can't wait to show my ring off to my aunt and uncle. He said they knew what he was planning and he even talked to my uncle beforehand to ask his permission. Isn't that so sweet? He is so respectful and considerate. He knows that my uncle is the closest thing to a father that I have. I am going to ask him to give me away at the wedding. I am not even going to think about what my mom is going to say because I don't want to ruin this happy moment.

Thank you, Kindred Spirit, for bringing Grant to me. I am not sure how all this works, but I like to think you had a hand in it. Well, you and God, I suppose. It's possible, right?

Until next summer,

Lindsey

Chapter 15

Sunset Beach
Summer 1992

"Daddy, Daddy, look at me!" Campbell's five-year-old daughter sang out from her perch on the deck railing. "I'm a bird!" She flapped her arms and nearly lost her balance. Campbell sailed across the deck and grabbed her off the railing.

"Nicole Amanda Forrester!" he yelled. "Don't you ever do that again!"

Crocodile tears filled eyes that were the identical shade of blue as his own. "I'm sorry, Daddy," she said.

Campbell softened and pulled her to him. "You just have to be careful, baby," he whispered. "Daddy couldn't stand it if something happened to you." He did not add what he was thinking: *You're all I have.* He rocked her back and forth until she stopped crying. "Daddy's sorry for getting so angry," he said.

She brightened and hopped down from his lap. "It's okay, I forgive you," she said. "The Bible says we should always forgive. Did you know that, Daddy?"

He nodded absentmindedly, barely listening. His mother had faithfully taken Nikki to church—something he couldn't help but respect—but he had always opted out. Lately, Nikki's mini-sermons had been getting to him more and more. He wondered if he should join her and his mother at church sometime.

"Daddy … are you going to forgive Mommy?"

Campbell was about to suggest they go for a walk on the beach. He stopped short. "What?" he asked her.

"When Mommy comes back. Are you going to forgive her for running away?" Nikki asked, blinking her saucer-sized eyes as she waited for his response.

His mind ran through a thousand answers, none of which he could repeat to his daughter. Ellie should have been grateful he stood by her all these years. Instead the thanks he got was her abandoning them both and running off to God-knows-where with God-knows-who.

"Mommy's coming back," Nikki said, matter-of-factly. It had been four months since he came home from work to a note left on his pillow.

"Is that so? How do you know?" He may have been twenty-three years old, but sometimes Nikki seemed wiser than him.

"She and the man talked about it," Nikki said.

"The man? What man? When?" He walked back over to her and picked her up. "Did you see Mommy?" His mind raced as he tried to decipher what his daughter was saying.

Nikki shook her head no. "Before Mommy went away, she and I went to visit the man. He got me french fries and they talked while I got to have as much ketchup as I wanted. You know how you only let me have a little bit so I won't get so messy?"

Campbell nodded, dumbfounded.

"Well, Mommy and the man said that they were going on a trip and that she would come back to get me after the trip was over. She said that it was a secret, that I couldn't tell you. So I didn't tell you." Her lip quivered. "But Mommy's been gone a long time." She paused. "Do you think Mommy will be mad I told?"

Campbell patted her back. "No, baby, I can promise you Mommy will not be mad." His blood boiled. He knew Ellie was capable of a lot of sneaky things, but he never would have imagined her involving their daughter in something like this.

As he carried Nikki inside, she brightened. "See, Daddy? Mommy will come back. And then you can forgive her, because the Bible says to forgive." She patted his cheek. "Then you won't feel so sad anymore. My Sunday school teacher says forgiving others makes our hearts happy. Do you want your heart to feel happy, Daddy?"

He nodded. "Yes, sweetie." He smiled at the miracle of his daughter and wished for a moment that Ellie would never come back.

Sunset Beach
Summer 1992

Lindsey sat on the beach towel, brooding. She hadn't felt well for several days and when she mentioned to Grant that she thought she might be pregnant, he told her she was just being dramatic. She wanted him to run out and buy a pregnancy test, waiting breathlessly by her side for the results. She wanted him to put his hand on her stomach and tell her how proud he was to be the father of her child. Instead he said he was going for a run and left her out on the crowded beach, feeling miserable and trying to remember when her last period was. She flopped down on her stomach and stared at the ocean, wondering if she would still be able to lie on her stomach for much longer.

Grant had been so distracted lately. A project at his new job was taking over their lives. He worked late and when he was home, he was distant. She had had to beg him to come down to the beach for their regular vacation time. He wanted to stay at work and even suggested she come down alone or invite Holly. They had compromised with him coming down for half the week and Holly coming down for the other half. He seemed only too happy to forego their precious time together. She didn't want to dig too deeply into why.

A little girl ran past her and she watched her with interest, wondering idly what it would be like to have a daughter. The girl had hair bleached platinum by the sun, caught into a ponytail on top of her head. She flung a Frisbee with all her might as Lindsey watched it arc into the air. She watched as the little girl's dad caught the Frisbee with ease and smiled, a smile she still recognized in an instant. A smile, she discovered, that still had the potential to make her heart skip a beat.

She pulled the ball cap she wore down onto her face so that he wouldn't spot her. She was thankful the beach was overflowing with people that day. Tucking the bottom half of her face into her elbow, she watched from a place of anonymity as Campbell threw the Frisbee back toward his daughter. Nikki. She had to be five years old now. She was, Lindsey admitted, beautiful. "I expected nothing less from you," she said aloud to him, even though he couldn't hear her.

Her eyes filled with tears as he scooped up his daughter and carried her into the waves with her giggling the whole way, the sound of her laughter carried on the wind. He clearly loved his daughter. He looked happy. He was just fifty feet from her. All this time and she was finally seeing him again. She wanted to freeze time. She watched Campbell put Nikki on his shoulders and make their way down the beach until they got too far away to see, staring in his direction long after he was gone.

———

Sunset Beach
Summer 1992

Ellie turned up just a few days later. She marched into Campbell's office, her whole body tense and ready for a fight. Even as his mind registered her presence, he thought again that it would be better if she just stayed gone.

"I guess this is a surprise to you," she said.

"Not as big a surprise as you might think," he responded. "Nikki told me you'd be back. Apparently you felt comfortable involving a five-year-old in your plans to run away from her."

She tapped her thumb on her thigh, searching for words. For a moment, he thought she would say she wanted to come back. And in that moment, he knew he would agree to let her. For Nikki's sake. He looked at her and, though she was undoubtedly beautiful, realized anew that he felt nothing for her and never had. Nothing romantic, anyway.

She continued. "Campbell, I am not proud of any of this. But the fact is there's someone else in my life now. And at first I didn't know what was going to happen with that. I didn't want to talk to you about it until I did. But we've decided to get married." She smiled just before she thrust in the knife. "He's a doctor," she said, letting it sink in. The unspoken words *He's better than you* hanging in the air between them.

"So he's fine with paying to file all the papers and make all the arrangements," she said. "He just wants it taken care of. We'll back-date the separation to the day I left, so that the year of waiting can be shortened and we can be divorced without dragging this out."

Campbell nodded, staring at her as though she were an alien that had landed in his office. "Campbell!" she yelled. "Quit looking at me like that! Say something!"

He stared at her for another moment. "Seems to me," he said, "that the first thing a good mother would do is ask about the daughter she hasn't seen in months."

He could almost see the smoke come out of Ellie's ears. "I hate you, Campbell!" she screamed before turning on her stiletto heel and clicking back out of his office. When the door shut behind her, he smiled. He had just been set free.

Summer 1992

Dear Kindred Spirit,

I saw Campbell yesterday. It took six years for it to happen, but it finally did. As much as I hate to admit it, my heart started flopping around in my chest like one of those fish Campbell and I used to watch the fishermen pull in at the pier. He walked right by me on the beach with his little girl, a cute blonde thing who looks like a girl version of him. He looked exactly the same, yet older somehow. Wiser, maybe. Experienced, maybe. He's someone's father.

I will only admit this here to you, because I tell you everything and because Grant will never see it. I did look at his left hand, trying to see if he wore a wedding ring, then I felt instantly guilty for looking.

I know our time together is over and we have both moved on, but in that moment, I felt drawn to him, the magnet in my chest pulling me in his direction just as it has since I was a teenager. Silly, I know. Certainly not the thoughts that a married woman should be having. And yet, there they were.

And for the record, I couldn't tell if he wore a ring or not.

I can only assume he does, since last I heard he had married Ellie. He told me himself that he had married her. But it doesn't matter now. It doesn't. I am married. And we have a baby coming. I took the pregnancy test today after Grant left. You, Kindred Spirit, are the first to know. I will tell Grant when I get home after I spend the weekend with Holly. I just hope he's happy about it. Lately he hasn't seemed like he will be. One year in and I feel like my marriage is coming apart. I hope the baby will make things better. Don't tell me how stupid that logic is, Kindred Spirit. I already know.

Until next summer,

Lindsey

Chapter 16

Sunset Beach
Summer 2004

When Campbell woke that first morning with Nikki back home with him and the smell of bacon and coffee mingling in the air, he lay in bed for a moment, allowing himself to feel that all was right with the world. He wanted to live in denial for just a little while before reality resurfaced. Slowly the facts emerged: He had just pulled his daughter from a hospital because she starved herself to the point of collapse. And later that day he had to take her to church for some pretty intense counseling. But in the meantime, lying in the bedroom he had slept in his whole life, with the beach just a few hundred feet away, all *was* right with the world.

He turned to check the time and stretched, a prayer forming. He closed his eyes as he lay comfortably in bed, quietly imploring his God for help.

He stood up and walked over to his bedroom window, feeling hopeful and positive and ready for whatever the day might bring.

Outside, the day was bright and sparkling, already hot. He could feel the heat radiating off the panes of glass. Another July day at Sunset Beach.

He headed downstairs, tiptoeing past Nikki's closed door, only to run smack into her in the hall.

"Hi," she said, blinking back at him. He let out an awkward laugh.

How long had it been since they spent the night under the same roof? She looked away, glancing down at her running shoes, shame etched on her face. What was she ashamed of? Him? The situation? Herself? Boney legs stuck out from her running shorts and stick-like arms sprouted from an old Nike shirt he remembered throwing away years ago. He absently wondered how she wound up with it. It was worn in places, looking as soft as a baby's blanket from years of wear. She wore her hair in a ponytail like her mother had that day at the hospital, and she had earbuds in her ears. He could hear faint music emanating from them.

He pointed at her ears. "Going somewhere?" he shouted.

She pointed down at the shoes on her feet in answer. "Running," she said, a bit too loudly because of the music.

In his mind he scanned the pamphlet about anorexia that the doctors had given him at the hospital. It listed constant exercise as a symptom. He wondered about making an issue and decided not to. He felt his stress mounting, the beautiful day sinking like a setting sun. His mind began to race with thoughts: I can't handle this! I'm not a police officer. I'm not a doctor. I'm not a psychiatrist. What if she gets worse on my watch? He forced the feelings back down and smiled in a way that he hoped looked convincing.

"Did you eat?" he asked, trying to sound nonchalant.

She looked back at him, one hand on her hip. "Dad," she said, "Grandma already asked me that. You two are quite a pair." She brushed past him and headed down the stairs. He heard the door to the porch slam and went to the window to watch her sprint away from the house.

When he walked into the kitchen, his mother looked at him warily. She shook her head. "I couldn't get her to eat a bite," she said, sounding defeated.

A thought occurred to him: What if she came to Sunset because she didn't want to get better and thought she could fool them more easily than her mother and Oz, who was, after all, a medical professional? He fought the urge to pick up the phone and call Ellie, to tell her it was all a mistake and he was bringing Nikki home that afternoon, when the phone rang. His mother answered, and he heard her tell the caller he would be right there. She handed him the phone. He expected to hear her say "Minerva" but instead she mouthed the word "Ellie." Speak of the devil herself.

"Campbell, is she there?" Ellie whispered.

He couldn't resist. "Why are we whispering?" he taunted.

She laughed nervously. "I don't know. I guess I didn't want her to hear me. Don't tell me how ridiculous I am."

Remembering the sight of Nikki sprinting out the front door, he swallowed before responding. "Well, to answer your question, no. She's not here. She just left." He paused a beat. "To go on a run." Ellie said nothing, deciding, he knew, whether to yell at him or let it go, give them time. She exhaled, the sound magnified by the mouthpiece like she was blowing in his ear.

He decided to forego her lecture by agreeing with her. "I don't think I can do this," he said. "I'm not cut out for this. I want to be her dad, not a policeman. I am scared to death I am going to screw this up. Maybe I shouldn't have agreed to this so quickly."

Ellie laughed, a bitter sound that lodged in his chest, close to his heart, his vulnerable, exposed heart. "Campbell, that's the part of raising her you missed out on. Being her dad *is* being a policeman sometimes. Don't tell me about doubting your ability to do this, Campbell. You are so doing this. Do you hear me? You have to. For ten years you have taken her for a few days here and there, plied her with ice cream and sand castles and then given her back. This time you have to gut this out." In the background he heard a sound, a door slamming and keys jingling.

"Think of it this way. You can't screw her up more than I have. I have to go," she said suddenly and then hung up. Campbell stared at the phone in his hand, the dial tone buzzing loudly.

His mom stood at the stove, pretending not to be listening. "Well," he said. "That went well."

She turned from frying bacon and smiled at him, but worry was clearly lurking just underneath. If they were in over their heads, there would be no deciding to send her back. Ellie wouldn't—or couldn't—take her back. He smiled back at his mom, going along with their charade. She put bacon on a plate and handed it to him.

He sat at the breakfast table after his mom urged him to sit at the place she had set for him, complete with fresh-squeezed orange juice and folded napkins. She had tried to make Nikki's first meal there special. He could see the street from where he sat, so he scanned it for a glimpse of Nikki. People walked back and forth, some coming from an early morning walk on the beach, their pockets bulging with shells, brushing the sand from their shorts. Others headed out for the day—renters intent on wringing out every bit of daylight they had to spend on the shore. They pulled wagons laden with beach chairs, radios, sand toys, and coolers. Their children walked or sat in strollers. They looked so happy, so hopeful, exactly like what he wanted.

He remembered when Nikki stopped coming to Sunset, back when she was in high school, and the horrible way he responded. Hurt and full of pride he had vowed not to go to her if she wouldn't come to him. It had started with a phone call from Ellie.

When the phone rang the day she was supposed to arrive to spend fall break with him, he expected it to be Nikki saying she was late leaving or confirming her directions. She had only driven to Sunset alone one other time, and he was nervous about her driving by herself. He picked up the handset and said, "Yellow!" instead of "hello" just like he used to when she was little and still thought that was hilarious. He hoped he didn't sound like an idiot to her and it could still make her laugh. His daughter, he reminded himself, wasn't six years old anymore.

"Campbell?" It was Ellie, not Nikki.

"Yeah, Ellie, everything okay?"

"Yes, it's fine. But Nikki just had a situation come up and she asked me to call you." Campbell could feel his pulse quicken. He sensed that what Ellie was about to say wasn't good.

Ellie went on. "Nikki got chosen to be on homecoming court at her school. Isn't that wonderful?"

He thought of Ellie on homecoming court years ago, a baby Nikki quietly growing inside of her before anyone knew. He stood beside her on the football field in a stiff suit feeling uncomfortable and thinking about someone else. "Sure," he said.

"Well, there is a lot we need to get done between now and then and, looking at our schedules, this long weekend is all the time we are going to have to get all her shopping taken care of."

"Oh," he said. "Well, I could take her shopping. Or my mom could."

Ellie laughed. "Campbell, she wants to go with me. It's what moms do, not dads. Nikki wants to stay here and shop with her friends and their moms. She'll really be missing out if she goes to Sunset." Ellie paused. "She feels just awful about it, Campbell. That's why she asked me to call for her."

Standing in the window looking for his skeletally thin daughter, he realized he had spent her whole life painting himself as the victim. Poor me, I got a girl pregnant but I didn't love her. Poor me, I'm stuck in a bad marriage. Poor me, my wife left me. Poor me, now my daughter's leaving me too.

It wasn't Nikki's fault that she had ended up away from him. He should have made more effort to be with her instead of demanding that she come to him every time. It was time for him to take responsibility for his actions and start making it up to the people he had hurt. At least the ones he was allowed to make it up to.

As he watched for his daughter, he decided to tell her how sorry he was and admit that even fathers have to grow up sometimes.

———

Nikki returned much later, sweaty and red-faced. If she had run all that time, Campbell thought, they were in dangerous territory. He went up to her room shortly after she had been home and paused before knocking on her door. He knew what a stalker dad it made him look like, hot on her heels like that. But maybe Ellie was right—maybe policing *was* part of his job.

He tapped lightly, hearing the *thunk, thunk* of her running shoes hitting the wood floor as she tore them off, one by one, still breathing heavily from her run.

"Yes?" she said, her words coming out in a huff.

"It's Dad," he said hesitantly. "Can I come in?"

"Uh, no. I'm like, getting ready to take a shower."

"Oh, okay. Well, I just wanted to remind you that we have your first appointment in about an hour. You've got just enough time to get showered and have some lunch before we go, okay?" he added hopefully.

"Ummm-hmmm," she responded through the closed door.

Feeling restless, he went to the front of the house and stood looking out, just in time to see Minerva's car pull into the drive. She got out of her car toting an assortment of bags from Food Lion. He moved to help her, grabbing the bags and then opening the door for her.

She limped past him. "Thanks, honey," she said and headed into the kitchen, hollering for his mother and huffing and puffing dramatically. "LaRae! Get out here and see what I brought," she yelled loudly enough for the people passing by outside to hear. She looked over at Campbell as he dropped the bags onto the kitchen counter.

"Don't y'all have a counseling appointment?" she said, he thought a little too accusingly.

He rolled his eyes at her. "Yup. We leave in an hour," he said with an overwide smile and began rummaging through the bags. "Um, Minerva? What's with the groceries? Chocolate ice cream? Oreos? Microwave popcorn with extra butter? Peanut Butter Captain Crunch? Are you crazy?" He said in a hushed voice as he looked over at her and raised his eyebrows.

She threw her hands up. "I just thought that I would inspire Nikki a bit. I know you and your mama keep all this health food stuff around, and I thought that maybe having some of the right"—she grabbed the bag of Oreos and waved them around—"*inspiration* would help the child." She waggled her eyebrows back at him, clearly impressed with herself.

He didn't have the heart to tell her about the literature he read that said that most girls who struggle with anorexia avoid junk food at all costs and the best way to get them interested in eating is by offering healthy alternatives. He reached into the bags and began putting the items away, wondering who would eat all that junk.

"Oh!" Minerva suddenly exclaimed, hitting the countertop. "Do you remember that girl that you were seeing that summer? You know, before Ellie?" she asked.

He cleared his throat and tried to steady his voice. "Uh, yeah, I do. Why?"

"Funniest thing," she said, looking pointedly at him. "I ran into her while you and your mama were gone to get Nikki. I found her standing in front of the house when I stopped by. I came to water your mama's flowers for her, and there she was, just looking up at the house." She laughed. "I think I scared her half to death! You know, she still looks just the same as she always did. Like no time's gone by at all. What was her name again? The old memory ain't what it used to be," she rapped on her head with her knuckles.

"Lindsey," he said. He found it hard to say her name out loud. It got caught in his throat, probably from being lodged inside for so long.

"Yes, that's right. Lindsey! Such a pretty name for such a pretty little thing like her. I remember—"

He interrupted her, betraying any efforts he might have made toward playing it cool. "Did you talk to her?" he asked.

"Well, of course, Campbell. Have you ever known me to meet someone and not strike up a conversation?" She laughed at herself.

"What did she say?"

"Well, not much about herself, actually. There seemed to be something not … right about her if you ask me. There just seemed to be a sadness hanging over her. If anyone knows people it's me, you know." She paused. "I'm sure there's a story there."

"I'm surprised you didn't drag it out of her," he mumbled under his breath.

"What did you say, Campbell? You know you have to speak up around me—these old ears just aren't what they used to be."

Just then, Nikki came down the stairs, calling out his name.

"I'll be in the car!" Nikki hollered as she raced out the front door in a blur.

He hastily shoved the sloppy sandwich he had made into a bag in a futile attempt to persuade her to eat on the way.

She was here, he thought as he made his way to the car. He suddenly felt closer to Lindsey than he had in years.

Chapter 17

Sunset Beach
Summer 2004

When Lindsey returned to the beach house after her morning run, she found the kids squabbling over whose turn it was to play a video game. She raised her voice to be heard over their yelling and ended up threatening to throw the whole game system into the ocean.

"You don't have to yell at us like that, Mom," Anna said. Lindsey restrained herself from explaining again why she had to yell in order to be heard over their shouting. Instead she just sighed and told them to get ready to go to the beach. Even coming so close to Campbell moments ago had not dampened the exasperating effect the children's bickering could have on her.

"We're tired of the beach," Jake whined. Already.

She leveled them both with her best Terminator Mom look. "Just go get ready," she said, in a voice that meant business. To their credit, they obeyed without further argument.

"If you're tired of the ocean, you better pack stuff to do! Because we are going to be out there for a while!" she yelled at their retreating backs. She saw Jake shake his head and knew Anna rolled her eyes.

She headed into her bedroom, which was her aunt and uncle's room when she visited as a kid. The best and largest room of the house, it featured a bank of windows stretching across one wall, each one filled with a sweeping view of the Intracoastal Waterway. She loved to lie in bed and stare out the windows, watching seabirds swoop down to catch tiny fish, studying the way the sunlight glinted off the water. She could tell whether it was high tide or low just by looking out, which made her feel natural and earthy, in tune with the tides, the pull of the moon, the way nature ebbed and flowed, dancing along to some unspoken rhythm. She felt more at peace there, close to the water, than she ever did in her landlocked home.

She stripped out of her sweaty running clothes and debated taking a quick shower, just to rinse the grit and sweat from her body. Instead she took the lazy way out and pulled on the first bathing suit her hand fell on—one that Anna hated.

"Mo-om," she said the last time she wore it to their community pool back home. "You have got to get some swimsuits that were made in, like, this decade."

"I like it," Lindsey retorted, defensive. "It hides everything in just the right way."

Anna looked down at the ground, shaking her head in utter despair. Her mother would never be the cool mom she hoped for. As a teen, Lindsey wore bathing suits that showed too much skin.

Now she admired bathing suits that covered up as much as possible without looking terribly matronly. She checked herself out in the mirror. She didn't have the body of a teenager, but she hadn't exactly let herself go, either. As she studied herself, she realized that the older she got, the more she liked herself. Sure she would never get rid of the stomach she gained from having kids. And her breasts didn't stand at attention like they once did. But she wasn't fifteen anymore, either. And frankly, from where she stood looking back over the years, she wouldn't want to be.

As she gathered up her sunscreen and headed to the kitchen to pack lunch, she noticed a devotional book she had been going through and tossed it into her bag to take to the beach, along with her journal and a pen. She wanted to do some journaling while the kids played. The image of sitting on the beach with a pen in her hand, alternating between staring at the waves and scribbling her thoughts contentedly, brought a smile to her face. She passed Anna in the hall, dressed in a bathing suit Lindsey bought her at the mall, a splurge to get her excited about the trip to Sunset without her dad.

She looked at Lindsey, noticing the wide grin on her face. "What's wrong with you?" she asked.

Lindsey didn't answer the question, but replied with, "That suit sure looks cute on you!" and kept on smiling as she made her way down the hall.

Lindsey ignored her daughter's reply: "Wish I could say the same for yours!"

About ten minutes after they got down to the beach Anna and Jake began to complain of hunger. Though Lindsey tried to stave them off for a bit, eventually she gave in and handed out sandwiches, chips, and Little Debbie Swiss Cake Rolls, a beach tradition from her childhood she attempted to pass along to her kids, even if Anna held up the treat and announced, "Mom, do you know how much trans fat is in one of these? Are you trying to kill us?"

Lindsey looked heavenward and told Anna she didn't have to eat it.

"Then can I have Anna's?" Jake asked hopefully.

They all ate their lunch in quiet happiness, accepting the sandy grit that inevitably worked its way into the sandwiches as part of the experience. After they ate, the children ran to investigate a tide pool that some other children had clustered beside. Apparently they had forgotten their earlier complaints about the beach being "boring."

With the kids preoccupied, she pulled out her journal. She opened to a fresh page and, though she had to fight with the wind a bit, she began to write about her jog and interaction with Minerva. She wrote about their conversation and how Minerva had seemed anxious for her and Campbell to see each other. Something about her brief encounter with the elderly yet enthusiastic woman made her feel like they would be friends if they could spend time together. She knew it was terribly psychological, but she did find herself gravitating to mother figures.

She then grabbed the devotional book and flipped to that day's date. She wished she had her Bible with her but feared what could happen to it out on the beach. A gift from Holly when they graduated from high school, her Bible had become one of her most precious possessions. She would have to go back later and read the verses that were printed in the book.

The book was given to her by a woman at her church back home who had become a mother figure for Lindsey—she was an older woman who actually reminded Lindsey a lot of Minerva, now that she thought of it. After learning that Grant had left, the woman had given Lindsey the book one Sunday morning when they passed in the church lobby. Lindsey remembered the woman wore a little corsage on her flowered dress. She imagined the woman's arthritic, age-spotted hands maneuvering the pin into the fabric as she stood in front of her mirror. Something about that effort filled Lindsey with equal parts of hope and heartbreak.

Lindsey knew that years ago the woman's husband had walked out on her for a younger woman, breaking her heart. Yet she seemed joyous. She hoped that the peace the older woman had could be discovered in the pages of the book she gave Lindsey. She had been scouring the pages looking for it ever since. So far, she had found no easy answers, no three-step plans to getting on with her life. Most of what she learned was about trusting God and being open to His next step for her. Instead she found herself sliding back into "If You love me why are You letting this happen to me?" conversations with God.

That day's reading talked about claiming a life verse and how the author had claimed several different life verses through the years, claiming different promises for different seasons in her life. As Lindsey read the words, she decided she should claim a verse for that season in her life. She thought about how Holly had challenged her to make this trip the best ever, to discover that she was worth loving. Perhaps she could find a verse that reflected her thoughts.

As she anticipated combing through the Bible to find a verse, she felt excited. After a bit of a spiritual dry spell, it felt like she had started to come upon an oasis. When Grant left, even reading the Bible was a mental effort she wasn't capable of. Instead of rising joyfully to have a quiet time before the rest of the house woke up as she once did, very often she slept until one of the kids tugged on her arm, pulling her from the deep blackness of sleep to stumble to the car and drive them to school.

Now she was finally beginning to emerge from the fog of his leaving, blinking and stumbling her way into the light of day.

That evening, as Lindsey and the kids made their way into the beach house, Anna noticed canned pears sitting near the kitchen sink and sniffed dramatically. "What are those?" she asked, pointing at the pears the way Lindsey did when one of the kids left their shoes on the kitchen counter.

"Anna, they're pears. We've had them a million times."

"But you know I like peaches." She paused, considering. "Or mandarin oranges. I hate pears! You know that!"

Even as the words came out of her daughter's mouth, Lindsey could see her just a few months before, fishing pears out of a jar with her fingers, smiling broadly at her when Lindsey caught her and asked her to please use a spoon or at least wash her hands before sticking them into jars other people were eating out of.

"But I love pears, Mom!" she had replied, her new braces glinting in the light and making her look at once youthful and mature. A little girl in a young woman's body, chocolate milk spilled on the ultracool shirt she had begged for earlier that day at the mall.

Who are you? Lindsey remembered thinking, amused at the sight of her little girl.

Lindsey's short escape ended. Sighing, she watched her irritated, growing daughter retreat to the back of the beach house, her little brother in tow.

After a quick shower, Lindsey, despite Anna's complaints, made corn dogs and canned pears for dinner, Jake's favorite—for now at least.

"Dinner!" she yelled toward the back of the house. She hoped to rush them through dinner so she could put on a movie for them and escape to the quiet of her room with her Bible and journal. She could hardly wait to be alone with God's Word and hear from Him. She hoped for as few interruptions from the children as possible.

As the kids dragged themselves to the table looking like they had been summoned to the gallows instead of dinner, she bit back her usual commentary on how there were many, many children in the world who would love to have hot, delicious food heaped on a plate for them. They knew there were starving children in the world. They knew they were—thankfully—not among those starving children. But they also knew their daddy was gone. And she would give them as much time as they needed to be sad about that without her preaching at them about having a good attitude all the time. She ruffled Jake's hair and kissed the top of Anna's head.

"Love you guys," she said, after she had blessed the corn dogs and canned pears.

"Love you," they both mumbled back through mouthfuls of corn dogs. The kids started a movie while they ate, and Lindsey made her escape.

She went to her room, shut the door, and settled down on her bed with her Bible opened on her lap. She prayed for the Lord to show her what He would have for her. She opened her eyes and focused on the fading light outside her window, watched the ripples on the water's surface and tried to clear her mind.

Instantly, a visual popped into her head: She was twelve years old, eating SpaghettiOs that she had heated up for herself in the microwave while her mom clomped around the house in high heels. Her mom smelled like a perfume factory and wore a too-short skirt and bra. Lindsey tried not to look at her mother in her bra, though her mother didn't seem to care if she did. Lindsey knew she wanted her to think that she looked beautiful and fancy, getting ready for her "hot date" as she called it.

Instead Lindsey thought her mother just looked sad and pathetic. Her "hot date" wasn't rugged or mysterious or good-looking. They watched *Magnum, P.I.* together and agreed that *he* was handsome—so why would she go out with this loser? She kept eating her SpaghettiOs, wishing that her mom weren't going out, wishing that she would cook a real meal for once. Instead she walked over to where Lindsey sat and bent down to air-kiss her before turning to leave. She had put on her shirt, the buttons straining against her chest like they would pop any moment.

"Don'twaitupdon'tstayuptoolatedon'tanswerthedoorseeyouinthe morning!" she hollered on her way out.

But something made her want to stop her mother for once.

"Mom!" Lindsey yelled back, before her mother could vanish in a trail of perfume.

Her mother stopped short, looked back at her with raised eyebrows.

"I-I," she stammered, looking down at the floor, her courage leaking out the soles of her feet and into the floorboards beneath her.

"What?" her mother asked impatiently. Lindsey was not supposed to interfere with her plans, an unspoken agreement.

"I just wish ..." She paused, searching her mother's face for some glimmer of recognition, some realization of what her daughter needed before she could even utter it, like Lindsey imagined other mothers could do. Finally she blurted out, "I just wish you would stay home and make me dinner and watch TV with me."

She had never argued with her about going out, never put up a fight. Even when old boyfriends of hers banged on the door while her mother was out, yelling, "I know you're in there!" Even when she lay awake until the wee hours of the morning, listening for her key in the door just so she knew her mom had made it home okay. Even when she heard her mother entertaining men in the living room, the clink of glasses, their deep voices and her loud, high-pitched laugh. In all of this, she never said a word. But on this one night, she did.

Her mother just shook her head, then turned to leave. "You'll be fine, Lindsey. You always are. Why don't you call one of your friends and talk to them?"

"But I don't want a friend!" she yelled, her mouth running ahead of her. "I want a mother! Why is that so much to ask?"

Her mother closed the door with a bang, marched over to where she sat in their tiny kitchen, pointed at the bowl of SpaghettiOs.

"Why you ungrateful little— Who do you think paid for this dinner you are eating? For this chair you are sitting in? For this roof over your head?" She gestured wildly around the room, jabbing at ordinary things as proof of her ability to mother.

"I just want a mom who makes me mashed potatoes," she said, staring into her bowl of SpaghettiOs. She was already sorry she said anything at all. Her mother didn't get it.

The last time Lindsey was at Holly's house, her mom made them the most delicious baked chicken and mashed potatoes swimming in butter. Later, her mom popped popcorn and carried it down to where they were watching TV, the white corn spilling over the edges of the giant blue bowl with the word "Popcorn" painted on the side.

Lindsey's mom marched back over to the door, throwing it open dramatically and turning to look back at her before leaving.

"You are lucky I come back at all," she said before storming out.

Lindsey sat at the little vinyl-covered kitchen table, staring at her half-eaten bowl of SpaghettiOs before she stood up and tossed them in the sink, leaving the red mess there for her mother to find when she returned. All Lindsey remembered thinking that night after her mom left was: *I will be a better mother than you someday. I will cook meals for my children. And I won't spend all my time chasing after stupid men.* Twelve-year-old Lindsey repeated the phrases over and over again, a litany of promises about the life she would lead just as soon as she could. That night she didn't wait up for her mother like usual.

The memory played in Lindsey's head like her own personal film clip as she lovingly laid her Bible back down on the nightstand. She looked up at the ceiling, half expecting to see God winking back at her. She heard His voice, gentle as a whisper: "I knew you'd get it."

Tonight wasn't about locking herself in her room to hear from Him. Tonight was about showing her kids His love.

She rose from her spot on the bed and headed back down the hall toward the den and the noise of the TV, where two little people needed their mother to make them a big bowl of popcorn and ice-cream sundaes. She knew that the verse God had for her would be there later. In the meantime, she felt a sense of urgency to be with her kids—to giggle with them over the silly movie and eat junk food. To be the kind of mom she once promised herself she would be. Did that make her any less holy and committed? As she sat sandwiched between her two children, she couldn't help feeling like it made her even more so.

*

The next morning, Lindsey rose from her bed in the still-quiet house, pulling her Bible out from where she stowed it on the nightstand the night before. As she flipped it open, a photo fell out. She had tucked it into the pages not long ago when her friend Brenda handed it to her at church one day. In truth, she hadn't wanted to look at it, didn't want to remember the happier time when the photo was snapped. In the photo ten-year-old Anna danced with Grant at Brenda's wedding. In her mind's eye, Lindsey could remember the scene: Grant lifting Anna up and swinging her around as Lindsey watched from nearby. Perfect timing allowed the wedding photographer to happen by at that precise moment, capturing the happy looks on their faces, her dress whirling out as she looked at her daddy with all the love in the world.

Lindsey remembered how Anna had pronounced happily, "Look, Daddy, I'm a princess!"

Grant had replied, "And whose princess are you?"

She responded confidently, "Your princess, Daddy."

He had swept her up in his arms, and Lindsey had been so happy she could give her daughter this thing—this father—she never had. Watching the two of them, her eyes had filled with bittersweet tears. Looking back now, Lindsey could see that she always feared Grant would leave her. She just never realized it meant he'd leave Anna too.

At the time Brenda handed the photo to her at church, she was oblivious to the feelings it would stir up later—it was just another reminder of what she had lost. But looking at it that morning, she saw more. She saw joy on her little girl's face. For the first time since she and Grant split up, she felt her daughter's loss in a profound way instead of merely focusing on her own. She had made this about herself for so long, yet she was not the only one who lost something when Grant left. Her children lost a parent, she lost a spouse, but they all lost a family.

One thing she knew for sure, united in their grief she and the children would move forward together, one tentative step at a time. God had shown her that He still had a few tricks up His sleeve—even if those tricks included a harmless encounter with someone from her past.

She propped the photo on the nightstand as a reminder to herself that this life-change affected more than just her. She went out to join her children, who were fighting over the last doughnut, their voices music to her ears.

Chapter 18

Sunset Beach
Summer 2004

Lindsey sat on the beach with her novel open while her children played, but she was distracted. Once again, she had made no progress in the story. And once again, thoughts of Campbell and Minerva stole her attention. She pondered the challenge Minerva gave her: Just walk down his street one evening. She imagined walking down his street, wearing—what?—her most flattering denim capris and a tank top that actually looked good on her with the weight she had lost since Grant left. Her hair should be in a ponytail so the beach gusts didn't blow it in her face, causing her to fiddle with it awkwardly as she was apt to do, while she talked to … him. She wondered if he still smelled like she remembered, a combination of salt air, sunscreen, and deeply tanned skin. After that first summer, he let her take a T-shirt of his home so she could inhale his scent buried in its fibers. She wondered whatever happened to that shirt. Her mother probably threw it out as soon as she left for college.

She tried to imagine herself slowing as she reached his house just long enough for Minerva to see her and push him nonchalantly out the door. She practiced looking shocked to see him. Would she say, "Oh, wow, you live here? I totally forgot!" Or would that be too obviously untrue? She tried to picture what he would look like now, but all that came to mind was him … then. Campbell skipping shells over the water. Campbell fishing off the pier, his wrist deftly casting the rod from years of practice. Campbell helping her cross Mad Inlet as they made their way to the mailbox, his hand reaching out to her, the sun glinting on his hair, lighting him up like an angel God sent straight to her. Snapshots her mind stored all those years. All images she thought she had let go of forever.

Her thoughts were racing. He wasn't married! He still lived here! Deep down she wanted to run to him, to burst through his door and say all the things she never got to say, to hopefully hear him say how sorry he was for ever letting her go. She caught herself short, scolding herself for reacting like a lovesick teenager. Hadn't nearly twenty years gone by? Had she grown up at all? She grinned stupidly and checked her watch. Nearly five o'clock. For Minerva's little plan to work tonight, she needed to make it back to the house, feed the kids, and then leave for her "no big deal, I do this all the time" walk.

She dusted off her hands and stood up, waving dramatically at the children until they saw her and dragged themselves out of the water, looking bereft. "Time to go!" she called merrily, trying to sound like leaving in the middle of all their fun was the best idea she had all day. "I'll bet you guys have worked up quite an appetite out there with all that boogie boarding!" She knew she didn't sound like herself and hoped they didn't notice. They gathered towels and bags and shovels and pails. Lindsey wrestled with her beach chair while Anna and Jake loaded up the rest of their things for the short trek home.

While the kids changed out of their wet suits, Lindsey popped open a Diet Coke and told them to stay out of the Popsicles before dinner. She had finally stocked up at the grocery store in town that morning, so they had plenty to eat. She picked the meat from a rotisserie chicken she bought and piled that on some bagged salad. She set out bacon bits, croutons, and shredded cheese, then announced "Dinner!" almost before they were done changing.

Anna and Jake emerged from their rooms, squinting as their eyes were still adjusting to the dim light of the indoors. They looked so healthy with the sun-kissed glow of their skin and sun-streaked hair. She hugged them both and, miraculously, they didn't complain or pull away. "Eat up!" she said, pointing to the food. She watched them eat with the satisfaction of feeding her children that only a mother could understand. When they were done, she told them they could take a Popsicle out on the porch while she took a shower. They cheered and immediately began arguing over who got what flavor. She shook her head and slipped away to the sanctuary of a long, hot shower.

As she pulled her blow-dried hair into a ponytail, her heart began to drum in a funny rhythm. If she felt absolutely queasy at the mere prospect of seeing him, how would she handle a conversation, should it happen? She considered not going, wondered if she was crazy to open up that can of worms when all the other pieces of her life were just beginning to fall into some sort of place. Seeing Campbell again could potentially change all that she had worked for, like a checkerboard that had been bumped. Just a small upset was enough to slide the pieces out of their strategic places.

But then again, her checkers weren't exactly in a winning position. So why not take a risk? She smiled at her reflection in the mirror and decided that a touch of gloss on her lips would compliment her lightly tanned face. Any more makeup than that and it would belie her act: that she was just out for a casual, aimless walk.

As she finished dabbing on her gloss, she whispered, "Lord, if You want this to happen, then it will. But one thing: If You could help me to not embarrass myself, I'd be grateful. And if I don't see him tonight, I'll probably need some help with disappointment."

The light over the mirror caught on her diamond wedding band, and she stared down at it. Just two years ago on their vacation to Sunset, Grant had surprised her with a new diamond ring as they sat at the mailbox together. He had held her hand and slipped on the ring, promising new beginnings. She hadn't had the heart to take it off since Grant left. She didn't want to stop believing in the things he had promised her.

But it was time. With a sad but resolved smile she slipped the ring from her finger and placed it in the bathroom drawer, shutting it with a small bang as she left the room.

She headed toward the porch and sat down in the empty rocking chair beside Anna and Jake, who were watching the first streaks of pink cross the sky as the sun made its way down for the night. They had thrown their Popsicle sticks down on the porch floor, but she didn't scold them. They sat in rare, companionable silence for a while before she bent over and began putting on her tennis shoes.

"Where ya goin', Mom?" Jake asked.

She tried to sound nonchalant. "Oh, just thought I'd go for a walk. Walk off dinner."

Anna rolled her eyes. "But you didn't eat much, Mom." Anna was right. Lindsey's appetite had left with Grant.

"Oh, I did too!" Lindsey retorted. She tousled her daughter's hair, which had nearly dried with the seawater still in it. She smelled like a combination of a child's skin and the beach, a magical concoction Lindsey wished she could bottle. "Why don't you two take turns taking showers while I'm gone?" She formed this as a question, but they knew a command when they heard one.

"We want to go on a walk with you, Mom!" Jake said, just before she could charge down the porch steps and make her escape. She stopped short. "We can take showers when we get back," he added, looking pitiful.

"Yeah, let us go with you, Mom," Anna echoed.

Of course, the one time I don't ask *them to accompany me on a walk, they volunteer. Go figure,* Lindsey thought.

She formulated excuses for not taking them. But before she could say, "Mommy just needs some time alone," she spoke something else entirely. "Well, okay. Go put on your walking shoes."

The kids raced inside while she wondered what had just happened and how dragging along two unpredictable children would figure into Minerva's plan. Lindsey hoped it would all work out somehow as she and her children set off on their walk, heading toward something she never expected, in a way she never would have planned.

Chapter 19

Sunset Beach
Summer 2004

If Campbell said he hadn't been watching for her, he would have been lying. Minerva and her scheming had set him up for an encounter that he had only dreamed of happening. Through no efforts of his own, the girl he never forgot could walk down his street after nearly twenty years any day now. Any minute now, in fact. So he continually watched for a glimpse, wondering if he would have the courage to actually talk to her when the time came. If the time came.

"Campbell," his mother scolded, "get away from that window. You look like a stalker, standing there scanning the street."

He shook his head. Minerva and her big mouth. He turned to face his mom. "So, Minerva told you about Lindsey?"

She washed the dinner dishes, her gray head bent down as she ran water over the plates. She looked up at him from across the room. "I always did like that girl. She made you happier than I've ever seen you. Before or since." She looked at Campbell without blinking.

Tell me something I don't already know, he thought. He smiled at her.

"What can I say, Mom?" he pointed up at Nikki's closed bedroom door, where loud music emanated. "I was hormonally challenged."

She threw her head back and laughed. His mom had the best laugh, but he'd rarely heard it since his dad died. "Well, it seems to me you might be getting another chance," she said. "Minerva seems to think she's here alone." She raised her eyebrows. "As in, no husband."

He walked into the kitchen and poured some iced tea, intending to carry it out to the porch. "Mom, let's just say, I hope Minerva's right. It would be nice for something to go well for once."

His mother dried her hands on a dish towel and changed the subject. "Well, at least Nikki ate some dinner tonight. I guess that first session did something for her. Did she tell you anything about it?"

"Nope, not a word. And I didn't ask a whole lot of questions either. I figure she'll tell me what she wants me to know."

"I suspect you're right," his mother agreed. She gestured up at Nikki's closed door. "Still, I think I'll go upstairs and try to talk to her." She winked at him. "Grandmas are supposed to be nosey."

He watched his mom go upstairs and enter Nikki's room before he took his tea and headed out to the porch. For the next hour he counted twelve people who walked past his house. Several couples with strollers walked past, probably out to walk off dinner and take in the night air. But no Lindsey.

His memory wandered to a night during the second summer they had spent together. They had walked out to the end of the pier, something they did almost every night. They loved how it felt isolated and dangerous and thrilling, with just the crash of the ocean waves under them and the expansive starlit sky above. They had taken Campbell's Sony Walkman and shared the headphones between them as "Boys of Summer" by Don Henley played. "This should be our song," she told him, her head pressed close to his as they listened. He took her in his arms and began to dance with her, the rickety boards of the Sunset Beach pier creaking underneath them.

I can tell you
My love for you will still be strong
After the boys of summer have gone

Campbell remembered how he never wanted that night to end.

Taking a sip of his iced tea, Campbell noticed a ragtag little crew rounding the corner from Main Street. A woman with two children. The boy and girl jostled each other and ran circles around their mom as she swatted at them playfully. She laughed and her voice carried down the silent street. A chill ran up Campbell's spine. He knew that laugh anywhere. Funny, he would have sworn he had forgotten it until he heard it again.

His heart thrummed wildly in his chest as they slowly approached. He stood and walked to the railing of the porch. The sunset had colored the sky a brilliant pink, wrapping her and her children in a rosy glow. He watched them like a voyeur, delighting in seeing her again, working up the courage to speak as she neared his house.

The girl—who was maybe twelve, thirteen?—looked like Lindsey probably had at that age. Her hair was the exact same color as Lindsey's when Campbell knew her, though he noticed that Lindsey's had darkened over the years. The boy, he imagined, must look like his father. The boy lumbered along beside Lindsey, alternating between holding his mother's hand and letting it go. He let it go when Campbell called her name.

The trio stopped and stared. "Hey," he said, working hard to appear confident and certain. Lindsey shielded her eyes from the sun and blinked back at him. "Fancy seeing you here," he added, which sounded much lamer coming out of his mouth than it did in his head. He smiled, trying to cover.

"Hi, Campbell," she said, pasting on a smile. "It's really good to see you." The kids looked from her to him and back to her, like an audience at a tennis match. She laughed nervously. "Wow, how long's it been?"

"Almost twenty years," he said, though he was sure she knew exactly how long it had been. He walked down the porch steps as she crossed the yard. They met in the middle and hugged awkwardly. She smelled—was it possible?—just the way he remembered, like aloe. He breathed her scent in and looked down to find the two children staring at them. He let her go. *Don't be so obvious, Campbell.* "So," he said, his palms sweating, "what are you guys up to?"

"Oh, nothin'," she said, her cheeks flushed from more than one day on the beach. "Just out for an evening stroll. You know, walking off dinner and all that," she said, laughing. "Plus"—she looked to her children—"I had to get you wild kids out of the house and do something!" She waved her hand at them both. "These are my children, Jake and Anna." Jake waved at him, but Anna turned away, embarrassed. "Can me and Jake, like, keep walking if you are going to stand here and talk?" the girl asked impatiently.

"Yeah, can we, Mom?" the boy piped up, looking excited. She glanced down the empty street and back at him.

Lindsey looked at Campbell with a smirk, then back down to her children. "I guess it won't hurt. I'll be right here catching up with my old … friend," she said, a fumble for the right word to describe him. What word would he have used?

The boy grinned and hit his sister in the back of the head. "You're it, Anna!" He took off running with the girl hot on his heels. They thundered away and left Campbell alone with Lindsey. He couldn't thank them enough.

"Nice meeting you guys!" he yelled after them. "It's great to see you," he said and smiled at her.

"Though obviously, no accident, our meeting like this," she said. Just like the Lindsey he remembered to always get to the heart of things. She looked down at the ground, kicking at a stray shell with her toe.

He decided to get to the heart of things as well. "So, you're here alone?" She looked up from the ground, blinking at him as if he had hit a nerve. "I mean, your husband isn't here?"

She sighed deeply. "No, he's not here this year." She paused, watching her children play. A resolute look crossed her face when she turned back to him. "The truth is he's not ever going to be here again. We, um … we split up a year ago. The divorce was final just this week. He said he wanted a different kind of life than—" she gestured to the kids—"this."

Before he could stop himself, Campbell reached out and took Lindsey's hand. He felt an electric current run between them. He felt a boldness he couldn't explain, but he went with it. "Well, I'd love to tell you I'm sorry, but I'm afraid I can't. That idiot just gave me the open door I've been waiting for, for a very long time." He smiled, hoping she wouldn't pull away. She didn't. They stood in silence for a few minutes, grinning stupidly at each other as the kids came racing back up. He discreetly dropped her hand.

"Let's go, Mom!" the boy, Jake, said. Campbell was not ready for her to go. He searched for a way to stall.

"Hey, kids," he said, his mind replaying the scene from that morning when Minerva stood in his kitchen, unloading bag after bag of junk food. "I happen to have a stash of great junk food in the house. Would you like to raid my kitchen? You can take anything you like. Load up!" He glanced over at Lindsey. "If that's okay with your mom, that is." He raised his eyebrows in question.

She laughed. "Well, as I always say, what's a beach vacation without a serious indulgence in junk food?" The kids looked at them unbelievingly for a moment before charging up the porch steps. Lindsey and Campbell followed behind them, smiling at each other.

Campbell helped the kids load two bags with the stuff that Minerva left behind. The boy kept asking, "Are you sure we can have this? For real?"

"Yeah, someone gave me all this stuff and I can't eat it, so why not?" he responded as he smiled at Lindsey again.

The girl scanned the house, checking the place out. She glanced at him, then her mother. "So, do you like, *live* here?" she asked skeptically. The thought of someone actually living at Sunset seemed foreign to her, something she never considered.

Lindsey answered her, "Yes, Campbell's lived at Sunset all his life."

The girl crossed her arms and sized them up. "So, how do you two know each other?"

Lindsey put her arm around the girl's shoulder, as if shielding her from the truth. "Well, when I was not much older than you are now, I came down here with Uncle Bob—whose house we stay in—and Campbell and I were friends back then."

"It was a long time ago," Campbell added, stating the obvious.

"So, where's your wife?" the girl countered.

"Well, I live with my mom, and right now my daughter is living with me too. Nikki." He looked around the house, willing them to appear. "They're around here somewhere," he added. He glanced up at Nikki's closed door and said to Lindsey, "I'd love for you to meet Nikki."

She nodded, her face reddening slightly. He scolded himself internally for his words. Nikki still reminded her of bad news and bad endings, of course. "I mean, eventually," he fumbled around like an awkward adolescent. For some reason, Lindsey's presence rendered him exactly that. He held up two full grocery bags. "Well, this look like enough junk food to get you two through at least a day?"

They giggled.

"You sure y'all can walk all the way home carrying these bags, or can I offer you a ride?"

Jake piped up, "Ride! We walked forever to get here."

Campbell looked at Lindsey. "Funny, it never seemed that long to me."

She smiled and looked away to the window, but not before he saw her cheeks redden. "I think a ride home would be nice," she replied quietly, still facing the window.

"Well then, one ride coming right up." He grabbed his truck keys and led the way out the door. The kids followed him, with Lindsey last. As he tossed the bags into the back of the truck, he saw her pause in the doorway, looking at the house before shutting the door. This was, he realized, exactly what she wanted. When he got the chance, he would tell her that it was exactly what he wanted too.

It was so "high school" to admit she was disappointed when the kids hopped in the car beside Campbell and she couldn't sit beside him. She wanted to be next to him, squeezed into the cab of his truck so close they could feel each other breathe. She wanted his warmth next to her, to breathe in his smell. No one said a word as they drove the short distance home.

"Wow," Jake said as he hopped out. "It doesn't seem that far when you drive!" Campbell handed each child a bag, and Lindsey shooed them inside to put the food away.

Campbell and Lindsey stood awkwardly by the truck, looking at each other without speaking. They stared at each other—it seemed neither one knew how to say good-bye or wanted the night to end.

"You really haven't changed that much," he said, breaking the silence.

She smiled. "I thought the exact same thing. I would know you anywhere."

"I'm sorry I said that about meeting Nikki," he said. "I didn't mean to bring her up. I realize that might not be something you're ready to talk about."

She put her hand on his arm. "Campbell, it's been almost twenty years. I hope I've grown up enough to handle meeting your daughter. She's obviously a big part of your life."

He smiled. "She's a cool kid. Of course, who am I kidding? She's not little anymore. She's starting college now."

The door to the house opened and Anna stuck her head out. "Mom! Jake's eating a bunch of Oreos even though he already had a Popsicle tonight!"

"Okay!" she hollered back. "I'll be right in. Tell Jake to stop eating and go brush his teeth." She paused for a moment. "You too!" she hollered just as Anna slammed the door. She looked at Campbell. "Sorry to yell." She laughed in a way she was sure sounded self-conscious. "I still don't think she heard me."

He smiled. "Your kids are great."

"Well, thanks. I think so."

"Guess this year's been hard on them."

"You know, I've put so much emphasis on me and my hurting that only now am I processing what Grant's—that's my husband—leaving did to them. This trip's been good for us in that way."

"How long are you here for?" he asked, a note of hopefulness in his voice.

"Well, my uncle hardly ever comes here anymore, so he said to stay as long as I wanted. I originally thought we'd stay a week, but now …" she let her voice trail off, hoping he would finish her sentence for her.

"Now, what?" he teased.

"Well, now I wonder if maybe we have some catching up to do," she answered, more boldly than she felt.

"I would say that's a correct assumption." They both stood there grinning at each other, the giddy feelings of youth rushing back to them as if no time had passed. "So, if I could get my mom to watch your kids, do you think that maybe we could go to dinner tomorrow night?"

She tried to imagine her kids with his mom. She couldn't help it. She thought of Anna or Jake telling Grant that she went out with a man, leaving them with his mom, a total stranger. She imagined that phone call, his disapproving tone. "I don't know," she said. "I mean the ink's hardly dry on my divorce papers."

He put his hand, warm and heavy, on her shoulder. "The last time I checked, old friends going out to dinner is okay. What if I promise not to make a move on you?"

Maybe it was because she felt young standing in the beach night air, or because seeing him again felt like a miracle, or maybe after losing a husband she just had less to lose, but she replied with exactly what she was thinking: "The problem is, I might want you to."

His laugh came out in a sputter. "Well then, that gives me much to think about tonight." They both laughed nervously. "So, is that a yes?"

She smiled at him, though it had grown dark and she didn't know if he could see. "Yes," she said, grateful he couldn't feel her heart beating ninety miles an hour.

As he got in his truck and drove away with the smile still on his face, she hurried inside the house and slumped inside the door, happiness rising inside her like bubbles in champagne, light and buoyant and never ending.

Chapter 20

Sunset Beach

Summer 1995

Lindsey sat on the beach watching Grant play at the water's edge with Anna, holding her chubby hand and trying to keep her from putting shells in her mouth. She waved at him but he didn't see her.

She watched as clouds gathered off the coast. The ominous gray color meant a big storm was brewing, and for a moment she wondered if she would be able to get to the mailbox tomorrow or if it would still be storming and she would be left inside with her family, staring forlornly out the window like a little girl unable to go outside to play.

She stared at the horizon and wondered if she should suggest that they pack it in for the day. Other beachgoers were collecting their blankets and balls, taking down umbrellas and throwing away trash. But she wanted to sit a bit longer and stare at the clouds. A memory flickered across her mind of her first summer at Sunset, a decade ago. This year was an anniversary of sorts, ten years of coming to the mailbox. She had allowed herself to remember Campbell more than usual in honor of the occasion.

She pictured her aunt Frances pacing in front of the TV set. "Bobby, Stephanie! I need you to be quiet so I can hear this weather report!" she said to Lindsey's cousins, her voice strained and sharp. Bobby and Stephanie stopped squabbling over the game they were playing and looked at Lindsey with fear in their eyes. Their mother never raised her voice.

Lindsey walked over to stand beside her aunt. "What's up?" she asked.

Her aunt shook her head and lowered her voice. "This hurricane is going to hit the coast. They've recommended a voluntary evacuation of the island. But please don't talk about it with the kids."

Lindsey nodded, her heart racing. "Does that mean we would leave early?" she asked, willing her voice not to sound as panicked as she felt. She looked over at Campbell, who sat with Bobby and Stephanie at the kitchen table. He raised his eyebrows and came over to join them.

"Hey, Lindsey, let's head over to my house to see what my parents are going to do. Do you mind, Mrs. Edwards?" Her aunt shook her head absentmindedly and turned back to the TV.

Lindsey followed Campbell out of the house. As soon as they got off the porch, she grabbed his hand. "I'm nervous, Campbell. If we have to evacuate, we won't come back," she said. "We only have a few days left as it is."

He smiled back at her, confident. "I've got a plan," he said and kissed her knuckles. "So don't you worry because you aren't going anywhere."

They walked into his house and found his mom. "Hey, Mom," he said. "Are you guys evacuating?"

Mrs. Forrester waved her hand in the air dismissively. "No, this thing's going to be nothing more than a bad storm. No need to go anywhere." She smiled at Lindsey. "Is your family leaving, honey?" she asked her.

Campbell interrupted before Lindsey could answer. "Well, that's what I came to talk to you about. Will you and Dad drop by and talk to Lindsey's aunt and uncle? They're nervous, and I think it would help for them to see that you guys aren't."

Campbell's mother nodded, looking from Lindsey to Campbell. "Well, sure, honey. Whatever you think would help. I'll go get your dad and we can drive you two back over there." She grinned at them. "I'll even offer to let Campbell stay with you guys for the night just to keep an eye on things. How's that?"

Lindsey couldn't imagine sleeping in the same house with Campbell, but she nodded before the offer went away. Her hopes were high as the group climbed into the Forresters' wood-paneled Jeep Wagoneer. Sitting beside Campbell in the backseat, she felt safe and secure, as if together they could handle any storm. She leaned into him and felt his warmth radiate through her.

A decade later she still remembered that feeling: She trusted Campbell completely. She believed then that the right person could solve all of her problems and erase all of her hurts. She had learned lately—thanks to Holly and, ironically, to Grant—that no person could be everything to her. She had recently learned that only God was capable of such a role. With Holly's encouragement, Lindsey had begun attending a Bible study and was actually starting to believe that only God could love her like she needed to be loved—plus, she had no idea where *else* she would find it. To expect a sixteen-year-old boy to do that for her had been her first mistake.

Raising her hand, she tried to catch Grant's eye, but he still wasn't looking. Disappointment lurched in her heart. How many years had she been looking to men to make her feel worthy, beginning with Campbell and now with Grant? If she depended on him to make her feel valuable, she would always be reaching but never taking hold. As the sky darkened, she put her hand down and waited for him to come to her.

Summer 1995

Dear Kindred Spirit,

We had a big rainstorm here last night. And today, the beach was covered in debris, reminding me of Hurricane Bob, the hurricane that hit my first summer here. I thought about how the skies looked that summer and how Campbell and I, along with a crowd of onlookers, marveled at the surfers, who refused to get out of the water even as the winds and rain whipped them around. Maybe you were there, Kindred Spirit. Maybe you were also in the crowd that gathered to watch those surfers. Maybe you saw me and Campbell and smiled at us because you knew that you and I were going to be friends.

I still remember how confident Campbell was as he comforted my family and convinced them not to evacuate the island. He stood in their kitchen leaning against the counter, the dishwasher humming behind him. "It'll blow over," he said, with a wave of his hand, dismissing the whole thing. Outside the window, I could see the people next door loading their car, heading for safer territory, their faces pinched with worry. "Wimpy tourists," Campbell had labeled them with a wink.

Looking back now, it seems silly that we trusted Campbell, but we did. He took us in with his demeanor: confident without being cocky, knowing without being a know-it-all. He made me feel safe when I was with him. I guess that's why what happened with Ellie still haunts me—because I had come to expect more from him. I didn't expect human weakness in him, which in hindsight was unfair. If I had the chance, I would tell him now that I forgive him. It's been ten years—ten years of feeling betrayed, cast aside. Abandoned.

Even as I say it—I forgive him—I can't believe I have reached this point. But there it is. I guess time does heal. Maybe not to the point that I can forget—because how can I forget?—but to the point that I see things as they were and not as I wished they'd turned out.

I can't help but wonder where he is now, what he's doing. Did he and Ellie work out? Did they have any other children? Now that I am married, I certainly can't try to find him, but I will admit to you—and only to you—that there is a part of me that still wants to stay connected to him. There is a part of me that would love to tell him how my *life turned out. That I am still waiting out the storms of life instead of running from them, even though I had to learn to do it without him. That gradually I am learning to trust God to be with me in the storm. I wonder if my newfound faith in God would surprise him or if he has taken a similar path. He knew how I used to feel about God. I would love to tell him how wrong I was.*

The night of the hurricane, my aunt and uncle let Campbell sleep at their beach house. With the wind howling and the rain beating the windows, he and I sat on the couch chatting with my aunt and uncle. When the house lost power, we lit candles and played cards. When the actual storm passed over, the wind gusted so hard that the doors of the house blew open by themselves and my aunt screamed. I think she second-guessed our decision to stay at that moment. I still remember her scream and the look on Campbell's face as he looked at us. "The worst is over now," he said calmly.

By morning, the storm had passed and we all went outside to inspect the damage. Tree limbs had fallen and lots of debris washed up on the shore. But nothing that warranted cutting our vacation short. I held Campbell's hand as we made our way down to the beach, barely talking, just happy to be together. "Thank you," I said as we walked.

"For what?" he asked.

"For talking my aunt and uncle into staying. If you hadn't been so convincing, I know we would have packed up and gone home early. And I would have had to say good-bye to you."

He smiled and took me in his arms. "Why do you think I told them to stay?" he said as he waggled his eyebrows up and down. That was when I realized that he was never certain that we would be fine—he had no special insight or prediction skills as we had all assumed. He was just a lovestruck teenager who didn't want his summer romance called off on account of weather. The fact that his parents weren't evacuating was reason enough for him to convince us to stay put. As I kissed him there, on the beach, I was so happy that it had worked and we had bought a few more days together, even if it took a dangerous gamble to make it happen. Even more, I knew that this was a person who felt safe in the midst of a storm, a person I could find shelter in. But people aren't made for that.

It seems strange to still miss Campbell as I sit here, all these years later. Maybe it seems strange to you, too. I'm a married woman, after all. But sometimes my memories of him are so thick that I can't push through them—especially when I come to the mailbox. Sometimes I just have to let the memories sit until, slowly, they dissipate and I go on with normal life.

Normal life for me these days is a whirlwind. It is only in rare times like these that I am allowed the luxury of a memory, the treasure of a deep thought. Anna is an active toddler who keeps me on my toes. She started walking at a year and running practically the next day! She is so inquisitive, which means I spend most of my time just following her around trying to keep her from hurting herself. I wish you could meet her. When she gets older, I imagine I will bring her here. Will she love the mailbox and you, Kindred Spirit, as much as I do?

Grant and I are doing fine. I wouldn't say great, but fine. The more I learn about marriage, the more I wonder if there are any truly great ones out there. Grant's parents have been married forever, but they bicker and fight so much it makes me uncomfortable to be around them sometimes. So, what is a great marriage, really? Can two imperfect people ever really love each other in a way that is mutually satisfying? Is it even possible for people to love each other completely? These are questions I try not to spend too much time pondering. Because the answers make me feel sort of sad and hopeless.

Grant is pushing for another child, which I am considering but very nervous about. I know that he would love to have a son. He wasn't disappointed that Anna was a girl, but he did say pretty quickly that he would like to try again for a son. Sometimes I would like to leave things the way they are—just surviving Anna's first year seems monumental enough. Although I don't want Anna to be an only child. I know firsthand how lonely that can be. Maybe that's why Campbell and I gravitated to each other the way we did—two only children reaching out to each other out of loneliness, and hanging on for dear life.

Speaking of hanging on for dear life, I should probably get going. Grant is alone with Anna and I am on borrowed time. The two of them do much better together than they did a year ago, but it's still better if I'm around. They both just seem to visibly relax when I walk in the door. I am the glue, Grant says, that holds our family together. Sometimes I wish someone else could be the glue for a while. Being the glue, I am discovering, is sticky business.

Until next summer,
Lindsey

Chapter 21

Sunset Beach

Summer 2004

All day Campbell thought of her. He had gotten up the courage to ask her out last night and, like a schoolboy counting down the hours to his first date, he now watched the clock. When he took Nikki for her counseling appointment, he knew she could tell he was preoccupied. Neither of them said a lot on the drive over, each lost in their own thoughts. Nikki acted like counseling was the last place in the world she wanted to go. Like if he gave her the choice, she would choose prison or the most boring class she'd ever sat through over that appointment. He knew that helping her needed to be his first priority. And in that way Lindsey turning up was bad timing. Thoughts of Lindsey filled his mind and tore him away from thoughts of Nikki. He was torn between Lindsey and his daughter once again.

When he dropped off Nikki, her counselor, Lisa, asked to speak to him alone for a moment. They stood out in the hall, next to a dilapidated, dusty ficus tree someone had stuck there and forgotten.

He wondered if Nikki could hear them through the door and guiltily stepped farther away. Lisa told him that helping Nikki build relationships with him, her grandmother, and her mom would be the basis of changing the destructive behavior patterns she had been engaging in. She asked if they would be willing to come to some of the sessions. He assured her they were committed to helping Nikki any way they could, yet inwardly winced at the thought of Ellie coming to Sunset, especially with Lindsey back in the picture.

Lisa told him that Nikki seemed committed to working toward her goals. But she also warned that, girls like Nikki were already proficient in achieving what's expected of them. His mind flashed to her graduation ceremony, the awards she walked up to the stage to accept, the blank smile on her face. He had brushed it off as nerves, but he now saw differently as Lisa spoke. Nikki wanted something out of those awards she didn't get. The awards, he knew, felt light in her arms, weightless, a lot of nothing. Lisa warned him that sometimes girls like Nikki had tricks up their sleeves, playing along for everyone's sake, yet continuing the behavior in new and secretive ways. He agreed to come in later that week alone to discuss details. He braced himself to hear whatever the counselor meant by "details."

While Nikki went for her hour of counseling, he wandered around the church, thinking about his daughter and how much work lay ahead for both of them if she would ever be whole and healthy again. He thought again of the things he needed to say to her, the apologies he needed to offer. Not that his words would make an immediate difference, but with time, perhaps she would let him in a little more. He couldn't shake the feeling that he didn't deserve to have a second chance with his daughter. And yet, she was in his life, his home, again. Maybe she needed the second chance as much as he did.

Eventually he made his way into the empty sanctuary, thinking of the many times he had sat through services, sung worship songs, prayed in the stillness for something … more. He took a seat in the pew and bowed his head.

"Lord," he said, "I wonder if You have brought Lindsey and me together for a reason. You know I have waited half my life to have a chance with her again. Please don't let me blow it this time. You know there are things I need to say to her. Things she might not understand. Show me how to tell her how much I already love her, how I have wanted to be a part of her life for longer than she knows. Give me the words to say. I don't know if I can handle losing her twice. Just please, please, please don't let this be anything but the real thing." Campbell finished his prayer by asking God to keep His hand on Nikki. He didn't want to forget his daughter in the rush of his anticipation about Lindsey. Nikki had to remain his priority.

He sat in silence for a while, waiting for that still, small voice to speak to his heart, to answer his prayer with divine reassurance. When he rose from his seat, he realized that God's answer already walked by his house the night before, looking just the same as she did years ago, as if no time had gone by at all. They had taken the long way back to where they started, but the timing of their encounter was no accident. He couldn't wait to tell her when he saw her later that night.

Chapter 22

Sunset Beach
Summer 2004

How do you fill a day when all you want to do is get to the evening? That was Lindsey's dilemma as she woke up the next morning.

She realized she must first find something to wear. After going through every possible combination of the clothes she packed, she determined a trip to the store was necessary. She bribed her kids with a stop at a fast-food restaurant for lunch, and then found a little boutique in Calabash with lots of beachwear that was perfect for a night out with an old friend—which she kept telling herself was all tonight was. She made sure to try on everything, even as her children sat in little chairs outside the dressing room looking positively miserable and voicing their complaints to her every time she walked out to view herself in the full-length mirror. She noted that she could wear a smaller size than the last time she bought clothes, thanks to her minimized appetite and renewed running habit. Lindsey swiped the debit card that she and Grant still shared.

Until she returned home from the beach and signed the forms, their accounts were still joined. She grinned, feeling thrilled at the thought of Grant buying her an outfit for her evening with Campbell: poetic justice.

Next, she had to inform her children that they were going to be staying at Campbell's house with his mother while she went out with him. She stressed several times to the children that she and Campbell were merely two old friends catching up, even as Anna raised suspicious eyebrows. Lindsey told herself the same thing several times an hour—she repeatedly had to push from her mind the fantasy of his arms around her, of kissing him again. A shiver ran up her spine as she let her mind wander. Was this wrong for a newly divorced woman? She didn't care.

She took her time in the shower that afternoon, using shower gel, shaving her legs, conditioning her hair. She hadn't taken that kind of time on herself in ages, and it felt good. She brought a radio into the bathroom and played it while she showered, dancing around under the steaming water as she washed and rinsed her hair to Barry White singing, "My darling, I … can't get enough of your love, babe." She smiled up into the stream of water, felt the force and heat cleanse her body. But it couldn't wash away her nerves. Her stomach coiled into a tight spring at the thought of spending an evening with Campbell. Alone.

Someone banged on the bathroom door. "Mom!" she heard Anna yell. "What are you doing in there? Why are you blasting that radio?"

She was glad Anna couldn't see her dancing around, a soapy mess. "Be out in a minute!" she called as she stuck her head under the stream one last time before shutting off the water and the radio. As she toweled herself off, she caught herself still humming the Barry White tune.

She opened the bathroom door to find Anna sprawling her lanky self across the bed, eyeing her skeptically. "What was that music you were playing?" Anna asked.

"Old music. Stuff from before you were born," she said.

"I could hear you singing," she said. "You sounded pretty happy."

Lindsey didn't reply, hoping Anna would drop the subject. She busied herself with putting on her makeup while Anna quietly watched. Some mascara ended up on her eyelid instead of her lashes. It never failed.

"Mom?" Anna asked.

"Hmm?"

"How come if this isn't a date you are making all this fuss about what you wear and your makeup and everything?"

Why did Anna's question sound like an indictment? Lindsey suspected it was her own defensiveness and not her daughter's inquiry that tensed her. Still, Lindsey had grown good at quick recoveries for her children's probing questions, a skill she had never wanted to hone. "Well, honey, I just haven't gotten to do something grown-up in so long, it feels nice to get to do something like this. I haven't 'made a fuss,' to quote you, over myself since—" she stopped short of finishing her sentence.

"Since Daddy was here, right?" Anna said.

Lindsey put her mascara down and sat down beside her daughter on the bed. "Well, yes. You know I loved dressing up and going out with Daddy."

"Yeah," she quipped with the emerging wit of a sarcastic teen, "and look where that got you."

"Honey, Campbell is just an old friend—"

"You've said that a few times," she said, smiling at her mother in a knowing way that made her look much older.

Lindsey smiled back. "Well, he is. And I enjoyed talking to him last night when we ran into him, so he asked me if we could keep talking. It's just that simple. Besides, I haven't seen the guy for like twenty years!"

"But you think he's cute, don't you, Mom?"

She had entered a new era with her daughter: talking about boys. "Why, do you?"

"Eww, Mom. He's old!"

She stuck her tongue out playfully. "Well, I guess he's old to you."

"But not to you, right, Mom?"

"Well, of course not," she said, returning to the bathroom to finish getting ready. The clock ticked away the moments to his arrival. "He's my age—and I certainly don't feel old," she hollered as she turned on the hair dryer.

But I'm sure I seem old to you, she thought as she finished drying her hair. She remembered when forty seemed ancient, now she could see it looming just ahead, a marker that snuck up on her while she cleaned house and ran carpool.

She shut off the dryer just as Anna rose from the bed. Her daughter stopped short and turned to look at her, a vision of herself at that age, a brilliant flash of what was. She knew that the thought of her as a young girl was as foreign to Anna as the thought of her as a grown woman was to Lindsey. She knew that her daughter couldn't picture her serious mom as a giddy teen with dreams and hopes and plans; couldn't see her in her mind's eye, dancing happily through this same house, singing the name of the boy who captured her heart at the top of her lungs.

"Mom," Anna stated matter-of-factly, "I think it's good you're going out to have some fun. And if you want to date this Campbell person, then you have my blessing."

"Well, now," Lindsey said, looking back at the mirror to avoid making eye contact. "Let's not get ahead of ourselves." She turned to glance at Anna before she left. "Thanks, though. It means a lot that you want me to be happy." Anna nodded and headed to her room to get dressed.

Satisfied that she looked as good as she could possibly look, Lindsey switched off the lights and walked to the kitchen, where Jake sat eating Oreos, again. "Hey, Mom," he said, his mouth stuffed with cookies, "if you marry this guy, does that mean we can live here at the beach?"

What was with these kids? Lindsey shook her head and picked the package of cookies up from the table, placing them up high in a cabinet, out of his reach.

He pointed, not missing a beat. "I can reach those with a chair," he said and grinned at her, his mouth ringed with chocolate and his teeth black. "Easy."

"A chair *better* not reach those, and go wash your face. You've ruined your dinner."

"It's impossible for me to ruin my dinner!" he said as he ran from the room to avoid her playful swat.

Lindsey barely heard Campbell's knock at the door over Jake's thundering feet. Just knowing he was on the other side of the door set Lindsey's heart racing. She took a few deep breaths and crossed over to open the door for him. The sight of him took her breath away.

He had looked good last night, no question. But tonight he had outdone himself. He wore khaki shorts that showed off his tan legs and a black T-shirt that contoured his body in all the right places. She noticed he'd had a haircut since the night before, and the thought of him preparing for their date thrilled her as much as the sight of him now. It was all she could do not to blurt out "You're perfect!" and throw her arms around his neck.

Anna and Jake slunk quietly into the room to say hello, both uncharacteristically shy. "Y'all ready?" Campbell asked, sounding a bit formal and nervous. They nodded and followed him out to the truck. She closed the door behind them. *Here we go*, she breathed to no one.

The truck was silent as they drove the short distance to Campbell's. As they parked in front of his house, he stopped Lindsey from getting out. "You don't want to go in there," he told her. "If you do, we'll be held hostage for hours—Mom and Minerva will talk your ear off. I'll get the kids settled and be right back." So, in the cramped quarters of the truck cab, she hugged Anna and Jake. Then they followed Campbell in without a backward glance, probably hoping to find more junk food awaiting them. He had found the way to their hearts.

"Be good," she said, waving until they disappeared into the house. She pushed the thoughts aside that taunted her: What kind of mother allows her children to stay with someone she hasn't seen in almost twenty years? And then doesn't even go inside to check out where they will be staying for the evening? And yet, God had given her a peace about the evening that she chose to rely on instead of succumbing to those nagging worries. She pulled down the visor mirror and checked her makeup. Again. When she noticed Campbell returning, she quickly pushed the mirror back up so he didn't see her primping.

He hopped in the truck and smiled at her. "It's a madhouse in there. They're going to have a blast." He gave her a sidelong glance. "Not to worry. They've got my mother and Minerva and Nikki to hover over them for the next several hours." He leaned over and took her hand. "And I have you all to myself." His words made her weak. She looked down at his hand entwined with hers and felt euphoric and nauseous all at the same time. He pulled the truck out onto Main Street, turning toward the pier and the old bridge they would cross to get over to the mainland, taking them somewhere they'd never been as they journeyed back to where they started.

Chapter 23

Sunset Beach
Summer 2004

Campbell resisted the urge to gush, to open his mouth and let all the silly, sappy things he wanted to say to her pour out. He struggled with playing it cool in normal circumstances, but trying to do so in a situation that he thought could only happen in dreams was darn near impossible. As they sat at the restaurant, he forced his hands under his knees so he didn't reach across the table and run his fingers through her hair. He wanted to grab her hand and pull her out of that civilized restaurant to a place where they could talk freely, finally say everything he'd waited years to say. He wanted to find a quiet place where he could hold her and whisper promises about nothing tearing them apart this time. He didn't want to make surface small talk in the middle of a crowded restaurant. Still, he knew it was a good place to start.

As they waited on the server to notice them, he complimented her on her kids. "You've done a great job raising them alone," he said.

She brushed aside the praise. "Well, I've only been a single mom for a year," she said. "So …" her voice trailed off, doubt lacing the edges of her voice.

"Do … do you mind me asking what happened with your husband?" he said. "I mean, if you can talk about it."

"You mean, if I can talk about it *with you*?"

He smiled. "Touché."

She smiled ruefully. "The truth is, I don't know what happened. I think he stopped loving me a long time ago, but hung in there for the sake of the kids." She paused reflectively. "You know, it's a sad old story that's been told a hundred times before." She paused. "But just because it's happened to countless other women doesn't mean it's any easier to take when it happens to you. Last year when we were here at the beach, I knew it was basically over. I—" she stopped again. "He agreed to come with us and I hoped …" She smiled. "He left the day after we got home. I've heard women say that they didn't see it coming, but that wasn't true for me. I saw the cracks in the foundation long before the building fell. You know how when you're swimming in the ocean and there's an undercurrent and you don't even know it's carrying you away until you look up and there's a whole new set of people up on the beach where your family sat?"

He nodded sympathetically. "Then you have to get out of the water and wander down the beach to find your family," he added.

"Well, he's the one who drifted, but I'm the one left wandering around trying to find something that looked familiar." She laughed. "The truth is, he found someone else," she said.

She added sarcastically, "But the good news is, he felt really bad about it." She rolled her eyes and shook her head.

The server approached the table to take their orders. They both ordered water, and the server retreated just as quickly as he came. She shook her head. "Sorry for dumping all of that on you right away."

"Hey, I asked," he said with a smile, hoping to make her feel comfortable. "You were just being honest."

"Yeah, but I don't want this evening to be about either one of our sad stories," she said.

"Well, then, can I say something?" he ventured.

She nodded and smiled. "Of course."

"I just wanted to clear the air between us, if that's okay." He watched a dark cloud cross her face, but he pressed on. "I wanted to tell you I'm sorry for everything that I did. I never got a chance to tell you that in person back then and it's always bothered me. I hated the way it all happened, and I've taken far too long to say it to you in person."

She held her hand up, signaling for him to stop, but he shook his head and continued. "No, I owe you this apology. I owe you a lot of things, actually. I know it couldn't have been easy." He paused and looked at her, willing her to understand. "It wasn't for me."

She looked back at him, the look on her face a mixture of resolve and sadness. "No, Campbell, it wasn't easy. It broke my heart. And it hurt for a long, long time." She smiled. The server placed two waters in front of them and receded into the background where he came from. She squeezed lemon into her water and took a sip. "But I found a way to move on." Another sip. "I have always wondered what happened to you, though …"

He charged forward. "I've wondered too. I wonder about you every day, Lindsey. I wondered during the ceremony when I married

Ellie. I wondered when I held Nikki for the first time. I wondered when Ellie left me. And when my dad died. I always wondered how you were doing, whether you thought of me." He lowered his voice. "I wondered, if I showed up on your doorstep, would you come away with me?" He stopped and smiled, suddenly self-conscious at his bold admission. "So yeah, I wondered too."

She smiled back, then looked down at her lap as she asked shyly, so quietly he almost didn't hear her, "Do you want to stay here?" She looked up at him expectantly. He realized what she had just asked.

He grinned back at her conspiratorially, like a couple of teenagers breaking curfew. "No," he admitted. "Let's get out of here."

She rose and began walking to the door. He paused for a moment before throwing down a few dollars for their sips of water and doing what he had waited to do for many years: He ran after her.

Chapter 24

Sunset Beach
Summer 2004

Sitting in the truck next to Campbell as they left the restaurant, Lindsey felt just the way she used to feel with him—giddy and breathless, both feelings she thought went the way of her aging metabolism and energy level. She was glad to know some things weren't lost forever, that a bit of her youth still lived on inside her. Despite the heat and humidity, Campbell rolled down the windows to let in the ocean breeze and smell. "The pier?" he asked her.

"You read my mind," she said.

They rode in silence, a million questions running through her mind as they drove, but none of them sounding like the right ones to ask first. As they pulled up to the pier and she started to open her door, he stopped her. "Allow me," he said as he scrambled around to the door and pulled it open with a debonair smile.

"Why, thank you," she said, trying to remember the last time

Grant held a door for her, or if he ever did. *Don't make this a competition*, she scolded herself.

"My pleasure, ma'am." As they walked to the pier, he took her hand casually. She wanted to go with the feeling, the moment, without obsessing over right and wrong. Though her heart soared, her head attempted rationalization. A verse kept running through her mind: "Above all else, guard your heart." She had tossed all rational thought aside the moment Campbell stepped down off his front porch the night before and smiled that lazy smile she had been missing all those years.

As if no time had passed at all, they headed to the very end of the pier. It all came back to her—the creaking of the ancient, weathered boards, the sound of the gulls swooping overhead, the angry crash of the waves below. She hadn't walked out there again since those two summers they spent together. Even when Holly dared her to do it back when Holly made the rules. She suggested that Lindsey write "I hate you, Campbell" on a piece of paper, tear it up, and throw it off the end of the pier for the waves and God to swallow up. But Lindsey was always afraid that going there would be too painful, stir up too many memories. She never dreamed that she would return one day, holding his hand.

"Still looks the same," Campbell said, interrupting her thoughts. "And so do you," he added.

She grimaced. "Hardly," she said.

"You never were any good at taking a compliment," he said. "Or believing one." Something in the way he looked at her told her he knew her better than she realized. He looked around. "I haven't been back out here since then."

She looked at him, caught off guard by his admission. "But you live here," she sputtered.

"Yeah, well. I just couldn't come out here without you. It seemed like, if I did come out here, that I would be betraying you even more than I already had. Plus, there was never anything worth coming out here for after you." He paused. "This was our place. Well, this and the mailbox."

He pulled her close, wrapped his arms around her. She wished she could ask for a time-out. She felt split down the middle. One side of her screamed, *I've only been divorced a week!* The other side reminded her, *You're not doing anything wrong.*

But her conscience won over, and she pushed him away. "I can't, Campbell," she said. "I'm not sure I'm ready to be—" she fumbled for the right word, embarrassed—"physical," she finished.

He bent down, his breath on her face, the scent of his skin and the warmth of his body so real she couldn't deny the feelings she had. Feelings, she realized, she had carried since she was fifteen years old. She didn't stop him as he covered her lips with his own, awakening in her something she had missed for most of her life. He eased away and looked down at her with his piercing blue eyes. "You mean like that?" he asked breathlessly. She pushed thoughts of right and wrong from her mind as she nodded and kissed him again. They were the only two people on earth and all bets were off.

He smiled down at her and pulled her close to him, resting his chin on her head as she rested her head against his pounding heart. "I'll take it as slow as you need to," he told her. "But I just needed to do that first."

They stood silently for a while and stared out over the waves.

After a few long, comfortable moments, without looking at his face, she spoke. "Tell me about your daughter." She wanted to hear about Nikki, and yet she didn't. To acknowledge his daughter opened up painful memories, yet not to acknowledge her excluded a huge part of his life.

He stepped away from Lindsey and looked at her with a questioning expression. She nodded her okay. "Well, the truth is," he began, "if you had asked me that question a few weeks ago, I would have told you all about her—what I thought was true about her. But now I'm finding out I don't know her at all." He paused, then continued to tell Lindsey about Nikki's recent hospitalization and struggles with anorexia. "I was so oblivious," he said, clearly grieving. "I saw what I wanted to see, I guess," he added.

She wanted to comfort him. "I think most of us do that with the people we love," she said, understanding. She thought of Grant and how much she didn't want to admit in the beginning that he could lie and cheat and ultimately walk out.

"Yeah, I suppose. But with your kids it's like, you want to know every little thing about them—even the stuff they are struggling with. The fact that she didn't let me in, didn't come to me when she needed me … well, I'm still processing that, I guess. And I take a lot of the blame. I wanted to be more of a father to her. But wanting doesn't make it so, does it?"

She shook her head, remembering all the tears she cried over the marriage she wanted. "No, it certainly does not. But the thing is, you're here now, and she's here now. Seems like you got a second chance to be the kind of dad you wanted to be."

He smiled warmly, looking every bit like the boy she once loved. "Seems there's a lot of that going around this summer," he replied, rubbing his hand along her back.

"Yes," she said, more boldly than she felt, "there certainly is." She giggled. Then Campbell started to laugh with her. They laughed self-consciously at first, then took one look at each other and broke into fits of louder, but still nervous laughter. As the darkness claimed the night, their laughter spilled out over the waves that churned below them, spreading out in ripples that carried out to sea.

Chapter 25

Sunset Beach

Summer 1997

Lindsey saw a man at the mailbox and her heart sank. She didn't want to share the mailbox with anyone today. She just wanted to enjoy some time there alone, write a quick note for the year, and head back to Grant and the children.

But she had come too far to turn back. She resolved not to make eye contact and just walk to the mailbox like always. She lowered her eyes and made her way up into the dunes, willing him to keep his distance. She busied herself with taking out a sheet of paper and a pen, then had a seat on the bench to write, telling herself not to look up. But the sound of a camera shutter made her forget her own admonitions. She looked up and saw the man aiming his camera in her direction.

She stood and held up her hands. "Excuse me!" she called. "Do you have permission to take pictures here?" What she really wanted to say was, "I don't recall giving you permission to take *my* picture!"

He let go of the camera, and it flopped onto his chest, suspended by an ornately embroidered strap. "Oh I am dreadfully sorry! I do apologize!" he called back, scurrying up the dune to reach her. His accent was British, or Irish, or Australian. She could never tell them apart. "I should have asked your permission first." He chuckled. "I am a bit of an artist with the camera, I guess, and I just forget myself when I get caught up in a bit of inspiration."

The man studied her for a moment, cocking his head as if he were sizing her up. "You just seem very connected to this place. The look on your face was so—" he searched for a word—"reverent." He smiled conspiratorially. "This place is special to you, no?"

She looked around to confirm that they were the only two people for miles. And yet something about how genuine the man was made her feel safe. *That's what victims probably think right before they're abducted*, she thought, smiling.

He took the smile as an invitation and extended his hand to shake hers. "Name's Roderick. Roderick Shaw."

She shook his hand and smiled. "Lindsey Adams," she said. He pulled out a small notepad from his camera bag and scribbled something in it. Her name, she assumed.

"Very pleased to meet you, Ms. Adams," he said, tucking the notepad back inside the bag. "So what brings you to the Kindred Spirit mailbox on this lovely day?"

"I come out here once a year around this time. It's a … habit, I guess."

"I'd say more like a pilgrimage," he said. "It's important to you." It wasn't a question.

She nodded, growing to like this strange man a bit more by the minute. "Yes, I always leave a note in the mailbox about the year I've had. Catching the Kindred Spirit up on all that's gone on in my life." She laughed self-consciously. "It sounds silly when I say it out loud."

"Not at all," Roderick said. "This place is special. There's no doubt about it. I think God listens to you better here than any place else in the world. I'd say, in fact, that He's the real Kindred Spirit."

"You think?" Lindsey ventured, curious.

"Well, of course."

She smiled, thinking of the church she had been attending, the way she'd been praying more and reading the Bible Holly had given her years ago when they graduated from high school. It was still so new that some of the pages were stuck together and it crackled from lack of use when she opened it. But she was breaking it in more every day. She had made some Christian friends at church who were helping her learn more about her faith, and she was trusting God more every day. "Perhaps that's true."

"Oh, Ms. Adams, I think you know." He motioned for her to take a seat beside him on the makeshift bench by the mailbox. "Might you have time to hear a story about this place?" Roderick asked.

She hadn't planned to be here long, but she told him she had time to hear his story. She was intrigued by the idea that there were other people who had been profoundly affected by the mailbox. Of course there were, yet she had never considered them before.

"I came here several years ago on assignment. I was hired to shoot some photos for postcards for the area. You know, like you buy there at the Island Market in town?"

She nodded. Though she had never bought one, she had seen them on the rack by the cash register. She never imagined meeting the man who took the photos, never really considered there being a person with a story on the other end of the camera.

"So they tell me that I am supposed to take pictures of this obscure mailbox stuck in the sand in the middle of nowhere, and so off I go, thinking this is quite possibly the most absurd thing I have ever done." He laughed. "To be honest, I thought it was someone's idea of a practical joke. I didn't believe there was a mailbox out here."

She remembered her first walk with Campbell, how she teased him about making the mailbox up.

He went on. "But nevertheless, I found it and started shooting pictures of it. It was a glorious day, kind of like today. But the difference was it had rained a bit earlier. In fact, I almost didn't come because I wasn't sure the lighting was going to be right. But when I got here, you know what I found?"

She had seen the postcards for sale at the market. "A rainbow," she answered.

He slapped his knee and laughed, pointing at her. "You have seen my photos! Yes! A gorgeous rainbow! It only lasted a few minutes, but I got the most amazing photo of this rainbow over the ocean with the mailbox in the foreground and the rainbow in the background."

He sighed and wiped at his forehead with an old-fashioned handkerchief. "After I finished getting the pictures and putting all my gear away, I decided to have a seat." His face changed as he looked off at the ocean. "The truth was, I wasn't in good shape," he said. "I was an alcoholic and my wife had left me just a few weeks before. I knew that I was heading back home to a mess, and that it was all my fault.

"So I sat right here, in this very spot and started talking to God about it. I told Him how I felt and asked Him to help me change. I gave my life to Him here at the mailbox. And all I can tell you is, after that day, I never had another drop to drink. My life turned around, and I've never been the same since." He smiled and winked. "Got my wife back too. I have never been assigned to come back and take more pictures, but I still come back whenever I'm in the area. And I always bring my camera, just in case." He paused and looked at Lindsey. "So when I saw you coming up to the mailbox, I recognized that look."

"That look?" Lindsey asked.

"The look of a person who knows how special this place is. Who appreciates it with a kind of reverence most people reserve for memorials and churches."

"Yes," she agreed. "I do love coming here."

"Well then, don't ever stop. And don't ever take it for granted either." His face took on a more serious expression. "And don't forget that God loves you very much, Lindsey Adams," he said.

The man stood up and brushed off his khaki shorts, smiling down at her. He patted her on the shoulder and her skin warmed under his touch. "Have a great day," he said. "It was very nice to meet you."

"You too, Roderick," she said. She watched as he made his way back down the beach, half expecting him to disappear into thin air. She wondered if he'd even been real. She sat for a long while and thought about what Roderick said before picking up her pen and beginning to write.

Summer 1997

Dear Kindred Spirit,

I met a man here today who reminded me that God loves me. I know God arranged for that man to be here. I can't explain it any other way. God seems to be pursuing me, Kindred Spirit.… He's showing me that He loves me in little, personal ways. Ways someone else may not even notice, but ways that speak volumes to me. I am learning that God knows me, and I'm trying to accept that He really does, as Roderick reminded me, love me anyway.

For a long time I have refused to believe that God loves me. I have pushed Him away and equated Him to all the people who have let me down—my dad who left when I was a baby … my mom who never had time for me … Campbell … and even Grant. But God just keeps chipping away at my walls, built not only by me but also by those who've hurt me. Someday I think He will finally knock them down.

The mailbox has always been a special place for me, but I always thought it was special because it held a sentimental attachment from my youth. I never stopped to consider that the presence I feel here has nothing to do with Campbell and everything to do with God—that the Kindred Spirit I am writing to isn't just some kindly person who I hope remembers me from year to year, but that the God who created me is waiting for me each time I come here. It makes me think of this place differently. It makes me think there is much more here than meets the eye.

I go home today changed by my time at the mailbox, this year more than ever before. Except maybe that first year, which will always hold a special place in my heart. Campbell, wherever you are, I wish you well.

Until next summer,

Lindsey

Chapter 26

Sunset Beach

Summer 2004

That night, after his date with Lindsey, Campbell went out to the garage and stood in front of several shelves full of red shoes. Starting with a tiny pair of red Mary Janes on the bottom shelf, Nikki's red shoes worked their way up to a pair she wore last when she was a freshman in high school. Red Converse high tops. Campbell stepped back from the shelves and stared, as if the shoes would speak to him, dispense wisdom for what steps he should take next with their owner.

Campbell and Nikki's red-shoe tradition started by accident when Ellie's lack of sentimentality got the better of him. He remembered finding the little red Mary Janes he had bought her in the trash can. He had brought them to Ellie, indignant. "Why were these in the garbage?"

"Campbell, don't be ridiculous. They're worn out, and she outgrew them." Ellie rolled her eyes, dismissing him. "Those nasty things belong in the trash." She started to reach for them, but he pulled them back.

"I'm going to keep them," he announced. He looked down at the shoes. "Her feet will never be this little again." He smiled at Ellie, perhaps trying to elicit some kind of emotional response. "I guess I'm not willing to let go of them yet."

Ellie waved them—and him—away. "Well then, go put them outside," she instructed, wrinkling her nose. He carried them outside to the garage and laid them on an empty shelf. That day he went out and bought his three-year-old daughter a little pair of red Keds to replace the Mary Janes.

"You're a big girl now," he told her as she sucked on a lollipop and nodded, her curls bouncing as she did. He laid his large hand on her small head, his heart filled with love for her. Right then he knew what he would do.

"I'll tell you what," he said as he lifted her into her car seat. He leaned into her and kissed her on the forehead. "I promise to always buy you a pair of red shoes. Every time you outgrow one pair, we'll take that pair and put them on the shelf in the garage." She looked back at him and blinked. He smiled and lightly tweaked her nose. "Before you know it," he said, "we'll have shelves full of red shoes, and I will be able to see how big you've gotten right before my very eyes."

As if she knew he needed her agreement, she nodded, her saucer eyes taking him in. "Is that a good plan?" he asked her.

She took the lollipop out of her mouth. "That's a very good plan, Daddy," she said and popped the lollipop back in.

Over the years, she lost interest in the red-shoe game but played along, even agreeing that she would wear red high heels in her wedding. He specifically remembered buying her first pair of high-heeled shoes in red when she was thirteen. And the time she wanted cowboy boots when she was eight and he managed to find red ones. And the time she declared that her red tennis shoes actually made her run faster and jump higher.

The more Nikki stayed away from Sunset, the less he had been able to keep up with the tradition. Over time he had all but forgotten just like she had.

When Lindsey asked him earlier to tell her about his daughter, an image had filled his mind: Nikki stomping around in red cowboy boots. After dropping Lindsey off, he went straight to the garage to check on the shoes. He surveyed them all, watching a little girl grow up before his eyes.

"How'd it go?" he heard his mother's voice behind him.

"Fine," he said, not turning around. He wasn't ready to talk about his night with Lindsey.

"I heard your truck pull in, but I didn't ever hear you come in. I figured you went for a walk on the beach or were up on the roof deck," she said.

"Nah. I just remembered these shoes and started thinking about our old tradition. I almost forgot these things were out here." He paused, running his fingers across the toes of the cowboy boots, remembering Nikki's smile when she opened them that Christmas. "I guess I just needed to make sure they were still here."

"They still are, Campbell. And so is she." His mother's words echoed Lindsey's. She patted him on the shoulder and, though he couldn't see her, he could hear her smile. "You're getting some pretty significant second chances this summer, Son. Don't shy away from the opportunities you've been given."

"But what if I don't deserve what I've been given?" he asked, turning to look at his mother in the dimly lit room.

She smiled again, her mouth barely turned up at the edges. "Honey, none of us get what we deserve. That's why they call it grace."

He blinked back at her, trying to absorb the weight of her words.

She crossed her arms in front of her and winked at him. "It's late. I'm going to bed, and you should do the same." He listened as his mother's footsteps disappeared up the stairs into the house. He flipped off the light and went to bed, thinking about red shoes and mailboxes, and how to believe that grace was meant for him.

———

That night Campbell dreamed of watching Nikki ice-skate as a little girl. He woke up with the vivid memory of how it felt to watch her glide and turn across the icy back deck. She didn't need actual ice skates—her little red tennis shoes worked just fine. He would stay outside as long as he could, but she always outlasted him.

"Beach bums aren't made for this kind of weather," he would tell her, then venture inside to the welcome warmth. Nikki didn't seem fazed by the cold. He would man his post at the window, watching her while he sipped coffee, thinking how there just wasn't a more beautiful sight in the world than that little girl. Standing there in the dead of winter, summer felt very far away. As if it would never come at all.

The idea to turn the deck into an ice-skating rink came one of those winter nights when the temperature dropped to below freezing. In his first weekends alone with her after the divorce he worried they would be like strangers without Ellie as their conduit. He worried they would run out of conversation, left with nothing to do but stare at each other awkwardly. As they bundled up in sweatshirts and wrapped themselves in blankets to stay warm, Nikki mused that it was too bad the ocean didn't freeze so they could ice-skate on it. Shyly she told him that she had been taking ice-skating lessons at her new home with Oz and her mother. She wanted to show him what she'd learned. In that instant, he knew what he needed to do. He told her to wait as he ran outside, lugging the old hose up the deck stairs and blasting the deck with water, which froze nearly on impact. Moments later he came in, bowed low, and said, "Your wish is my command. Skate away, my lady."

From then on, whenever she stayed with him on winter weekends, she would anxiously watch for the temperatures to dip low enough to freeze, though it didn't happen very often. He installed a thermometer just outside the window, which she watched intently anytime it got the slightest bit cold. Just like that, they had something that united them that was theirs alone. He foolishly thought it would always be enough. That somehow she would always see him there, in her mind's eye, watching her through the window, delighting in her every move as she skated her problems away in red tennis shoes.

Campbell lay in bed for a few moments, trying to savor the purity of the dream, not wanting real life to fully wake him up. He heard the morning sounds he had heard all his life—gulls outside the

window, his mom banging around in the kitchen, the coffee perco-
lating. He rolled over and buried his head under the covers. And that
was when his night with Lindsey came back to him. He smiled wide
at the way the night ended: the awkward kiss he planted on her cheek
in front of her kids, the rowdy children she wrangled up the stairs
after he dropped them off, the sight of her waving apologetically as
she closed the door. The evening had been as close to perfect as he
could have dreamed of, a beginning to build on. Before he started his
day, he thanked God for new beginnings.

He rose from his bed and pulled up the shade to find the day
glorious, the sky a perfect blue, the kind a child would draw in a
picture, complete with fat, fluffy clouds.

"Dad?" he heard Nikki calling him from the hall.

"Just a sec, honey." He threw on his pajama pants and T-shirt
and opened his door to find her at the top of the stairs. "Yeah?" Her
thin body still startled him. How could she think that was beautiful?

"Um, can I talk to you?"

He waved her into his room and pointed to the easy chair. "Sure,
have a seat." Next to her elbow sat a stack of papers he needed to
remember to put away. He had pulled them out the night Lindsey
came by his house and had fallen asleep reading through them.

Nikki sat, nervously glancing around.

"Hey, Nik, thanks for helping out with Lindsey's kids last night,"
he told her. "Grandma said you were great with them."

She shrugged. "Yeah, I like kids. They aren't so complicated, you
know?"

He laughed at those words coming from his own daughter's
mouth. When he looked at her, a kid is exactly what he saw. "I agree."

"So you really like that woman, huh?"

"Um, well, it's kind of complicated with Lindsey. We knew each other a long time ago, so I guess you could say that we're just getting to know each other again." An image sprang to his mind of the way she looked after he kissed her. His face colored as he pushed the thought from his mind.

"Dad, you can't fool me! It's written all over your face!" She laughed and slumped back in the chair, her elbow knocking the papers to the floor. He didn't move to pick them up for fear he would break the spell that had her talking to him, laughing in his presence.

He hung his head in mock shame. "I guess I'm found out then," he said. He looked up. "Does that bother you?"

"Actually it's a relief."

He laughed in shock. "A relief?"

"I don't want you to be alone. I've always felt sorry for you here, with no one except Grandma for company. I mean, she's great, but I always wanted more for you. When I was little, I felt bad leaving you here after I would come for a visit. I knew you were lonely, and I never understood why you chose to remain alone. I wanted you to have a life like Mom did—someone special to be with, maybe even other children, all of that stuff." She looked away, out the window at the clouds floating by. "I used to cry when I had to leave, because I felt so sorry for you. Though I couldn't have explained it then—I felt like you deserved happiness." She looked at him, and for the first time since she'd been there, he caught a glimpse of his daughter—the person behind the diagnosis of anorexia. His heart filled with hope like sails catching the wind.

He choked on his words before he could force them out. "Thank you, sweetheart. That's good to hear."

"Anyway, Dad, I came to ask you if you would come to my counseling session today. Lisa thought it would be a good idea." She paused and then added, "I mean, and I do too." She cleared her throat. "If you want to, I mean."

The wallflower was finally being invited to dance. He could almost hear the door to her heart creaking open, the rusty hinges groaning with the effort. She had only cracked the door, but it was enough to let in the air and light. He couldn't walk through it yet, but he was getting closer.

Chapter 27

Sunset Beach
Summer 2004

All day Lindsey fought the urge to just "happen" by Campbell's place. She busied herself with cleaning up the beach house, attempting to distract her mind from dwelling on him—the way he looked at her, how familiar he seemed. She'd replayed last night's events countless times. A schoolgirl all over again, she stopped just short of doodling his name in her journal.

Finally, after resisting the urge all morning, she put on running clothes and sheepishly headed toward his house. She knew he would see right through her little ruse, but she didn't care if it meant they'd be in close proximity. The point was to be with him again. How she made that happen didn't really matter.

She jogged the distance to his house, the sound of her feet keeping time. How often had she orchestrated this kind of encounter when she was fifteen and sixteen years old? Turns out she had not outgrown the behavior.

When she rounded the corner to his house, she noticed his truck missing from the driveway. Disappointed, she decided not to turn around but to complete her run down his street. Running past the house, she heard a familiar voice call out, "Lindsey!" She slowed down slightly and shielded her eyes to see LaRae waving at her from the front porch. LaRae set down her watering can and waved Lindsey over, grinning ear to ear. Before Lindsey had even made it up the porch steps, LaRae began talking. "I'm so glad you and Campbell had such a lovely time last night," she said, seeming as giddy about the whole thing as Lindsey felt.

"It's nice to see you, Mrs. Forrester," Lindsey said with a smile, not wanting to seem too eager. "Thank you so much for watching my children! They had fun with you."

She waved her hand in the air. "Honey, that was nothing! I'll watch them anytime if you'll take Campbell off my hands! He's the real handful."

Lindsey laughed, and LaRae grinned back at her. "Now don't get me wrong. I love Campbell and I don't know what I would do without him. But I do wish he'd meet someone and move on with his life. He's been alone too long." Her eyes got a wistful look. "Campbell's daddy and I were so happy. I hate that he never saw Campbell find that same kind of love. It's what he wanted for him, and I keep hoping for it still." She looked at her meaningfully. "But he never seemed interested. And I finally understand why."

Lindsey stared back at her blankly and answered, "Why?" before she could stop herself. Her heart pounded in her chest even though she had stopped running.

"Well, honey, because of you, of course. I think he's been

hoping he'd find his way back to you, or you to him. Whichever."
She gave her a once-over. "Come on inside and I'll get you some
water," she said. "It's awful hot to be running right now."

Lindsey followed her inside, wondering if LaRae had guessed
that her run was really a ploy to see Campbell. "I guess he's not
here, then?" she asked.

LaRae frowned slightly. "No, he took Nikki to her counseling
session. You know about all that, right?" she asked.

Lindsey paused before nodding, not wanting to drag anything
shameful or embarrassing out of Campbell's mother, yet hungry to
know more about his life, all the parts she had missed out on.

"Well, then you know that Nikki has anorexia. She nearly
starved herself to death and now she's in counseling. He takes her
every day." She handed Lindsey a glass of ice water and gulped
some down herself. Setting the empty glass on the counter, she
added, "She has emotional issues to work on."

"Don't we all?" Lindsey blurted out.

LaRae smiled and nodded. "Yes, honey. I suspect you're right
about that. Nikki's problems are just more—" she searched for the
right word—"urgent than the rest of ours."

"You must be crazy about her," Lindsey said, noticing the tenderness in the way LaRae spoke her name.

"Absolutely smitten, yes. She may not have come into the
world the way I would have wanted, especially not for my son.
But we pulled together and made the best of it. Because that's what
families do.

"I guess it was especially around the time that Ellie took off
and we had Nikki to ourselves that I got so crazy about her. She

had always lived with me, but Campbell and Ellie took care of her. When Ellie took off, we had such a sweet time together." She smiled. "I even took her to church, 'cause Lord knows her parents never did. I thought it might make a difference in the long run if I could get as much of the good Lord into her while I had the chance."

"I'm sure it did," Lindsey offered.

LaRae nodded and swiped at her brow, laughing nervously. "Well, maybe. But it ended up doing the most good for Campbell. He started going with me and Nikki every Sunday—mainly, I'm thinking, because he didn't know what else to do—and he's never quit going since. As a boy he always seemed resistant, rebellious, to anything to do with God or church. But that boy soon became a broken man who'd made a wreck of his life. He knew it was time to start cleaning things up, letting God put things back together for him." She smiled. "He's made a lot of progress, but he still struggles with shame over what happened. He still wonders if God really does give second chances. In spite of what He seems to be doing this summer. I think God's up to something. Don't you?" She raised her eyebrows as Lindsey nodded and tried to stop the color from rising in her cheeks.

"Mrs. Forrester?" Lindsey impulsively asked her, an idea coming to her mind. She felt buoyed by the news about Campbell's faith. Could it be possible that they had both drawn close to God over the years? "Would you mind if I left Campbell a note?" She wanted to write down what she felt, to tell him he did deserve a second chance, and leave it for him to find when he came home. She hoped to somehow capture how hopeful she felt. She had come to Sunset to write about endings and in a few days' time the subject had changed to new beginnings. She shook her head in amazement.

"Well sure, honey. Now let's see … I don't have any paper down here, but I know that Campbell does a lot of writing and reading upstairs. Why don't you just go on up to his room and you should find a bunch of paper right there on his desk. Besides, if you leave it down here, he might never see it. Lay it on his desk; that's a safer bet." She waved in the direction of the stairs. "I'll be outside messing around in the yard if you need me," she said as she tromped out the door in her heavy gardening clogs. The back of her shirt read "Sea Turtle Rescuers Do It In The Dark." Lindsey smiled as she watched her go.

Lindsey climbed the stairs, remembering the only other time she'd ever been upstairs in Campbell's house. Campbell's parents were gone one night that second summer and the two of them came there, despite the fact that his parents had told them not to. He held her hand as he led her up to his room, both of them nervous over the potential of what could happen in his empty house, in his empty bedroom. She remembered they sat on his bed and kissed, their hearts thrumming so loudly in their chests each could hear the other one's.

It was Campbell who stopped them; Campbell who asked if she wouldn't mind just going to find the other kids at the arcade. They both nearly ran out of the house, grateful for the reprieve from what could have happened. She smiled at the memory of two nervous kids somehow doing the right thing. That night, Lindsey remembered, she had felt that she had never loved him more. He protected her. He respected her.

Campbell's room looked different than she remembered. The paraphernalia of a teen boy—rock-star posters and sports mementos—had disappeared. Instead a queen-sized bed dominated the small room, along with a desk, a dresser, and an easy chair with a table beside it. She imagined Campbell sitting there to read or think. Did he ever think of her?

A painting of a beach scene graced one wall. As she looked at it closer, she realized it must have been an original watercolor. It featured the mailbox, with a girl sitting on the bench beside it, writing. The girl looked remarkably like … her. Lindsey stood in front of the picture, remembering, and realized that the resemblance was no accident.

She saw a pad of paper on the desk and moved toward it to begin her letter. Still wondering about the picture and also wondering what to say in the letter, she noticed a pile of papers scattered on the floor near the easy chair and bent down to pick them up for Campbell. She assumed they had been blown off the desk by the breeze from the window. As she picked up the pages, her heart began to beat wildly in her chest, as if her body already knew before her brain could register it. She recognized her own handwriting as she flipped through the papers. Summer 1992, Dear Kindred Spirit. Summer 2000, Dear Kindred Spirit. Summer 1986, Dear Kindred Spirit.

A lifetime worth of letters. Her letters.

The room started to spin, and she sat down on the easy chair. How? Why? Questions floated through her brain with no answers attached. She looked down at the letters in her hands, noticed them trembling. Her heart pounded as it brought rise to a sense of injustice. How could he have betrayed her? Again?

Not thinking, she began to fling the papers all over the room, scattering them like large bits of confetti, the mess a calling card that she'd been there. She had seen what he was hiding, what he took without permission. Turning from his room, she ran out the door, down the steps, and out of his house. She bolted past his mother in the front yard and didn't even wave when LaRae hollered good-bye. Lindsey ran and ran and ran until her body gave out. But when she stopped to take a breath—about halfway to the beach house—the horrible feelings were still there. It seemed she couldn't outrun those.

Summer 2003

Dear Kindred Spirit,

I feel a sense of urgency today, Kindred Spirit. I really need to talk to you. I just wish we could sit across a table with a cup of coffee between us and have you tell me what to do. As I walked here, I noticed several happy couples laughing together, their hands all over each other—some to an embarrassing degree. Grant says I have become a religious fuddy-duddy, but come on, *people. There are children on the beach.*

Maybe I am just jealous. Jealous that I don't have what those couples have. Did I ever? Did Grant and I ever look at each other that way, laugh hysterically together, share the deepest parts of our hearts? I am sure we did once upon a time, but it has been so long ago and we have moved so far past that time that I can't remember anymore.

I have come to believe that you, Kindred Spirit, get the best part of me. And I am left wondering who you are ... and not wanting to know at the same time. I assume that you are probably one of those old women I see tottering along with their Sea Turtle patrol T-shirts on, visors tucked smartly over their eyes as they scan the beach for nests or tracks or whatever it is that they look for. It would be great if that were true—I could so use a mentor.

My fear is that you don't really care like I think you do. That my words are lost in an abandoned mailbox that holds neither the mystique nor the allure I have attached to it since I first came here as a lovestruck teenager. Have you followed these letters through the years, looking forward to reading the next installment as much as I look forward to writing it? I really hope that you do. That I really do have a Kindred Spirit somewhere on this earth, someone who knows the truth and loves me anyway.

I know that I have One in heaven. But earth would be nice too. I don't think that's too much to ask.

This year has been rough for our marriage. Grant is cheating on me—again. I knew before I had evidence. It was not what I saw, but what I didn't see. The absence of lingering looks, kind words, tenderness. The silence between us. We used to talk, didn't we? We used to laugh. We used to have conversations about more than payments and plumbers and pediatricians. We used to be more than just me and just him. We used to be us.

Instead we have been slowly drifting apart, almost as imperceptibly as the steady erosion of this very beach. One little particle at a time—a cross word said out of frustration, a night of sleep instead of sex, a forgotten little something that we used to do, and now don't even remember. Other than the hassle of divorce and what it would do to the children, I can't say I really care enough to fight. And that's the awful truth. The awful, awful truth that

I have told no one except you. What wife doesn't want to fight for her husband? What Christian woman doesn't want to make her marriage work?

Maybe one that is too tired to care. One that is tired of fighting for the things in life that should come easy—someone to love you, a mother who cares about you. These things should be a given, but they aren't to me.

That is what I thought as I stood outside the closed door of our laundry room and overheard Grant talking to another woman, making arrangements for a hotel room. He used his sexy voice—one I vaguely remember as being laced with innuendo and confident in tone. He thought I had gotten in the shower but didn't count on me first coming downstairs to get a clean towel out of the dryer. I listened outside the door and was there when he opened it. His expression betrayed his otherwise calm demeanor. "Hi," he said, plastering a shyster grin on his face. He pointed to the phone. "Business call. I'm meeting a customer and needed to make arrangements."

I looked at him, in shock that he would actually try to cover it with a lie. "Oh? And is this customer a woman?"

He waved his hand in the air and laughed, dismissing me. "A woman? No! Why in the world would you ask that?"

"So you're secretly gay now?" I shot back, my blood pressure rising along with my decibel level, my attempt to stay calm evaporating like water on hot asphalt.

He brushed past me, collecting his briefcase. "Gay?" he asked with his back to me. "No." He turned back to me, smiled his shyster smile a second time, ruffling my hair like a silly child and air kissing my forehead as he headed for the door, suddenly in a hurry to leave. "What a weird thing to say. I don't know what you think you just heard, but your imagination must be running away with you." My mouth opened and shut like a fish as I fumbled for a comeback. But he never made eye contact as he walked out the door, hollering about how he'd be home in time for dinner. Like that was some sort of gift to me.

As the door slammed shut, I hollered back, "I'm not making dinner." An act of rebellion. He ate cold cereal that night while I ignored him and worried over what our future would look like.

Which brings me to now. Grant moved out just before we left to come down to the beach. He agreed to come here together so that the kids could have one last family vacation. I had high hopes that a miracle would occur while we were here, but it hasn't happened. At night I lie in bed and try not to obsess about who the other woman is and what she looks like and if she's young and incredibly thin and beautiful. And I don't cry. This much I promised myself. I pretend my heart is made of steel, hard and tough and impenetrable. I pretend that none of this hurts and that I can just move forward without being crippled by the realization that the family I worked so hard to build is crumbling at my feet, like a house that has burned down with only the chimney left standing.

I know that we will not be back here together next year. I know that the marriage I thought I had is a sham. I know that I am going home to his half of the closet empty. I wonder if there's any hope. I wonder if during our separation, he will realize what he had and come back. I wonder if deep down he feels any love for me at all. Most of all I wonder, what did I do wrong? And will I ever do something right?

Until next summer,

Lindsey

Chapter 28

Sunset Beach

Summer 2004

After Nikki's counseling session, Campbell asked her if she wanted to grab lunch. To his shock and delight, she said yes. Neither of them mentioned the session as they drove to the restaurant. She commented on the heat. He nodded in agreement. He commented on his hunger. She nodded in agreement, though he couldn't help but wonder if she was just being polite. In the session, Lisa talked about how he could support Nikki through this. He felt funny talking about her as if she wasn't even there. But she just sat stoically. His heart went out to her.

"Have you talked to your mom?" he asked her as they made their way into the little coffee shop that served Campbell's favorite sandwiches. He didn't want to talk about Ellie but felt obliged to feign interest.

"A few times," she said. "She's worried. Wants to know if I'm happy here."

Before he could stop himself, he asked, "Are you?"

She sat down across from him at the table. "Dad, don't worry. If I didn't want to be here, I wouldn't." She looked around. "I can't think of a better place to …" She paused, unsure of what to call it. "… get better." She gave a small smile. "I might just stay indefinitely," she said, twirling a piece of her hair around her finger, a nervous habit he recognized from her childhood. "How would you feel about that?" She gestured toward the counter where a girl her age stood, taking orders from a steady stream of customers. "I wonder if they're hiring?"

"Well, if you need a job, you know I could always work something out for you down at the company."

She smiled. "I hoped you'd say that." She took a deep breath. "Because I'd like to stay here. I'm not going to college this fall. Lisa has helped me decide that."

He started to panic inwardly. College was always Ellie's dream for Nikki. Since Ellie didn't get to go, she decided early on that she would make sure Nikki did. "Have you told your mom?" he asked, trying to keep a poker face. He didn't want to let on that this felt like the worst news possible.

"Not yet," she said. "I hoped you'd tell her for me. That you would explain how the counselor and I reached that decision."

He imagined that conversation with vivid clarity. Accusations about the counselor being a hack. Accusations about how he projected his beach-bum mentality on their daughter. Accusations about how badly he had bungled the one and only thing he'd been asked to do. He smiled at Nikki. "That sounds like fun," he managed. She grinned back broadly.

He would not let her down. He sighed dramatically and, even

though it was the last thing in the world he wanted to do, told her, "Okay, I'll call Ellie and break the news."

"Thanks, Dad!" She seemed genuinely happy. Or perhaps just relieved. "I just can't deal with Mom right now. I don't want to hear her lecture."

"Oh, so you're going to make me have to hear her lecture?" he teased.

"Well, you're not required to listen the same way I am. You know?"

"Yeah, I have an idea …" he said. He imagined what her life had been like being Ellie's child.

"And, Dad?" she continued. "Thanks a lot for coming with me today. I liked having you there."

He watched with satisfaction as she took a healthy bite out of her sandwich. "You're very welcome. I liked being there. I want to be there for you more than I have been in the past. I owe you an apology for not visiting you in Charlotte like I should have. For always expecting you to come to me. I should have been there for your school events. I should have put your needs ahead of my own, and I didn't. I haven't been the father I should have been." He swallowed. "But I am glad God's giving us a second chance."

She nodded and looked down at the table, staring at the food on her plate like it was something new and strange. "Someday I'll be ready …" she began, "to tell you the whole story about how this all … happened."

He reached across the table and brushed the top of her arm. "You take your time," he said and smiled at her. "We have plenty of it now that you're not going anywhere."

On the way home, he asked Nikki if they could make one more stop. "I'd like to buy you something," he said.

She raised her eyebrows. "Me?"

"Yes, you. Who else?"

She shrugged her shoulders. "Okay," she said. "I never turn down a gift!"

He parked the truck in front of Wings and got out. She followed him inside. "I don't need a bathing suit, Dad," she said as they entered the beach shop. He hadn't been inside the place in years, but it hadn't changed much.

"Just follow me," he said as he wound his way through the aisles to find the display of flip-flops. He spotted a pair in red and looked for women's size 7s. "These look like they'll fit," he said, handing them over to her.

She took them from his hand. "Dad—" she began in protest.

He held up his hand. "No. No arguing. You don't even have to wear them. I mean, they're just cheap beach flip-flops. But I've been thinking about our old tradition, and I just wanted to buy you a pair of red shoes like I used to. I haven't done that in a long time." He paused, looking around to see if anyone was watching. "Will you let me do that?"

She studied him, taking him in with her wide blue eyes that were the same shade and shape as his own. She nodded just like she had when she was three years old. "Sure," she said.

"It's a good plan," he said, remembering.

"What?" she asked, following him to the cash registers.

He laughed. "Nothing," he said. He forced himself not to say any more, to let Nikki decide when or if she would wear the red flip-flops. For now it was enough that he had bought them, resurrecting something that had been dormant for far too long.

———

When he and Nikki returned home, they found LaRae slumped on the couch holding a glass of ice water to her forehead. She eyed them as they came in. "It's too hot out there for human beings," she said.

"You look terrible," he told her. Her face was red and splotchy, and her hair stuck up in sweaty clumps all over her head.

"Well, that's what happens when you spend time gardening in the heat of the day," she retorted, the fire not entirely gone in her. She grinned at Nikki. "Honey, gardening makes you ugly. Don't ever start." She looked back at Campbell. "I take it you ate lunch already, 'cause it's way past time."

He nodded absentmindedly, already itching to find a place to be alone and call Lindsey. "She came by," his mother said, reading his mind.

"Lindsey?" he asked, as if other women were in the habit of stopping by his house.

She gave him a sarcastic look. "Of course," she replied. "No offense, Campbell, but you don't exactly have a ton of women flocking to your door."

"Touché," he admitted. "So what'd she say?"

"We chatted for a bit. I offered her something to drink. She was out jogging in this heat if you can imagine."

He pointed at his mom and smiled. "Did she look like you?"

She waved her hand in the air. "You be quiet. She looked very nice, just like you'd expect. We had a nice talk …" She paused, suddenly hesitant, nervous.

"Mom … what did you do?"

"Campbell, you assume the worst about me." She pointed Nikki in the direction of her bedroom. Nikki got the hint.

"I need to, uh, check my email," Nikki said.

Campbell watched his daughter scale the stairs then repeated, "Mom …"

"Well, it was the strangest thing. I explained a bit about what's going on with Nikki and we just chatted a little about the past. She was just as sweet as ever, real charming. Then she said she wanted to leave you a note. So I told her she might as well head upstairs and leave it in your room. I went back out to the yard, and the next thing I knew she flew out of the house and ran down the street, her feet barely hitting the ground. She didn't even say good-bye!"

Campbell's heart hammered away in his chest. He paced around the room, running his hands through his hair, saying the same words over and over again, a refrain. *"Oh no, oh no, oh no, oh no."* He took one look at his mom before bolting out the door, chasing Lindsey even though she was long gone.

Chapter 29

Sunset Beach
Summer 2004

Lindsey was about a hundred feet from the beach house when she noticed the familiar silver sedan sitting in the drive. Her heart, already pounding, began to somehow pound harder, a new round of adrenaline flooding her veins, making her stomach rumble with nausea.

She stopped and put her hands on her knees, stared at the pebbles and shells littering the ground, willing her eyes to focus, her breathing to slow down, her head to stop spinning. She looked up to a flash of movement on the porch. A vision she had seen so many times before: her husband and children sitting together. He sipped a Diet Coke and smiled like he belonged there. It could have been a scene from any previous year. Just not this one.

The children were waving wildly at her, smiling like their dreams had come true. Which, she supposed, they had. Oddly enough, had Grant shown up just two days earlier, his appearance would have meant her dreams had come true too. Instead the sight of him on her porch, with her children, made her angry. How dare he ruin the brief bit of happiness she had allowed herself to grab? And yet, with the turn of events that had happened at Campbell's place, she wasn't sure she was happy anymore. She didn't know what to think or feel. And thanks to Grant showing up, she had no time to process, to pray. She pasted a polite smile on her face for the sake of the kids and walked toward the house.

As she climbed the porch stairs, questions ran through her brain. Why was he there? What was his intent? And then there was the nagging thought of Campbell. How could she possibly get to the bottom of what he did with Grant around? She had a hard time meeting Grant's gaze, couldn't look at him sitting on the porch like he belonged there, like he had the right. She focused instead on Anna's and Jake's faces. Anna sidled up to her. "Mom," she said, almost shyly, "Dad's here."

"Yeah, he came to visit us. Isn't that cool, Mom?" Jake echoed his sister.

Anna examined her mother's face closely, nervously awaiting her reaction.

Lindsey made her head nod in response, grasping for the right words to say. "Wow" was all she could eke out.

Grant stared at her; she could feel his eyes boring into her even though she wouldn't look at him. She mumbled something about showering and bolted inside the house, away from the three of them and their happy little reunion. She closed the door to the master bedroom, stepped into the master bath, and closed that door as well, locking it. A double barrier. Stripping out of her sweaty running clothes, she ripped the ponytail from her hair and turned the shower water on to cold. She could feel the heat radiating from her body as she stepped under the cool water, letting it wash over her and mingle with her tears. She leaned her head against the tile as the water pounded her skin, a cold shock after the intense heat. From outside, she heard knocking on the bathroom door, but she didn't respond. She mouthed words that she did not say: *Go away. Go away. Go away.*

When her teeth started to chatter, she switched the water over to warm and sat down in the tub, letting the water calm her. She lathered her hair and then sat with the suds on her head, allowing the water to pound down on her tired, aching legs. She couldn't remember the last time she ran that much in one day. She fought the desire to climb into bed and shut the whole mess out of her life through sleep, the great escape.

When the hot water was gone, she reluctantly climbed out, toweled herself off, and wrapped the towel around her. She brushed her hair and stared at herself in the mirror. She wondered what Grant saw when he looked at her. She wondered what Campbell saw.

She wished Holly were there. She tried to picture her friend laughing over her predicament: "Two men, Linds, wow! Two men are fighting over you!" Closing her eyes, Lindsey could hear Holly saying it, see her dimpled smile. She wanted her friend there, helping her figure out what to do next. But calling her at that moment was out of the question. Most likely she would call Holly later and beg her to help her figure all this out while Holly made jokes about her being a vixen, a minx.

Lindsey secured the towel around her body and stepped into the bedroom to dress, running smack into Grant as she did. He put his arms around her and kissed her forehead before she could push away from him. She noticed the closed bedroom door and was grateful to be away from the children so she could speak her mind, yet she also didn't like the assumption he had made by closing the door behind him. He scanned her body up and down with an appreciative look on his face. She attempted to pull the towel tighter around herself, as if that were possible.

"Grant, you have no right to be in here," she scolded him, not liking the way his eyes proprietarily lingered on her body.

He laughed. "No right? I'm with my family on vacation." He reached out for her again, playfully attempting to grab the towel from her body, just like he would have done if things were normal. As if nothing had changed, when everything had.

"Grant, no. This isn't right. We are divorced, in case you forgot. And you're confusing the kids by being here." She looked at him and narrowed her eyes. "Why are you here, anyway?"

He gave her a puppy-dog look that had worked many times in the past but no longer affected her. The realization was a shock.

"I missed you guys," he said, shrugging his shoulders. He sat down on the bed, the bed they'd shared during every beach vacation since they'd married. How many nights did she sleep next to him in that bed? How many times had they made love there, giggling and whispering so the kids didn't hear? She shook those thoughts from her head and attempted to steel herself from the emotion, from going backward. "I wanted to see my family. I wanted to see you," he continued. He chuckled to himself and stared at her as though the towel was not there. "I have to admit I didn't think you had it in you to do this trip with the kids without me here to help. And then, when you did, well, I started feeling left out. Like you guys had forgotten all about me."

"That's generally the idea when you walk out on your family, Grant. They tend to go on without you. What did you think we would do, stop living?"

He hung his head in what she knew was mock humiliation. "I guess I did," he said to the floor.

She noticed a bag by the door of the bedroom. The same duffel she bought for him ten years ago at a discount store, so proud of the bargain she had found for him. *That duffel,* she thought, *will last longer than we have.* She pointed at the bag. "You can't stay here with me, Grant."

He stood and began to move toward her again. "And why not?" He put his index finger under her chin, raising her eyes to his. He looked sad and broken and entirely trustworthy. "Let's be a family. Let's make memories here, this year, together."

He spoke words her heart had longed to hear for a year. But as he spoke, it wasn't his face that filled her mind. She saw Campbell on the pier the night before, listening to her, smiling at her. Then she saw the pile of her letters in his room. She backed away from Grant and sat down on the bed, her head in her hands. Grant came over and put his arm around her shoulders, pulling her to him. She stiffened even as she allowed him to be so close.

"I need time to think," she said into his shoulder. He wore a golf shirt in a hideous green hue that she would never choose, evidence of another life apart from her. Evidence of another person who had perhaps picked out his clothes, shared his bed, felt his touch. She sat up. "Don't think that you can just waltz back in here and the last year is gone—" she snapped her fingers—"just like that."

He nodded. "Baby, I know that. I do. I didn't think…. To tell you the truth, I didn't really even know I was coming here today." He smiled. "I just started driving and ended up here. It's where I belong. I hope you will see that."

She willed herself not to smile, not to be sucked in by his charm. But even as she hardened herself on the inside, she felt her heart flutter with hope. In her heart this was still her husband. *Their* children were outside. The family was together again in a beach house that was chock-full of family memories. And with all the tears she'd cried over the end of their marriage, what she had begged God for was exactly what was happening. She just hadn't expected Campbell to come back into her life before Grant did. She didn't think it was possible to love anyone else besides Grant—even Campbell, who had seemed a lost cause for so many years. Her rational side said that what she felt for Campbell couldn't already be love anyway. That it would be foolishness to send Grant—her husband—away over some guy she used to know, some guy she used to love. She recalled the pile of letters on the floor, and a rush of betrayal rose up within her all over again.

"How about I take the kids out to the beach for a while? They've been begging to go since I got here and it would give you a break." He patted her head like a child, like his child. "It would give you the time you need to think," he added.

She nodded, choking back the tears that had suddenly collected in her throat. His small act of kindness, of gentleness, so welcomed she wanted to weep with relief. She didn't realize how much she had missed the little things he used to do. Making him a monster in her mind—overlooking the side of Grant that was what made her love him—was easier than admitting what she had lost: his goodness. His potential to be the husband she desired. What if she said no to him this time around? Would she be making a huge mistake? What if the biggest fool in all of this turned out to be her?

"I'd like to take you and the kids to dinner tonight," he said. "You know, like we used to do. Go to Calabash." He chuckled. "Gorge ourselves on fried shrimp and hush puppies." He reached out to tickle her as she clutched at the towel to keep it from falling off. "Will you think about it?"

"I'll think about it," she said.

"That's all I can ask," he said, smiling like the Cheshire Cat.

Immediately after he left the bedroom, she heard his voice calling out to the children to get ready for the beach, followed by excited whoops of joy. For a moment it felt like it always had between them. Her challenge was to decide if that was a good thing.

Chapter 30

Sunset Beach
Summer 2004

Campbell did not go straight to Lindsey. He started to head in her direction, then realized that he simply could not see her until he had time to think about what he would say, to determine the right way to explain what she had found. Instead of running toward her house, he detoured to the pier, jogging past the grizzled fishermen and families who had gathered in hopes of seeing one of the fishermen pull in a big catch.

As a child he had spent hours on the pier as his dad taught him how to fish. He had great memories of the hours spent with his father out there, away from his mom, away from his dad's work. He remembered what it felt like to be the sole focus of his father's attention as he helped him bait the hook and carefully cast it out to sea. Sometimes they talked, sometimes they just sat in silence. What Campbell would have given to have his father there now. To ask him, "What would you do?"

He imagined his father's response. "Well, boy, I wouldn't have been foolish enough to land myself in this predicament in the first place." His father, who fell in love with his mother in high school and married her right after graduation, never understood the pain of letting the love of his life slip away because of his own stupidity. He had loved one woman his whole life, never veering from the course set before him. His greatest disappointment, though he never talked about it, was not being able to have more children. Campbell's parents, he knew, had planned to have a houseful. Several miscarriages into the marriage, they had Campbell. They had hoped their trouble was behind them after he was born, but more miscarriages followed. Though they were satisfied—even grateful—for their life as a family, it always seemed there was someone missing. Campbell knew if he felt it, his father did too.

Campbell made his way to the end of the pier and found an empty spot to stand and take in the waves, the sky, the seagulls. A crane flew low over the waves for a moment before plucking a fish from the water in an effortless, graceful swoop. Campbell closed his eyes and tried to rehearse the words he needed to say to win her trust, to convince her he was not who she thought he was. Words ran through his mind: *stalker, creep, deviant.* He prayed they were not the same words that were running through her mind. Lifting his eyes to the sky, he wondered what God thought of him, what He would say about that moment in his life. That he deserved it? That he mismanaged everything He had ever given him? That he had lived his life as a coward, never once doing the right thing at the right time, always recklessly allowing things to unfold and pushing the blame on others?

If that's how God saw him, then God was right.

Campbell spotted a ship out on the horizon and foolishly, instinctively, wished he was on it, bound for someplace far, far away. That he would stumble upon a way to escape having to face her, having to see her disappointment in him etched on her face. But once again, he knew it was time to stop running.

"Sounds like you gotta be the man here," he could hear his father say, the same thing he had said when Campbell broke the news of Ellie's pregnancy. Campbell turned and began walking back, praying the simplest prayer. It was just one word, repeated over and over: *Please. Please. Please.*

———

It was time for Lindsey to write the letter she had put off since they arrived. She had composed so many different versions in her head, the pendulum swinging from despair and desperation to hope and happiness and back again. Lindsey took a pad of paper out on the porch and propped it on her lap to write. Normally she'd write at the beach, but she just couldn't deal with the trek. Plus, her entire experience with the mailbox seemed anything but normal to her now.

The words came in staccato phrases, alternating between anger and affection. The letter, she knew, would sound choppy and disjointed, would reflect the confusion she felt as she sat and tried to get the words from her head to the paper. The flow didn't come as it had in years past. Writing that letter wasn't as natural as breathing. It was as hard as labor, as hard as exercise, as hard as staying in a marriage that had died long ago.

A rare breeze blew through the screen, ruffling the papers at the edges and cooling her skin. She lifted her chin, closed her eyes, and let the breeze caress her face, pretending it was Campbell, come to say good-bye. When she opened her eyes, she saw him standing on the tiny strip of lawn in front of her uncle's house as if she had conjured him.

He shifted his weight from one foot to the next; his eyes were the saddest she had ever seen. For the second time that day, she willed herself to feel nothing, pretended her heart was made of steel and not flesh. She watched as he approached the stairs hesitantly, intending to join her on the porch.

Before he could climb the first step, she rose from her chair and headed down the stairs to meet him. Something about him being so close to the house felt wrong with Grant around. She met him on the grass, carefully avoiding the sand spurs that lurked there, threatening her bare feet. They stared at each other, neither one of them sure what to say first. "I'm sorry," he said, "about the letters."

She put her hand up in the space between them and shook her head. "You have to leave," she told him, even though it was not, she discovered, what she wanted to say.

"If you'd just let me explain—" he started to argue.

"Campbell," she said. It hurt to say his name out loud. "Grant came back. He was here when I came home earlier today. He wants to work on things. With us. He's gone with the kids right now, but they could come back at any time. So I would really like it if you'd go. I don't want—"

"You don't want what?" he interrupted. "You don't want him to see me? You don't want him to know? Why? Have you forgotten he walked out on you? What gives him the right to waltz in here and expect you to give up everything—"

"Campbell, it's not like there's anything to give up. You and I went on one date. And with what I found earlier, well, I think it's best if I just keep things simple right now. Grant and I have children to consider. We have something that's worth saving."

He looked at her with sad eyes she had to fight to resist. "And we don't? That's what you're saying?"

She shook her head and turned away from his stare, looking off in the direction where Grant and the kids would be walking back, guarding those few moments she had alone with Campbell. "I'm saying that I learned not to trust you a long time ago. To think that's changed since then was foolish of me. I don't know what you were doing with my letters and I don't even want to know. When I got home and found Grant here, everything changed."

"Including us?" he challenged, grabbing her arm so that she would be forced to look at him, his blue eyes flashing, sending unspoken signals to her heart, a kind of Morse code that had always, she realized, existed between them. "You're really ready to let go of us that easily?" His eyes pleaded with her.

She looked away again. "You need to go now," she said. Even though his leaving was the last thing she wanted. Even though staying with Grant frightened her, she knew what she had to do. She had a chance to give her children their father. What kind of mother would pass that up to stay with a man who had never done anything but betray her? What kind of woman gives up her family for a silly childhood wish?

Campbell didn't move. She fought the urge to wrap her arms

around him, even as she turned to walk back up to the porch where her letter waited to be written. "Please, Campbell. Just leave. We made a mistake by thinking we could rewrite the past and expect a different ending."

She climbed the stairs resolutely, listening for the sound of his retreating footsteps, his truck engine cranking up and driving away. She did not turn around until she heard him go. She did not trust herself to stay strong if she looked at him again.

Chapter 31

Sunset Beach
Summer 2004

After Lindsey sent Campbell away, he headed home. Thankfully, his mom and Nikki were gone when he arrived. He couldn't handle his mom's prying eyes or Nikki's questions. He guessed that his mom treated Nikki to dinner somewhere and, though he knew that he should be thinking about finding some dinner himself, he couldn't imagine eating and didn't feel the slightest bit hungry. As he passed by the kitchen, he pictured Anna's and Jake's faces as he loaded them down with Minerva's junk food. He imagined them eating the Oreos and Popsicles with Grant on the same porch he had seen Lindsey, and he felt inexplicably cheated on, replaced. How foolish he was to let Lindsey and her children into his heart so quickly, to envision them as part of his life for much longer than a few days at the beach. He had moved too fast, wanted too much. Just like always.

He climbed the stairs to his room and flopped down on the

bed, forcing himself not to look at the letters scattered on the floor. He pictured Lindsey flinging them to the four corners of the room in anger just before she ran from the room. He thought of the moment when Nikki knocked them down and he didn't stop to put them back in the place they had occupied for years. Just putting away the letters might have changed the way his whole life had turned out. He tried not to think about it. The last time he stood in his room, everything seemed so hopeful, so possible—Nikki's progress, Lindsey's presence in his life. He foolishly believed that nothing could change that. And yet one moment, one decision had altered everything. It was a lesson he would keep learning over and over until he got it, he supposed.

Oh God, what have I done? Help me. Please.

He began to gather up the letters, putting them in order of years, just as he had always kept them. Whether it was obsessive behavior or a romantic notion, he couldn't just leave her letters flung all over the room like trash. He bent down to retrieve them and wondered idly just how many times he had read each one. Some he had memorized—especially one. Should he have revealed the identity of the Kindred Spirit she faithfully wrote to all these years? That it wasn't the same Kindred Spirit that tended the mailbox for everyone else, that Lindsey had her own personal Kindred Spirit? Better yet, should he have left her letters alone?

There were times he thought about going there to wait for her so he could tell her. She was such a creature of habit that he could usually time her arrival at the mailbox to the hour. He used to imagine sitting down on the bench in the sand and waiting as long as it took until he saw her approaching. He even thought about what he might say, what it would feel like to see her face again, to have her stand in front of him.

But he always chickened out, reasoning that she wouldn't want to see him, that she surely hated him and the letters were the only bit of her he could ever hope to have. He feared if she knew about him, she would stop writing her letters, that in his admission he would steal the magic of the mailbox from her. He didn't want to be the one to take that away from her. Most of all, though it was hard to admit, he was scared of what would happen to him if he didn't have her letters to look forward to each year. Telling her the truth might have resulted in the end of what was the highlight of each passing year: reading Lindsey's latest letter, gaining a glimpse into her life, her heart, knowing her in a way that no one else did, having her in part when he couldn't have her in whole.

You didn't fight for her. He felt the insistent tug on his heart for the second time that week. He had let Lindsey slip away in a haze of bad decisions and misplaced allegiance a long time ago, back when he didn't understand about listening to God's voice in his life, when he didn't know that God cared about giving a guy like him a second chance. He couldn't go back in time and change the course of their lives, but he could stand up, be a man, and fight for what he wanted now. He didn't have to bow out quietly again.

He knew what he had to do. Taking a pen and some paper out of his desk drawer, he attempted to write some of his thoughts down. Though everything in him said to walk away, give up, move on, and let go, something wouldn't let him until that one last thing was done.

His pen scratched over the paper as he filled the space inside him with words. Words of apology. Words of truth. Words of promise. Words of love. The words tumbled out, linking him to her just as they always had, yet this time in reverse. He knew that once he said what he needed to say, that would be all. Or it wouldn't. He prayed she would make the choice he had waited for most of his life.

They looked like any other family as they stood in line to be seated at the restaurant in Calabash. Lindsey told the kids to stop climbing on the gate outside, reminded them to be patient when they asked how much longer it would be, and made polite conversation with Grant. To a casual observer, there was nothing amiss. But a casual observer could not see into her heart or discern the roiling emotions that churned within her. She smiled, she chatted, she scolded. But she didn't relax.

As irony would have it, Grant chose the same restaurant she and Campbell had been to just the night before, a new place that did less greasy fried fish and more upscale menu items. She eyed their table with longing, wanting to rewind the clock and be sitting there with Campbell again, safe in her not knowing what she knew now. As her family made their way to the table, Anna caught her eye, a question on her face: Is this real? Lindsey pretended not to see it.

When they sat down, Jake slid up next to Grant, his eyes taking in his father's every move. He looked like a puppy, wiggly and eager to please. He clearly adored his dad, and the joy on his face was unmistakable. Lindsey couldn't pretend not to notice that. "Are you guys having a great vacation?" Grant asked after the server had taken their drink orders and walked away.

Anna and Jake nodded and blew their straw wrappers at each other. "No spit wads," Lindsey warned Jake. He rolled his eyes and dropped the wadded-up wrapper.

Grant smiled at her. *You're such a good mother,* his eyes said. She felt nauseous.

"What was the best part?" he asked, trying to draw them out, make the kids trust him, create a happy family experience that would sway Lindsey. "The boogie boarding? The sand castles?"

"We didn't make any sand castles because you weren't there," Anna said. She put her elbows on the table and propped her chin on her hands, leveling him with a glare.

Inside Lindsey cheered her daughter on.

"Well, maybe we should do that tomorrow," Grant offered, clearing his throat.

Jake piped up, "I know what the best part was, Daddy."

"What?" Grant tousled his hair.

"When you came," he said.

Grant caught Lindsey's eye and she looked away, but not before he saw the look on her face, one that surely revealed that she was struggling and that he could use it to his advantage.

———

She heard the beeping when they walked in the house. She had plugged her cell phone in to recharge after she tried to call Holly earlier that day but had found the phone dead. She followed the beeping sound back to her bedroom where the phone rested on her dresser. She wondered when she would have a moment of privacy to call Holly. She had so much to tell her.

She picked up the phone, expecting to see Holly's number on the missed call log. Instead she saw five missed calls from her uncle. She felt panic rise in her throat. What if he was calling to tell her they had to leave? It was his house after all. With her heart racing, she selected his number, hit Send, and hollered at Anna and Jake to quiet down as they chased each other down the hall outside her room. She closed her door and sat down on the bed.

Her uncle answered on the first ring. "Lindsey?"

"Uncle Bob, I saw I had some missed calls from you. Is everything okay?" She knew the unsteadiness of her voice was giving away her panic.

"Lindsey, I've been calling you about your mother," he said.

She was ashamed at the mixture of feelings that flooded her. She knew it must be bad news if he was calling, yet she felt relief wash over her that he was not going to tell her she had to leave. "What happened?" she asked.

"It seems she's had a heart attack. She's not doing too well. She needs surgery and …" he paused. "She's been asking for you. I told her I would do my best to get in touch with you."

"Oh," she said, pathetically. She glanced around the room, a million thoughts pinging around in her mind.

"I know you are on vacation, and I know you're alone with the kids—"

"No," she said, "Grant's actually here." The minute it was out of her mouth she regretted saying it. No sense alerting her family, such as it was, to a new development that may or may not mean anything.

"Well, uh, that's nice," he said.

"I mean," she offered, "he's here seeing the kids." She exhaled, hoping she had thrown him off thinking that she and Grant were reconciling. Were they reconciling? She shook her head and tried to focus on the conversation.

"I'm sure that's good. For the children," he added.

"Mmm-hmm," she said.

"Would you please call your mother?" he asked, his words coming in a rush. "I know things haven't been exactly good for you two, but she's not doing very well. She's going into surgery, and she's awfully weak. There are—" he searched for the right words—"things she wants to say to you."

Lindsey nodded. "Sure, Uncle Bob, I'll call my mom."

"It's too late to call her tonight, but it would be good if you called first thing in the morning, before her surgery."

She wrote down the number on the back of her hand with a pen she kept in her nightstand. After they hung up, she stared at the ink that marred her skin, remembering her mother telling her not to write on her hand, that it would give her ink poisoning. She remembered being surprised by how maternal that advice had been. Then, as now, her mother surprised her. She willed herself to cry over her mother, but no tears came. Instead she checked on Grant and the children before selecting another number. She had never needed to talk to her best friend so badly.

When Holly picked up, she skipped the pleasantries. "You

can stop praying now for this trip to be memorable or whatever it was you said you were going to pray for!"

"What?" Holly laughed. In the background at Holly's house she could hear a *Baby Einstein* video and Josie's little giggles.

"Let me just cut to the chase," Lindsey began as she fell onto her bed and kicked off her shoes. "Just this week I have run into Campbell, gone on a date with him, discovered he's kept all the letters I've ever written to the Kindred Spirit, and best of all, Grant showed up today." She paused. "And apparently, he wants to try again. Oh and … to top it off, I just found out my mother has had a heart attack. And she's asking to talk to me."

"Wait a minute. What? Can you say all that again? I don't think I heard that right," Holly said. Lindsey heard a door close and the background noise faded. "Okay, I gave Rick the baby and I am outside on the porch so I can focus. Seriously, say it again and say it slower this time, please!"

Lindsey smiled. "Ohhhkaaay. I will say it slooower," she joked, thankful for the moment of lightness.

"Look, don't make fun. My life is about strained carrots and diapers, not old love affairs and two men chasing me. Two men, Linds! Seriously, two men!"

Lindsey laughed. She knew her friend well. "Okay, I will be serious now. Because I really need your help. First, I went on a date with Campbell. Remember him?"

Holly snorted. "Duh."

"Well, it turns out he's divorced from Ellie and he's still living here. His daughter, Nikki, is seventeen. And she's here too. She has anorexia and it's—well—it's a long story, but he's just the way I remembered and we had this amazing time and things were going so well and—"

"Remember how we're going slow?" Holly interrupted. "You're speeding up again."

"Sorry. So, then yesterday I went by his house and was going to leave him a note and just, you know, thank him for the date."

"Aka, stalk him."

"You say *tomayto,* I say *tomahto,*" Lindsey said.

"So what happened when you went to his house? He has your letters? What do you mean?"

"He has my letters. The ones I've been putting in the mailbox for years? You know—"

"Yeah, of course I know, but how did he end up with your letters?"

"Well, that's the question of the day," Lindsey said, stretching her legs up into the air and back down again. "I didn't get to find out, because when I got back from his house, Grant was here. Campbell came by this afternoon, but I sent him away. To be honest, I wasn't ready to talk to him. I feel completely betrayed."

"Again," Holly quipped. She heard Holly blow a bubble and then pop it. Holly was a serial gum chewer. "So what are you going to do?"

"I was hoping you'd tell me."

"I'm afraid you're in uncharted waters here, girl."

"Gee, thanks, Holl. I didn't know that already."

"I'd say I'd come down there, but I would bring a screaming, teething infant with me, and I'm not sure that's what you need right now."

She could hear Anna and Jake wrestling with Grant in the den. "Yeah, we have our share of screaming here already," she said.

"I guess the kids are thrilled Grant's around," Holly said.

"Of course. They're ready for him to move back in tonight."

"Any idea why he picked now to come back?"

"No. Of course I did ask him to come, if you remember."

"What's the old saying, 'Be careful what you wish for'?" Holly teased.

"Don't remind me."

"Well, Linds, maybe you should first get to the bottom of why he's really there. And, Lindsey, would you do me a favor?"

"Of course," she replied.

"Don't let Grant come back just for your kids."

Lindsey thought of the way Jake looked at Grant at dinner, the flash of longing she saw in Anna's eyes as they got back in the car afterward. She would reconcile with Grant if it would make her kids happy, if she could have a guarantee that the family she wanted waited on the other side of this mess. "That's easier said than done," she said. "My kids mean the world to me. How could I take their father away from them if he's willing?"

"It's about more than being willing. I don't want to see you sell yourself short." Holly giggled and her voice took on a different quality, one Lindsey hadn't heard since they were teens. "So—I have to know—what does Campbell look like now?"

Lindsey lowered her voice. "As good as he always did," she said.

"Ah, too bad. If he was fat and balding, this might be much easier on you." She could hear Holly's lips part into a smile. "Let me pray for you before I go. Okay?"

"Definitely. I need prayer right now. A lot of it," Lindsey quipped. "Just no more prayers for eventful weeks at the beach."

Across the miles, connected by technology, the two friends closed their eyes and bowed their heads as Holly prayed for Lindsey, just as she had so many times throughout their friendship. Even years ago when Lindsey refused to believe that prayer worked. She knew different now. She listened as Holly prayed for God to give Lindsey clarity in what she should do and for Lindsey to be able to see both Grant and Campbell for who they were.

After Holly said "Amen," Lindsey said, "If I didn't know better I would think that you're pulling for Campbell."

"I'm pulling for *you*," Holly answered. "I want you to be happy. And I want you to know that you are precious and either one of them would be lucky to have you. Okay?"

Lindsey laughed. "Okay. Thanks, Holl. I love you."

"Love you too. And I can't wait to hear what happens," Holly said.

"Me either," Lindsey said and laughed in spite of herself. "You'll be the first to know."

"I'm going to hold you to that. Remember your boring old friend stuck in housewife world. I need some vicarious excitement."

"Glad to provide it," Lindsey said, rolling her eyes even though Holly couldn't see her. "And, Holly?"

"Yeah?"

Lindsey could hear *Baby Einstein* as Holly went back inside her house. "Boring sounds good to me right about now."

"You know I wouldn't trade my life for the world," Holly said. "I'm just trying to make *you* feel better!"

Lindsey giggled as she said good-bye and closed her phone, then took a deep breath and went to join Grant and the children. They needed a referee for their wrestling match. Just like old times.

Chapter 32

Sunset Beach

Summer 2004

Early that morning Lindsey slipped from her bed and carried her cell phone past Grant, who was snoring on the couch with his feet propped up on the arm and his arms splayed over his head awkwardly. It had been a year since she had seen him asleep. He looked like a stranger. She opened the door to the screened-in porch without a sound and took a seat in one of the peeling wicker chairs. The ink on her hand was smudged from sleep, but she could still make out the number as she pressed it into her phone. Her mother's voice was soft and weak as she answered, far from the commanding tone Lindsey remembered.

"Hi, Mom," she said feeling incredibly unsure of herself. "Uh, how are you? Uncle Bob said I should call early before they take you to surgery."

"I'm glad to hear your voice," her mom answered, her voice faint and breathy. "I told Bob to try and find you. He said you were with your family at the beach."

"Yes, we're here at Sunset." She tried to sound positive. "It's my twentieth year here." An image flashed in her mind as she spoke: her mom in the apartment parking lot, waving good-bye without a trace of sadness, her smile radiant. "Do you remember when I came here that first year? I was so mad at you for making me come. Now I guess I should thank you."

"I wanted you to have some time with a real family," her mother said. "My brother could give you what I could not."

Lindsey pulled the phone away from her ear and stared at it for a moment. Had that admission just come from *her* mother? She put the phone back to her ear. "Mom," she said, "I always thought—"

"That I didn't want you?" her mom finished.

She grimaced. "Yeah."

"I know. That was my fault. I could never admit the things I failed at." She sighed, her breath ragged. "I never knew how to tell you how I felt. So I let you edge me out of your life. I deserved it. It was me who first alienated you. All these years …" her voice trailed off.

Lindsey felt exactly like the time she got hit in the stomach by a basketball in gym class. She caught her breath. "Mom." She stopped, her eyes panning the water, searching for words. "I never—" She laughed. "I don't know what to say," she said.

"Say you'll come see me. After my surgery. I always thought that I had plenty of time to get back in touch with you. But I know now that none of us know how much time we have. I'd like the time I have left to include my daughter."

A tear leaked from the corner of Lindsey's eye as she nodded her head. "Yes. Of course we'll come. I'd love for you to see Anna and Jake."

"I'd like that very much," her mother said. "I have some lost time to make up for. What I'd like more than anything is to get to know you, and my grandchildren." Lindsey heard a voice in the background. "Oh," her mother said, "they're coming to get me prepped for the surgery. I need to hang up now."

Her mother sounded very old, so far from the young woman who flitted around their apartment in her bra and high heels. Lindsey rested her forehead on her palm, letting her tears flow. With every ounce of courage she said, "Make sure Uncle Bob calls me after the surgery. And … I'll be praying for you."

Her mom was quiet for a moment. "Thank you. I will," she said politely before hanging up. Lindsey closed the phone and turned to find Grant standing on the porch.

"What's going on?" he asked, putting his hand on her shoulder.

She shrugged her shoulders. "That was my mom."

"Your mom?"

"Yeah," she said. "This trip just keeps getting weirder." The corners of her mouth turned up slightly. She felt the heaviness of Grant's hand weighing on her.

"Why'd you call her?" Grant was still confused. She hadn't told him last night about her uncle's call.

"She had a heart attack. My uncle called and told me. She asked to speak to me before she went into surgery." She paused, feeling a slight breeze blow through the porch. She inhaled the sweet sea air and silently thanked God that she was at the beach. She realized that the beach had become a constant in her life, just as she'd always considered Holly. Now she wondered about her mother—could she trust her mother's words? Were they too good to be true? The only constant she had ever known from her mother was *in*consistency. Lindsey looked at Grant, sure that he could see her fragility. "She wants me and the kids to come see her."

He pulled her into a hug. "Let me take you. We'll go right now."

Lindsey shook her head and stiffened against him, not wanting to fall into the lull of his attention and care. "No. She said to come in a few days. I'll wait until the week is up at least."

Grant wasn't deterred. "Okay, sure. Just let me know if there's anything I can do. I know it will be hard for you to see your mother again, but you'll do great. You're the most forgiving person I know." He backed away. "The kids want me to make pancakes. Would you like some?"

She had missed his famous Saturday-morning pancakes. She nodded and wiped her eyes.

After he went back inside and she listened to the kids cheer over his pancakes, she knew that her forgiveness was what he was counting on. She could forgive him—had forgiven him—but she also wondered if she could ever love and trust him the way she wanted to love and trust her husband. As she listened to her kids singing "The Pancake Song," a song they made up years ago that was nothing more than a repeated chorus of "Dad makes great pancakes, great pancakes, great pancakes," she felt more confused than ever.

She began to pray. Should she open up her heart to people who had hurt her in the past? And if so, who? She remembered Holly's prayer from last night and hoped that God's answer came soon.

Later that morning Grant didn't argue when Lindsey told him she wanted to walk to the mailbox alone. She thought it would be obvious to him that this wasn't an ordinary trip, that she had a different agenda. She worried that the truth was coloring her face like a sunburn. That after all these years he would be able to look right into her head and see the thoughts of Campbell she carried around. So when he smiled and said to not only go but also to take her time, she was surprised. She pushed away the thought that he didn't know her as well as she wanted to be known and plastered on a smile. He was playing Sequence with Anna and Jake, and she waved to them all, grateful to escape the beach house and head down the desolate shore with only the seagulls and her thoughts for company.

Her letter was in her pocket, finally written, though not even close to the letter she had come there expecting to write. So much had changed since their arrival at Sunset just a few days earlier.

Grant hadn't slept with her the night before, though it wasn't for lack of trying. After the kids were in bed, he stole into the master bedroom. To have him standing there after she had come so far made everything feel off center. Though something inside her wanted him there, something else wanted him gone. She looked up from the book she pretended to read and blinked back at him as if she hadn't already discerned what he was going to say next. He pointed to the bed. "Can I join you?" he asked and raised his eyebrows.

"Grant," she said, laying the book in her lap and smoothing the covers so she wouldn't have to look directly at him. "It's too soon. I need a lot more time."

He exhaled loudly, revealing a hint of his impatience. "Well, then where should I sleep?"

She stifled a smile, her small revenge. "On the couch?" she offered sweetly.

He wasn't to be deterred so easily. He strode across the room and sat down beside her on the bed. He smelled different. Like someone else's detergent, someone else's soap, cologne someone else had chosen. She wrinkled her nose. He leaned in and kissed her cheek, tangled his hands in her hair. "Your hair's gotten so long," he said. Grant always liked her hair cut in a certain style, kept as neatly manicured and predictable as the life they once had. She had let it grow wild and long in his absence, an act of rebellion.

She shrugged her shoulders. "I like it," she said.

"Mmm, I do too," he whispered in her ear, in a husky voice she knew all too well.

She took both her hands and placed them on his shoulders, pushing him away with all the force she could muster. He looked back at her, his face giving away his shock. Apparently he had thought he could seduce her with enough effort.

"Grant," she said, "I told you it was too soon. You've been away for so long, you can't possibly just expect to pick up where we left off."

She saw the disappointment etched on his face as he rose from the bed. "No, Lindsey, I wasn't expecting that at all. The truth is, I don't want to pick up where we left off. Because where we left off was a terrible place. I wanted to start something new here, this week, with you and the kids." He walked to the door and turned back to face her. "I hope somehow you'll let me do that." And then he was gone.

This morning, as they ate pancakes together around the table, Lindsey almost let herself get lost in the moment. But the thought of her letter and getting to the mailbox kept her firmly planted in reality. She barely made it through breakfast and a round of Uno with Grant and the kids before she bolted from the house.

She walked so close to the water that it lapped at her feet. As she breathed in the salty air, she placed her hand in her pocket and rubbed her letter just as she saw the mailbox in the dunes up ahead, her own personal lighthouse. Her heart quickened to be this close to it even as it sank with the knowledge that there was no Kindred Spirit for her, no magic attached to the place as she had once believed.

She paused before she opened the mailbox to place her letter inside. Her pulse quickened with her assumption that Campbell had followed her year after year and lurked in the dunes, watching her. Even though the temperature climbed and the sun beat down on her, she shivered at the thought of being watched. She looked around, peering into the dunes, trying to catch a flash of movement, a glimpse of him. But nothing was there. As she opened the mailbox, she realized that what she was feeling was, strangely, disappointment.

Inside the mailbox was the usual assortment of loose paper, watermarked notebooks, and pens with missing caps. Sitting on the stack of notebooks she found a folded sheet of paper with her name on it. She reached into the mailbox to retrieve it and noticed that her hand shook, keeping time with her trembling heart. She took the letter over to the bench in the sand and sat down to read it. Her eyes filled with tears as she began to read.

Dear Lindsey,

I just saw you a few minutes ago at your house. You sent me away, and for that I can't blame you. I know you are angry with me for what I kept from you. I know you must have a million questions that you need for me to answer. And believe me, I want to answer them all. For the rest of my life I will answer your questions, if that's what it takes.

I know that with your husband back in the picture, things are more complicated. But I don't feel that his arrival has to mean that there is no chance for us. I have to believe we have a future. Because if I stop believing that we have a chance—as I have believed every time I read one of your letters—I will stop existing. It is the possibility of you that has kept me going every day of my life, ever since I was sixteen years old and kissed you on this very beach.

I have made huge mistakes. And the knowledge of how I have broken your heart is what's kept me from coming to find you all these years. But the truth is, I was always there for you, even when you couldn't see it. All these years you wrote faithfully to the Kindred Spirit. I have to ask you now, are you willing to accept the fact that your Kindred Spirit is me? That I am the one who has kept your letters for you, recorded your history, felt every pain and every joy you've experienced year after year?

You can choose to leave me here, at this mailbox, in your past, or you can choose to move forward, beyond this place,

*into a future we can build together. I think you know what
I hope you choose. I will wait as long as it takes for you to
decide.*

All my love,
Your Kindred Spirit,
Campbell

She refolded the letter and slipped it into her pocket, removing
the letter she brought with her so she could reread her own words.

Dear Kindred Spirit,

*Of all the letters I have written to you through the years,
this is the hardest one. Because I know it must be my last. How
I have loved coming here every summer. How many memories
are tied to this simple act of writing a letter each year about my
life and placing it in this mailbox?*

*Is it any less magical now that I know the recipient was you?
In some ways, yes. But in other ways, absolutely not.*

*But, as with all things in the world of grown-ups, it's time
to admit that magic is an illusion. A long time ago, we loved
each other. And, if circumstances were different, we might have
had a future together. But the truth is, circumstances aren't different. My husband wants to work on our marriage. You have
a daughter who needs you now more than ever. We must go
on with our lives and stop living in a distant past that we are
trying in vain to retrieve.*

*I will never be that fifteen-year-old girl again. And you will
never be that sixteen-year-old boy. Please know that, though I*

won't be writing to you anymore, I will carry those two people in my heart. Always.

Lindsey

She held the two letters, hers and Campbell's, weighing them in her hand like gold on a scale. Which one was real? Which one was worth more? She stared out at the sea, wishing she could blink and see Campbell there, skipping shells across the water. Or Holly, dancing fearlessly in time to the rhythm of the waves. She wanted to ask them both: What would you do if you were me? "Help me," she whispered to no one.

Before she could talk herself out of it, she tore her own letter to shreds, admitting to herself for the first time that—Grant or no Grant—she wasn't ready to say good-bye to Campbell yet. She knew that she and Campbell hadn't said everything they needed to say. She didn't know when or how she would see him again, but as she started her walk back to the beach house, she knew that somehow the mailbox would unite them, just as it always had. Both Campbell and Grant would have to wait on her to sort it all out. She had certainly done her time waiting for them.

Chapter 33

Sunset Beach

Summer 2004

"Can I take Nikki to her appointment today?" Campbell's mom asked. He was still lying in bed, his arm slung across his face to block the intrusive rays of the sun. He had been trying to come up with just one reason to get out of bed. Driving Nikki to her appointment was the only thing he came up with.

"You just took my reason for getting up this morning," he responded, not bothering to remove his arm.

He heard her bustle into the room, opening the shades and picking up his discarded clothes with a sigh. She sat on the very edge of the bed, so close she looked like she could slide right off. He didn't move over to give her more room, though. He was being selfish, sulking like a child. He could sense his mother gearing up to call him on it. He didn't want to give her room to do it.

"Campbell," she said.

"Oh no," he said from under his arm. "Here it comes."

"I think I know what's bothering you. And it isn't Nikki."

"Tell her what she's won, Bert!" he said, removing his arm and looking at her for the first time, offering a meager smile.

She shook her head. "I don't know what happened between you and Lindsey, but I do know this. She makes you feel like a kid again—in a good way. She might even be your soul mate. Whatever she is, I know she's something special."

He turned to look out the window. "It's too late, Mom," he told her.

"Has she gone home yet?" she asked.

"No, she'll finish out the week with her husband." He looked back at her, hoping she could see the hurt on his face and let it go. "He came back. And I screwed up. Case closed."

His revelation did not deter his mother. "Well, then it's not too late. You have to go to her. You have to chase after her. Maybe that's what she's been waiting for all these years. For you to follow after her. Maybe she just needs to know she's worth the pursuit." She raised her eyebrows at him, and he couldn't help but grin back.

"Did Dad chase after you, Mom?" he asked, even though mentioning his dad could still stir up fresh pain for both of them, like pressing on a bruise.

"Every day, honey," she said as she rose to leave. "Every day."

———

When Lindsey walked into the beach house, she could hear Grant's voice in the master bedroom. The kids were outside by the canal, throwing pebbles into the water. They were so engrossed in their activity, they barely acknowledged her arrival. Something in her quickened as she tiptoed toward the door with an extreme sense of déjà vu. She stood just outside the open door where he couldn't see her, but she could see him. He had his back turned to her and looked out the window, keeping an eye, she supposed, on Anna and Jake.

"I know," he said. "I do too." A long pause followed.

"Of course," he said. "Yes. You know that." His tone was the same tone he used when he tried to seduce her last night. Her blood ran like ice through her veins, and her heart pounded so loudly she could barely focus on his words.

"This is just something I had to do. For the kids. No, no, not for her. I told you it's over with her." He paused, then chuckled, a deep throaty laugh.

In the next moment, she no longer thought of Anna or Jake, of what they wanted or what might or might not be right for them. She didn't think about the photo of their family that hung in the foyer back home, the picture of perfection she strived for every day, with every decision. Instead she thought of herself on the beach an hour earlier, the satisfying sensation of the shreds of letter slipping from her fingers as she tossed them into the ocean and watched the waves pull them out to sea. All her life she did what was *right,* what was *expected,* what others wanted her to do. And it had gotten her nowhere. In a few short seconds, Grant had just convinced her that taking a chance on Campbell was less risky than settling for more years of disappointment with him. Five years ago, one year ago, one week ago, she would have overlooked this in the name of keeping their family together. But everything was different now.

She stalked into the room with her adrenaline pumping and took the phone out of Grant's hand, hardly noticing the angry, shocked look on his face. She didn't bother to note what the woman on the other end's voice sounded like as she told her that Grant would have to call her back when he was on his way home. She just knew she had to get him out of the house as fast as she could.

"I don't know why you came here or what you're up to," she said. "But I want you out of here. Now. I will call the police if I have to, Grant. But I will get you out of here one way or another."

He sputtered and fumbled for words. "I—it's not what you think—I—she's just someone I had taken out a few times and she wanted it to be more. I—she—I was just trying—I had to let her down easy."

"Grant," she said, nearly feeling sorry for him as she spoke. "You don't fool me. I know this woman is more to you than that. And I know it's really over between us. Now you can make someone else miserable with your lies and deceit. But it won't be me. Not anymore." She could feel Holly cheering for her as she walked out of the bedroom and into the den where his duffel bag lay opened. She shoved his few things into it and handed it to him. "I can't do this with you anymore. You have put me through enough. So, go tell your kids good-bye," she said. "Tell them that you enjoyed your visit and I'll make up an excuse as to why you had to leave."

He took the bag from her hands and picked up his keys, resigned to leaving, the fight gone out of him. "I'm sorry you heard that conversation," he said sullenly.

She laughed. "I'll bet you are."

"I just … I couldn't stand the thought of you moving on with another man. Something in me wanted to stop it, to prove I could."

"But … what are you … how did you know about that?"

"Anna called the night you went out. To tell me good night. She said she was afraid I would call the beach house and get worried because they weren't there. She said you were out with an old friend named Campbell." He smiled ruefully. "Of course I remembered who he was. And I guess I couldn't accept it."

He paused, twirling his keys around on the ring, the jingling the only sound in the house. Outside she could faintly hear Anna and Jake laughing. The thought of what was being decided for them, once and for all, broke her heart, but made her no less resolute.

"I wanted you to let me go," Grant said, "but I guess I never considered I would have to let you go in the process. How's that for irony?"

She nodded. She knew that Grant would probably never be faithful to anyone, and she couldn't be one of his casualties anymore. Instead of sadness or loss, relief vibrated through her like a tuning fork. The sound of the door closing behind Grant felt less like an ending and more like a beginning.

Chapter 34

Sunset Beach
Summer 2004

Before Nikki and Campbell's mom left for Nikki's counseling session, Nikki milled around in the kitchen while LaRae finished a load of laundry in the other room. Campbell brooded at the kitchen table in front of a half-eaten bowl of cereal with soggy flakes floating in the now warm milk

Nikki eyed him suspiciously. "Dad?" she asked. "You okay?"

"Fine, thanks, honey. Uh, I'm probably going to go into work today," he said, even though she hadn't asked about his plans.

Nikki cocked her head, studying him. "Grandma told me about Lindsey. I'm sorry," she said, sounding so much like an adult he almost wanted to shush her.

He tried to muster up a smile. "Lindsey isn't the point. You are."

She shook her head. "Dad, seeing you with Lindsey made me happy. It even gave me a little hope for my future. I've worried that there was some sort of genetic code for loneliness that I inherited from you."

"But, Nik, we only went on one measly date."

"Dad, come on. You and I both know it meant much more than one measly date." She paused, seeming to ponder whether to say more before continuing. "Do you know what has helped me most to work through this whole ordeal?"

He shook his head. "Counseling? Being near the ocean?"

"Sure, those have been super helpful. But mostly it was opening my eyes in that hospital and realizing you came all that way to rescue me. I didn't know until I saw you there how much I needed you to come after me." She straightened up, shaking her index finger in his direction, grinning as she reversed their roles. "Now, Grandma and I are going to be gone all day and you have nothing better to do than to go find her. Give it one more chance. If it doesn't work this time, I'll leave you alone about it. But I can't believe that Lindsey wants to be away from you any more than you want to be away from her. So go try to talk to her again."

"You sound a lot like your grandmother," he said and rolled his eyes.

"I will take that as a compliment," she said. "Did Grandma tell you she's sitting in on my counseling session today? And then we're going to have lunch and drive to Myrtle Beach to shop. I might even go with her to her turtle-watch meeting tonight," she said, her words coming out in an excited rush. "So, do you think I have a future as a turtle lady?" she asked.

He laughed at the image of Nikki wearing a turtle T-shirt, wandering down the beach surrounded by little old ladies in visors. "You have a future as anything you want," he told his daughter.

"Dad?" she asked.

"Yeah?"

"So do you."

He turned to say something smart-alecky back to her but was silenced as he saw that she was wearing the red flip-flops. His heart lifted, and for a second he let himself believe that the future was open with possibility. Maybe he would take his daughter's advice.

Chapter 35

Sunset Beach
Summer 2004

The morning after Grant left, Lindsey decided to go for a run before the kids woke up. This time she decided to run on the beach instead of the road, hoping that being near the water would clear her head and help her process all that had happened in a few short days. While her decision about Grant had been made, she still wasn't clear about Campbell. She could see him standing in the yard the day she found the letters, the way his eyes bored into her, imploring her to give him another chance. She couldn't get his face out of her mind.

She ran toward the pier, enjoying how deserted the beach was at that time of day. Only a few beachcombers—avid shell collectors and old men with metal detectors—populated the coast. She forced herself to smile at them when she ran past. It was Sunday after all, a day for goodwill. As she ran, she talked to God: *Show me what to do,* she prayed silently. *Please speak to me. I need to hear from You, Father.* She thanked God for answering Holly's prayer that she would see

Grant for who he really was, but reminded Him that she didn't have her answer about Campbell.

When she reached the pier, she saw a small crowd gathering beside the pilings. Worried that something was wrong, she decided to check out whatever it was they were paying attention to. Perhaps they had found a turtle nest or someone injured—a surfer trying to catch some early-morning waves. She quietly approached the edge of the crowd and waited for her breathing to return to normal. It was too late by the time she discovered that the crowd wasn't gathered for a turtle or an injury. They had gathered for the sunrise service, a weekly tradition held at the base of the Sunset Beach pier. Several pairs of eyes turned to look at her, and she felt trapped. Only a heathen would walk away now.

The cluster of people listened as the preacher greeted them, their eyes at half-mast, many sipping coffee from travel mugs. She wished for one of those travel mugs filled with steaming hot coffee. When everyone else bowed their heads, she caught herself scanning the faces in the crowd for Campbell, scolding herself for wanting to see him. Did she want to see him? What if she did? What then? Questions followed each other like cars on a train. She quieted her thoughts and concentrated on the hymn they sang next, even if she didn't know the words or the tune very well. In that crowd, neither seemed to matter.

The minister, a young man who hardly looked old enough to drive, announced that he would be speaking on Psalm 139 that morning. He cleared his throat and began to read the familiar words, his Adam's apple bobbing up and down as he spoke. She had heard the psalm so many times before that she almost stopped listening.

But her ears perked up as the minister said, "This psalm shows us that God knows us intimately but loves us anyway." He read the verses that spoke of how deeply God knows His creation—the words thought before spoken, the secrets. The preacher said that even though He knows the ugliness, the embarrassing stuff, the parts no one else sees, He doesn't turn away. In fact, He loves people all the more. Lindsey's eyes filled with tears as the feeling set in. She thought again of Campbell standing in her front yard. The minister's words echoed in her mind: "He knows us intimately but loves us anyway." Without warning, God had provided her with the life verse she had forgotten to find.

After the service was over and the people wandered away, Lindsey took a seat on the sand, wrapping her arms around herself to break some of the cool breeze. Her thoughts were as turbulent as the waves, one after another, each one crashing in on the next. Campbell had no right. He had violated her trust. He knew so many things about her that no one else knew. And yet, he had begged her for another chance. He knew her intimately but loved her anyway.

———

Lindsey found it more than fitting that Campbell found her on the beach only minutes after the service. Even as he flopped down beside her, she still had no idea what to say to him. They sat quietly for a few minutes, their bodies nearly touching. She held her breath; waiting, she realized, for an explanation that would make everything all right again. An explanation that would make her laugh with relief. The Kindred Spirit had delivered the letters to him each year like a miracle, she hoped he would say. *Please*, she thought, *let me be wrong about this.*

He looked down at the sand spread out below them like a soft gray blanket, ran his fingertips over it as though he just had to see what it felt like, even though the feel of sand beneath his fingers had to be as familiar to him as the feel of his own skin.

"Where's your family?" he asked her tentatively, breaking the silence.

"The kids are back at the house watching TV. They didn't want to come out here, but I needed to."

He nodded. "And your husband?" His voice cracked like an adolescent's.

She turned to him and suppressed a smile. "I asked him to leave when I got back from the mailbox yesterday." She took Campbell's letter from her pocket. "I overheard him talking to another woman when he thought I was gone."

He sighed. "I'm sorry."

She looked away from him, focusing on a ship far out at sea, making its way across the horizon. "I'm not. It helped clear things up for me without dragging out some sort of false reconciliation. He knew about you. That's what this was all about." She grimaced as he shook his head at Grant's audacity. She took a deep breath before plunging ahead. "But I don't really want to talk about Grant. I need you to help me understand this, Campbell," she said, shaking the letter a little for emphasis.

He took a deep breath and exhaled loudly. "Look, I never meant for it to happen like this. Any of it. You have to know that I was going to tell you about the letters. I really was."

"But when? Why didn't you tell me when we went out? It's not like there wasn't opportunity."

"Well, in hindsight that would have been best." He closed his mouth. Opened it. Closed it again. "I wish I had told you then. But I wanted to give us time."

"Time for what?"

He brushed the hair away from her face and looked at her so intently a shiver ran the length of her body. "Time for us to remember what we once had. I didn't want to wreck that possibility by telling you something that could make you run from me."

She shook her head. "So tell me now." Families were beginning to crowd around them, the noise and commotion of another day on the beach impeding their conversation. She wanted to be alone with him to talk. As a nearby child began to cry, she stood. "But tell me while we walk," she said, willing him to get up and follow her.

They fell into an easy rhythm, walking close enough to the shoreline that the waves splashed against their toes, their feet sinking into the wet sand. As he began to speak, she braced herself. "Okay, so the year you wrote that first letter at the mailbox, I couldn't wait to see what you wrote about me. So I went back the next day and got it out. I just had to have it. It was wrong, and I knew it. The fact is, I could probably just have asked you and you would have given me the letter. But instead I snuck around behind you." He stopped speaking and looked at her face, to gauge her reaction. "And then the next year I did the same thing again. Things had been so strained between us that summer. I figured you'd tell the truth in that letter about how you were feeling about us. Which, of course, you did."

Lindsey once again felt naked, exposed. "I always told the truth in my letters. But I could do that because no one was supposed to see them." She paused and corrected herself. "Well, I mean, no one I actually knew." The incoming tide caused a wave to splash them a little too forcefully, and she darted away from Campbell. He quickly closed the gap she'd created and attempted to grab her hand. She pulled away, crossing her arms over her chest, as he continued his explanation.

"So then everything happened with Ellie and—you have to know—that year was just hell for me. All of a sudden it was like I had made a wrong turn and ended up in someone else's life. Who was this girl? Where was the girl I really loved? How was I married? How was I someone's father? Yet, I had this sense of what I thought was honor, of doing the right thing.

"This summer I've learned that I need to take responsibility for my part in all of it. For my daughter's sake. For yours. But back then I didn't want any of it, so I just got through it as best I could. And what got me through was hoping that the next summer you would come back to the mailbox and I would be able to hear how you were. I had the idea to continue reading your letters when I wrote you the letter saying I had married Ellie. I felt like I was losing you, and I was desperate to hang on to you somehow." He smiled. "I thought I knew you well enough to guess that you'd come back. And I was right."

"So, I'm predictable is what you're saying," she said with a small smile that she couldn't contain.

"Only to me." He smiled back.

"Continue."

"So, every year after that, I knew to look for a letter in the mailbox the last week of July. I didn't follow you or anything. So don't think I'm some kind of crazy stalker. I just knew when you usually went. You are," he said, reaching up to brush a strand of hair from her face, "a creature of habit. I would usually go on a Saturday evening and there it would be, waiting for me like a promise that you were still around. I might have lost you, but with those letters you weren't gone." He looked up at the sky, pausing to watch a large heron swoop down and land on the beach with a kind of reverence, before speaking again. "I had to hold on to those letters so I could hold on to a piece of you."

"But those letters were private … and personal. They weren't yours to have. No one's supposed to know all of that stuff about me."

"Except the Kindred Spirit, right? You didn't mind the Kindred Spirit knowing all that you wrote."

She looked away in embarrassment, but he put his hand under her chin to face him.

"Lindsey," he said, "you wrote those letters to the Kindred Spirit, right?"

She nodded.

"Every year you poured your heart out to this Kindred Spirit that you so desperately wanted to believe was out there for you. And I was right there, reading every word. What I've always thought as I read them is that you were always writing to me, whether you knew it or not. I think deep down you knew it, here." He rapped lightly on his own chest, just above his heart. "What you didn't know is that you were my Kindred Spirit too."

She looked at him with furrowed brows. "I was?"

"I wouldn't have sought God without reading your letters and seeing your faith grow every year, Lindsey." He paused. "It was you who ultimately made me believe that God really did care, that He really did love me … the messed-up coward that I was."

She stopped and looked at him. "I thought—" She shook her head. "I thought that you got close to God when Ellie left. That's what your mom—"

"Yes, I went to church when Ellie left. That was the beginning. But it was watching you battle your doubts and come to trust God that made me want to trust Him too. You made Him real for me."

He reached for her hand, and she let him take it. Kissing the knuckles of her hand with his warm lips, he looked at her with all the love in the world and not a trace of deception in his soft, kind eyes.

"I almost didn't come here, to try again with you. I didn't think I had the right to ask. But you said it was a summer for second chances, and I'm learning that even a guy like me might have a shot." He grinned. "So I was hoping you'd find it in your heart to forgive me for reading your letters. I promise that all I ever wanted was to tell you the truth and give you the letters back. They're a part of you, and they belong with you." He pulled her into a hug and whispered in her ear, "And so do I."

Chapter 36

Sunset Beach
Summer 2004

Campbell and Lindsey walked back to the beach house hand in hand. His grip was so tight she had to pull her hand away and rub it to get the circulation going again. "I'm sorry," he said and winced as he watched her massage her hand.

She grinned at him and took his hand again. "Don't be sorry," she said and looked at him, catching his eye. "Don't be sorry," she said, louder and firmer.

He nodded, understanding that she meant more. They walked a little farther in silence. As they reached the driveway of the house, she turned toward him. "So, let me ask you a question," she said.

"Shoot."

"So you're not the Kindred Spirit … but do you know who is?" Her voice was teasing.

He laughed. "No."

She narrowed her eyes as though she doubted him.

He held up his free hand, laughing. "I promise! I have no idea who the real Kindred Spirit is!"

She smiled warmly, and he thought about the inroads he still would need to make with both Lindsey and Nikki. He was up for the challenge. Created for it, in fact.

"Okay, I have one more question for you," she said.

"Anything," he said, though his heart beat a bit faster with the way she posed the question.

"Who painted that picture in your room? Of the girl sitting by the mailbox? I mean, I think I might know where it came from, but it just seems impossible that you of all people ended up with it."

He smiled and looked off down the beach, not realizing she was going to hit him with that question—and searching for a way to answer it. He let out a long breath before he started. "I had taken Nikki to a fair up in Wilmington. I was letting her walk around the craft booths, though I was thoroughly bored, I might add. She liked looking at all the T-shirts and begging me for junk. You know."

Lindsey nodded.

"So I found this booth with this guy selling prints of the beach. Some of them were pretty spectacular. I saw that he had done one of the mailbox, and I asked him if he had any more. The one he had was in black and white, but I wanted one in color."

A little boy pedaled by on a bicycle, and Campbell stopped talking as he waited for the boy to pass. "So," he resumed, "the guy gets this funny look on his face and says in this British accent, 'Well, I do have one other, but it's not quite ready to sell. But I suppose I could let you see it.' So he goes and digs around in his things and comes back with this photo—just an ordinary print from a camera."

She looked at him without blinking. "So, I look at the picture and there you are, sitting there, writing a letter that I would eventually go and get. I couldn't believe it." He reached out and stroked her face. "Lindsey, I swear to you in that moment it felt like a sign. That I was meant to do what I was doing. That I was supposed to be connected to you." He looked at her hard. "I mean, what are the odds?"

"Roderick Shaw," she blurted out. She shook her head, amazed.

"Yes! That was his name! I asked him if he knew you, how he knew you. He told me he met you at the mailbox. So I bought the print from him right there. Then I paid him a lot of money not to sell that picture to anyone. Ever." He laughed. "I didn't want anyone else to have it. It was my picture. So he sold me the negative. He said that he could tell you were very special to me and that he would pray for us." He laughed. "And then I bought Nikki a bag of cotton candy."

"And the painting?" she asked.

His face reddened. "I paid a local artist to recreate the print for me." He shrugged. "It made me feel closer to you to have it on my wall where I could see it every day."

Just then, Jake came out to stand on the porch. "Mom?" he called. She held up one finger.

"I better go," she said.

"I'd like to take you out tonight," he told her. She started to argue with him, but he held up his hand. "Nikki said she'd come and watch your kids." He paused, knowing the implication of what he was about to say. "She really likes your kids. I think that's a good sign, don't you?"

She nodded, shifting her weight from foot to foot. He put his hand on her shoulder and pressed his forehead to hers. "Pick you up at six?" he asked.

She nodded again and turned to run up the stairs. As he watched her go, he did not see thirtysomething Lindsey. He saw Lindsey at fifteen: laughing, vibrant, and full of life, especially when they were together.

That night Campbell dropped off Nikki and picked up Lindsey at the beach house. Anna and Jake seemed thrilled to see Nikki walk in the door. He heard her promise Jake a duel on some video game and Anna a makeover. He put his arm around Lindsey as they headed to his truck and pulled her close. "They sound like they're going to be just fine without us."

She grinned. "I think they're actually ready to be rid of me for a while." She swallowed. "They haven't said so, but I think they fault me for Grant leaving."

He evaded her mention of Grant. The evening wasn't about him. "I think Nikki wanted to have an excuse to get out of the house for an evening. Even if it's just to spend it with two kids. It's better than my mother and Minerva."

She laughed as he opened the truck's passenger-side door for her and braced himself, watching her as she registered the stack of her letters, which he had arranged in order of years and tied with a red bow with a single rose threaded through the center. She looked at him. "Is this okay?" he asked her.

He watched her eyes fill with tears as she nodded and let her fingers flutter through the stack. "I never thought I'd see them again."

"They're all there," he said, tapping the bundle and shutting her door.

He drove them straight to the pier. But before walking to the edge like he normally did, he asked the question he'd wanted to ask for years. "Will you dance with me?"

She laughed, then looked at him like he was crazy. "Dance?" she asked, as if she heard him wrong.

He turned on the truck's stereo, which had already been queued to a track number. As the first strains of "Boys of Summer" began to play, Lindsey looked at him and shook her head incredulously.

"Remember this?" he asked her.

"How could I forget?"

He got out of the truck and walked around to help her out. He held her in his arms in the parking lot at the pier, and they swayed to Don Henley, both of them remembering a couple of kids dancing slow to a fast song. Though much had changed, their dance stayed the same.

Some surfers walked past them, oblivious. A teenage couple walked by, looking very much like Lindsey and Campbell once did. The couple smiled and leaned into each other as they continued toward the pier.

Campbell sang to Lindsey softly, "I can tell you my love for you will still be strong, after the boys of summer have gone." He held her close until the song ended, then took her hand to lead her to the pier.

"I have to say, I can't believe we've made our way back here in spite of everything," she mused as they walked.

He chuckled. "Me either. We have a lot of lost time to make up for."

"But was it lost?" she asked.

"What do you mean?"

"I mean, it wasn't what we would have chosen, but I'm starting to believe it was what was supposed to happen. It looks like we made wrong turns with the wrong people and yet, I look at Anna and Jake and Nikki—"

"Nikki?" he interrupted with a playful grin on his face.

"Yes, Nikki!" She laughed and shoved him slightly. "Anyway, I know they are supposed to be here, and that wouldn't have happened without those wrong turns." She looked over at him, and he nodded his understanding. "I have to believe that the way it all played out was part of God's very interesting plan for our lives. That for whatever reason we could only be together now, after we grew up."

"I still wish we could have grown up together," he said, squeezing her hand.

"And yet I love who we've both become," she added. "I wouldn't change that. The way you are with Nikki. How we both found a relationship with God through our struggles. I'm not sure we would have reached the same conclusions without those struggles."

He just grinned. And as they reached the end of the pier, he asked her, "Can I see you tomorrow?"

Her answer was a given. "What did you have in mind?"

He smiled. "I thought we'd take a walk out to the mailbox. You still have a letter to write this year, if I'm not mistaken."

She thought about the letter she wrote but never left and knew he was right. She leaned closer to him, kissed his cheek. "Let's write a letter together this year. Start a new tradition. I'm tired of writing letters alone." He wrapped his arm around her, and they stood in the same spot where they had danced and dreamed and decided to love each other always. They couldn't see the mailbox from where they stood, but it was, always, near. The gulls shrieked and the waves crashed, and they had never heard any music more beautiful than that.

The Kindred Spirit Mailbox
Sunset Beach
Spring 2005

She gathered with the small group of guests to watch the couple exchange vows in front of the mailbox. Being there with other people felt foreign, unnatural. She liked the anonymity of coming and going undetected, savoring the contents of the mailbox without sharing them. She tried to stop thinking about where she was and focused instead on why she was there.

She watched the groom, who looked happier than she had ever seen him as he took his place beside the pastor. Beside him stood the bride's son, who looked stiff and uncomfortable in his starched white shirt and tie. The boy tugged at his collar and stared off at the ocean as though he were about to jump into it. She smiled and winked at the groom's mother, her dear friend. She felt the pang of keeping the secret of her identity from her, but it was part of the job description.

A violin began to play the strains of a song she didn't recognize as the bridesmaids—the bride's daughter and the groom's daughter in matching pale pink sundresses—came down the shell-lined aisle. They held bouquets of beach roses mixed with baby's breath. As the bride came in behind them, stunning in a simple white sundress with a sheer white wrap over her shoulders, the Kindred Spirit rose with the rest of the guests. She watched as the bride winked at a woman with a walker in the front row. The woman winked back and gave a thumbs-up. The Kindred Spirit noticed the resemblance between the two women and wondered if they were perhaps mother and daughter.

Of course, everyone there knew the story of how the mailbox brought these two people together—but no one knew the thousands of other stories she was privy to each time she made the trek down the beach to retrieve the notebooks and letters. Watching the wedding was her own celebration of what being the Kindred Spirit was all about.

The mailbox wasn't just hers. It belonged to many. Though she could share her secret with no one, she could share this moment with those who gathered there. She could thank God for seeing fit to let her be the Kindred Spirit. The mailbox might not change the world, but it had changed these two people's lives—and hers in the process—revealing a place where soul mates are discovered, hope is salvaged, and love finds a way back to where it started.

... a little more ...

When a delightful concert comes to an end,

the orchestra might offer an encore.

When a fine meal comes to an end,

it's always nice to savor a bit of dessert.

When a great story comes to an end,

we think you may want to linger.

And so, we offer ...

AfterWords—just a little something more after you

have finished a David C. Cook novel.

We invite you to stay awhile in the story.

Thanks for reading!

Turn the page for ...

- **Author Interview**
- **Discussion Questions**
- **Visiting the Mailbox**

Author Interview

Q: How much of this novel is actually true?

A: The assumption is that a first novel is going to be autobiographical, but in this case it's not true. While there might be brief references within the novel to things that happened to me or feelings I have had—especially as a mom, friend, wife, etc.—the overall story and situation is completely made up. But the setting ... that's entirely true. There really is a Sunset Beach, North Carolina, and it's my most favorite place in the world. So it makes sense that I would set my first novel there. I have been visiting the mailbox for years and believe that it is a special place. A place where, as the photographer Lindsey meets says in the book, God hears you better.

Another true aspect about the novel is that I did first visit Sunset Beach, like Lindsey, at fifteen years old in 1985 (telling my age). I have very vivid memories of that trip to this day, which is how I was able to recall the details, the music, etc., of that time. In the acknowledgments, I thanked an old friend of mine, Holly, who took me with her on that trip. I also named the character of Holly after her as a little tribute. She couldn't have known then that that trip sparked a lifelong love of Sunset Beach for me. When we left that year, I vowed I would come back when I was a grown-up. And I do go back every summer. I also named the characters of Uncle Bob, Aunt Frances, and cousins Bobby and Stephanie after my real aunt, uncle, and cousins, as it is their beach house we stay in every summer. That was my way of giving them a little shout-out.

Q: So the mailbox is real? Do you know who the Kindred Spirit is?

A: Yes, the mailbox is real, but I don't know who the Kindred Spirit is. No one does. That's part of the mystery and folklore of the mailbox. If you are ever in North Carolina, I highly recommend a visit.

Q: You have said that the book changed quite a bit from the original to the version we see. How so?

A: In the original, there was a letter to the Kindred Spirit for every year from 1985 to 2004. My editor didn't feel we needed a letter for every year—that the letters were slowing down the flow of the story, which was true. So we left a few in so that the reader would know that Lindsey was writing letters every year, but not get mired down in every detail of every year as I originally planned. I think we have a happy medium now, a better mix between narrative and the glimpses into Lindsey's past via the letters.

Also, in the original, Holly died. That seems so weird now because she became so much a part of the story, helping Lindsey process what's happening to her like good friends do. The story of Holly's death was told through the letters, so when we pulled those out, we had to figure out what that did to the storyline. I ended up adding her back and I am so glad I did! Oh, and in the very first manuscript, Lindsey's name was Lucy, but I quickly discerned that she was so not a Lucy. Lindsey suits her much better!

Q: Did you experience a powerful summer romance like Lindsey and Campbell's that you drew from for this story?

A: No. I had a few summer romances, but none that were enduring like you see in this story. Regardless of whether we've had a great summer love, I think it's a notion that resonates with all women: this idea that we are unforgettable, that we are worth pursuing at all costs. God puts that in our hearts because ultimately He is the great Pursuer, the One who never forgets us. I liked that in this story, Lindsey discovers that about Him first, then finds it in Campbell. She was never forgotten. None of us are.

Q: You deal with a tough subject in this book: a Christian woman in the midst of a divorce and rebuilding her life. What made you decide to focus on this?

A: Honestly, it's just how the story came to me. I didn't really think about the aspect of her being divorced until I was well into the first draft and a friend of mine had pretty much the exact same thing happen to her that was happening to Lindsey. What was so interesting is that I went back and read what I had written from Lindsey's point of view and it was nearly verbatim what I heard my friend saying. I knew then I was on the right track of tapping into the feelings and emotions of what Lindsey was going through in a way that would ring true. We have had so many friends go through this; I know there are women everywhere facing what Lindsey faced. And I often think, *But by the grace of God, go I.*

Q: You dedicated this book to a friend, Ariel Allison Lawhon, saying that this book wouldn't exist without her. Why is that?

A: For most of my life I have had story ideas pop into my head. I would see something happen and think, *What if …?* So when I met Ariel, I was chewing on this idea for *The Mailbox,* and had been for some time. At that point she was trying to find a publisher for her novel, *eye of the god,* and she really encouraged me to try writing fiction. I was so nervous about it—I didn't know if I had the stick-to-itiveness to actually finish a novel. With her continued encouragement, I kept putting words down—though I knew next to nothing about what I was doing. Finally I got about sixty thousand words in and quit. I had written myself into a corner and couldn't get out. So I closed that file and moved on to other projects. A few months later I received this random email from Ariel encouraging me not to quit and begging me to just finish it. She said, "No one writes sixty thousand words and quits. You have to finish this book." So I did. If she hadn't persisted, I am convinced the book would still be sitting in a forgotten file with sixty thousand words written. So that (and her continued friendship and listening to my rambling on a daily basis) earns her a dedication for this book. I also dedicated it to my husband, who puts up with a whole lot when I am writing and deserves a dedication too!

Q: Now that you have written one novel, do you think you will write more novels?

A: Yes, I plan to write more novels. I keep a running list of ideas and add to it often, so I hope that list will keep me going for quite some time. I am working on a new novel that comes out next year and is totally different from *The Mailbox*. One thing I have learned through this experience is, I will always have more to learn about the craft of writing. I will continue to learn for the rest of my career as a novelist, and my hope is my work will reflect what I am learning with each successive book. That's the plan at least.

Discussion Questions

1. Lindsey is recently divorced. If you have been through a divorce and have kids, do you sympathize with her feelings as a newly single mom? If not, did seeing her character struggle affect how you view divorced women?

2. Lindsey struggles with her role as a mom, especially in light of the new dynamic of her family and her daughter's transformation into a preteen. Campbell struggles with staying connected to his daughter from a distance. They each make efforts to connect with their children. Why do their efforts work or not work? Are they doing all they can as parents? Why is God's grace so important to both of them?

3. At the beginning of the story, Campbell discovers his daughter has passed out at work. His mind goes down paths of worry even though he tries not to be irrational. Have you ever experienced that happening? How did you control your tendency to worry?

4. Lindsey's daughter, Anna, says to her, "If Dad loves me like you say, he wouldn't hurt me like this. I don't think that he really loves any of us. I think that he loves himself and doing what he wants is all that matters now. But that's not what real love is. If he loved me, he wouldn't make me feel this bad. 'Cause when you love someone, you care about how they feel too." Why is this true of Grant, and what does it say about his character?

5. What are some of the things Lindsey learns to appreciate about her new life as a single mom while she is at the beach? How do these little realizations affect her perspective and influence her actions?

6. Ellie shocks Campbell by telling him that he can take Nikki with him to Sunset Beach. Why does she allow him to? Is Campbell prepared to be a father to a teenage girl with issues? Does he think he is? Does Ellie?

7. Both Holly and Grant's mother, Jane, encourage Lindsey to move on with her life. Do you think that encouragement has something to do with Lindsey's decision to take Minerva up on her offer to walk by Campbell's house? If you were Lindsey, would you have done what Minerva suggested?

8. Running is a great outlet for Lindsey. How does it help her heal? Is there a physical activity or hobby that helps you like that? If not, are you inspired to find one?

9. All Lindsey wanted her whole life was a hands-on, involved mom. How do you think that lack affects her mothering?

10. Lindsey and Campbell leave the crowded restaurant and end up at the pier. Why do you think they both agreed to do that?

11. The photographer Lindsey meets at the mailbox plays a role in both her and Campbell's lives. Do you believe God puts people

in our lives to accomplish His purposes? Have you ever had an encounter that could have been orchestrated only by God?

12. What do the red shoes symbolize to Campbell? What does it mean to him when Nikki decides to wear the flip-flops he buys her?

13. How would you describe Campbell's journey as a father? As a child of God?

14. How would you describe Lindsey's spiritual journey? What does she learn about herself by the end of the book?

15. Would you have been able to trust Campbell after you found the letters? Would you have been able to forgive him? Why does Lindsey?

16. Why does Lindsey make Grant leave? Was she right to do so? Did he deserve a second chance? Why, or why not?

17. Holly prays for Lindsey to see Grant and Campbell for who they really are. Was her prayer answered?

18. What do you think happens between Lindsey and her mom after the wedding? Was Lindsey right to stay and deal with her situation with Grant and Campbell, or should she have gone to her mother's bedside?

19. Forgiveness and second chances are big themes in this story. The saying goes that unforgiveness is like eating poison while waiting for

the other person to die. To whom do you need to ask forgiveness and a second chance? To whom do you need to offer your forgiveness?

20. Do you know who the Kindred Spirit is whom we see in the beginning and ending of the book? At what point in the story did you figure out her identity?

Visiting the Mailbox

"Slightly hidden among the dunes on Bird Island is a plain rural mailbox, containing an assortment of notebooks, pens, and pencils. The outside of the mailbox is marked 'Kindred Spirit.' Visitors use the notebooks to record inconsequential statements, special thoughts, and sometimes private prayers. Visitors have the opportunity to make public statements in complete anonymity." (Source: Wikipedia, "'Kindred Spirit' Mailbox," 1/27/10)

Finding the mailbox:

If you decide to visit the mailbox, you must first start at Sunset Beach and head toward Bird Island, a nature preserve of pure, undeveloped coastline kept by the state of North Carolina. The mailbox is on your right, tucked into the dunes before you get to the jetty of rocks that jut out into the ocean. If you get to the old shipwreck on the beach, you've gone too far. And if you have trouble finding your way, just ask one of the nice people you see walking along the beach. They're sure to help you get where you're going.

Do you love Christian fiction?
Then She Reads is the place for you!

She Reads is an exciting division of Proverbs 31 Ministries that provides access to the best of the best Christian fiction.

She Reads exists to honor Christ by connecting readers with novels that inspire through excellent writing, explore deep issues of faith, and initiate change in the reader's life.

Readers who join *She Reads* receive a number of benefits, including:

- **Connection** with other readers on the *She Reads* blog who are passionate about great fiction and uplifting stories.
- **Information** via the *She Reads* newsletter that will keep readers up to date on their favorite authors, and books, with a few surprises thrown in for fun.
- **Reviews** of newly released titles written by a variety of readers, writers, and industry professionals.
- Options to create a *She Reads* book club or bring an existing club under the *She Reads* umbrella.
- **Relationships** developed within the intimate setting of a regular book club meeting.
- **Online Community** for those who can't participate in a monthly meeting (or don't live near an existing club), via the *She Reads* blog and Facebook group.
- **Pre-selected novels** they can trust and appreciate—an important aspect in today's economy where every buying decision requires a second thought.
- **Free books** from time to time via contests, giveaways, and publisher promotions.

Find us at www.SheReads.org.
We'd love to see you there!

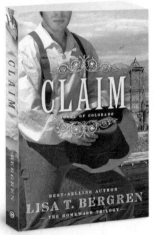

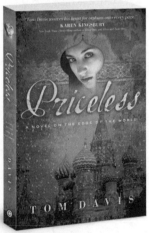

EAGLE VALLEY LIBRARY DISTRICT
P.O. BOX 240   600 BROADWAY
EAGLE, CO 81631   (970) 328-8800